BLACK PIANO

Dawn Lowe-Watson has been a journalist and feature writer, written plays for television and is widely known as a radio dramatist. She has won several awards for her novel writing.

She lives in Hampstead and Norfolk, where she reviews fiction for the Eastern Daily Press, writes, walks on the marshes, gardens and sails with one of her three sons. Her London interests include the theatre and art exhibitions. Her youngest son, to whom she dedicates *Black Piano*, is himself a concert pianist and composer.

Dawn Lowe-Watson

BLACK PIANO

A·PIATKUS·PAPERBACK

First published in Great Britain in 1986
This edition first published in
Great Britain in 1987 by
Judy Piatkus (Publishers) Ltd of
5 Windmill Street, London W1

British Library Cataloguing in Publication Data

Lowe-Watson, Dawn
The black piano.
I. Title
823'.914[F]   PR6062.0893

ISBN 0-86188-904-5

Paul Wilding/The Gallery: cover illustration

Printed and bound in Great Britain by
Biddles Ltd, Guildford and King's Lynn

Grateful acknowledgement is made of the use of poetry taken from *John Betjeman's Collected Poems*, first published by John Murray Publishers in 1958.

I would like to acknowledge the following for their assistance and information whilst writing this book:
    The Hallé Concerts Society
    Messrs. Ingpen and Williams, Concert Agents
    The Royal Opera House, Covent Garden
    Charterhouse School
    The Brighton Pavilion
    Confederation of British Industry

For my youngest son, Andrew

Chapter One

The South Bank complex in London froze the soul that day. The wind seemed to blow straight in from Siberia. Jethro Manning wore gloves, sheepskin-lined, as he arrived at the Artists' Entrance while even then, in his dressing room, he had to rub his fingers together and hold them under warm water.

Irritable gusts of wind blew the incoming audience along the draughty terraces, picking their way over the puddles where the rain always collects, past the inhospitable slabs of New Brutalism, the giant steel rampant sculpture, over the concrete cavern where the children used to skate-board a while ago when it was all the rage, along the wind funnel, and into the foyer of the Queen Elizabeth Hall. Expressionless men in green uniforms tore the tickets at the glass doors. Within, those already arrived thawed through, many still huddled in coats, looking around the austere and charmless interior to see who might not be here.

Already there were queues for the loos in the ladies' lavatory, and plenty of concert-goers stood around in groups, meeting and greeting and complaining about the cold.

Away through the window, lines of motor cars edged the pavement, parked right across Waterloo Bridge, almost to the other side, the Festival Hall audiences; and the river chopped away, grey-green and surly, bearing desultory craft.

It was a Sunday afternoon in February, not a particularly tempting time – three p.m. – to turn out from the fireside or the central heating; but people always came to hear Jethro Manning. It was an event. And nowadays he graced London

1

audiences seldom enough to keep them on their toes, so that even if other recitals and concerts, and theatres too, were embarrassed by rows of empty seats, a date like this would be sure to be well booked, considerably ahead.

John Sorensen took his camel-coloured teddy-bear coat to the cloakroom and exchanged it for a ticket. A short, chubby little chap, he was not the sort to excite notice, although musically he had his own following, too. Those who knew considered him, increasingly, as a cellist of merit. He could still be called young. And he was a friend of Jethro Manning's. Although Jethro played little chamber music nowadays, and could afford to be choosy about whom he played with, his name could be seen from time to time coupled with that of John in the *Radio Times*.

It could be said, on two levels, that John had a foot in the door of the Manning establishment. Except, of course – today that establishment hardly existed. At any rate, it had been thoroughly rocked. Nothing thought John, who was a traditionalist by inclination, is ever safe in this world. Nothing stays the same. And with this disquieting thought he bought himself a coffee. He would have preferred something stronger, but this was the afternoon.

Then he sat and watched the audience flow in through the doors. He was waiting, with pleasant anticipation, for Tatiana.

Theo Bristol swept in, wearing a long musquash coat, his beard damp with freezing rain. John saw him shake the coat hard, then leave it in the cloak-room, look around the foyer and take himself to the vast plate glass window where he stood, staring out across the river, over the cheerless water, at the dear old Savoy, so solid, so affluent. With every stiff movement he registered that what he saw was redolent with nostalgia for such as him, who remembered receptions in The River Room or dancing to Carroll Gibbons and the Savoy Orpheans.

John thought – as he always thought – that the foyer of the Queen Elizabeth Hall looked more like an airport lounge than a place with any pretensions to culture. Its leather benches jutted out at awkward angles so that those seated there had no way of forming a group or chatting intimately to each other, but were forced to sit in rows obliquely, as comfortless as travellers on the underground. Glumly, now, they sat there, solitary concert-goers reading their programme notes, wondering where to put their drinks.

'The English at leisure, taking their culture,' he thought. And then, hearing two German women passing him, discussing Jethro in Bavarian accents, he modified that. They had grey hair like wire wool – and knitted stockings. There was, he decided, something a little drab about concert-goers. They had less style than other audiences, but more integrity. A lot of them were plain ugly. But perhaps that was just this damn hall, with its hygienic absence of any character. The audience took on the aura of the space itself, stern, disapproving of self-indulgence. The Wigmore Hall he much preferred to play in; audiences there smiled more readily, wore brighter coloured clothes. The ambiance was altogether jollier and compensated for the scrum in the bar.

The doyng-doyng-doyng began to toll and the synthetic voice informed the audience that the recital in the Queen Elizabeth Hall was about to start. John looked at his watch. No Tatiana yet. But come she must – surely. He made his way towards the doors of the auditorium and just missed Kitty making her entrance, her grown-up children at her heels like three Borzoi hounds.

Kitty Manning had dressed in black for Jethro's Queen Elizabeth Hall recital, as though in mourning. She made her point and it did not go unnoticed.

From his place, John smiled quietly and fingered the ring on his hand, registering it all as she and hers came in procession down the gangway to seats mid-centre, from the stiletto-heeled black boots to the ebony beads (her great-grandmother's) around the jet stand-up collar. Even her knees, he could see as she crossed them, sitting down, were encased in sheer black – was it silk, rather than plebeian nylon? Nina had her arm now, Antony in front. Tatiana walked alone, a step behind. John was pleasantly stunned, as always, by her beauty.

Four rows in front of him sat Arthur and Irene Heygate,

whom he had already seen while buying their coffee tickets for the interval. Irene, a first violin with the Royal Opera House orchestra, was now nudging Arthur, a small slight man with pale blue eyes and a neck too small for his collar. He worked for the British Council.

'Kitty's making an exhibition of herself,' Irene was saying, but he disagreed on principle as he habitually did.

'She may have lost an elderly relative,' he was suggesting.

'Nonsense,' said Irene. She saw Theo and waved her programme at him. 'Well, there's Theo, anyway. Looking remarkably spry.'

'Why shouldn't he be?' asked Arthur.

'He's not young.'

'Neither are any of us,' commented Arthur, lugubriously.

Way behind, in the much cheaper seats, Bridget Scoyle sat with Sally MacKinley, and Sally's brother Alerick. Alerick was a pupil of Jethro's, and Sally a childhood friend of Tatiana's, with whom she now shared an office in the administrative department of the Royal Opera House, Covent Garden. Bridget claimed a slight acquaintance with the Mannings which she was eager to preserve against odds – they never seemed to recognise her however frequently she was introduced to them, so that she was constantly having to repeat her name. Not an attractive girl, she was inclined to acne and a lumpy waist. Not to mention dandruff. Sally, whose thick autumnal hair sprang from her brow in waves like her brother's, was not the kind of person people forgot. Carelessly, she accumulated hangers-on. It irritated Alerick, who had not wanted Bridget with them that evening, but Bridget was difficult to lose. She kept contact with people, very assiduously. She wrote letters and made telephone calls and invited her friends and acquaintances round for chilli con carne.

Jethro made his appearance and lumbered up on to the platform to a warm reception. The applause died down to a last, ostentatious handclap. Someone coughed. Jethro waited. Someone dropped a programme. He frowned, bent his head, raised his hands and began.

The first half of his programme was a surprise to some who had not bothered to examine it closely before booking, had

4

simply come because it was Jethro. Schumann *Waldscenen*, three Field Nocturnes, and the Grieg Lyric Pieces – *Papillons, Notturno* and *To The Spring*. A rum offering to a public who expected fireworks and brilliance from the man. Today he seemed to be playing for himself – or so Irene whispered to Arthur between the Field pieces. He pretended he hadn't heard.

Kitty thought – to herself – this is a message. She caught it. Pride quivered.

He had played the Grieg as an encore for that début, so many years ago, when they had been young, when she had come dressed in white to give him the support he had so desperately needed on the night. What a night! Jethro taut, ashen but stoic, relying on her. It had been the most cruel timing. Until then his father had been the person at the forefront and then, so suddenly, she had stepped forward and taken his place. The occasion had brought its own strength in the way crises do. As Jethro had begun the first opening bars of his programme she had relaxed her stiff position and known he would be all right. She had been with him up until ten minutes before he had come on and then, with hauteur, walked down the aisle of the Wigmore Hall between the waiting audience. She knew eyes were upon her. People had realised her significance. They knew, the discerning, that one era had finished and another had begun.

The Lyric Pieces could be no other than a message. A call. A beckoning. Kitty felt restored.

She sat upright, shrouded in her black, between her daughters. Antony was neat and fair, to the left of Nina. Each of the girls wore a fine gold chain around her left ankle. Nina was in grey, very soft, dove-like, and Tatiana in deep crimson. Antony looked essentially Charterhouse. It was, after all, mid-quarter. His finger nails were very clean and his shoes polished.

Now Jethro sat straight as a board at the keyboard, lean, tall, taut. There was a luminosity about his white dinner jacket.

When he came to the end of the Field, he walked off for a moment or two to applause, and Kitty slid her eyes surreptitiously around the hall to see if 'that woman' was there.

5

Everybody seemed to have a cold. The snorting and coughing was quite appalling and no doubt kept Jethro waiting in the wings for a little longer than normal. They had to have their little cough and splutter.

'Bring out the Benylin!' whispered Sally.

'He drinks gallons of water,' said Alerick. 'He has a consuming thirst. Then a pee-ing problem.' It was Alerick's pleasure to be familiar with the more intimate details of Jethro's life style. He bathed in the great man's reflection so that even his bodily functions took on an awesome significance.

'His lady friend's here!' said Sally, pointing.

Alerick shot a look across the hall.

And then, to a background of applause, Jethro stalked on again, inclined his head briefly to the audience, and sat down to begin the Grieg.

'Short first half,' muttered Irene as people rose and began to stumble across each other to get to the bar.

'I don't know,' said Arthur.

'Where's she sitting?' asked Bridget, craning myopically over the bobbing heads. She was more interested in Jethro's private life than his performance.

'I'm surprised she's come,' said Sally.

'She's not the most sensitive female,' sniffed Alerick.

'Where is she?' asked Bridget again. She had rather hoped to be an oboe player once, but was doing a secretarial course now.

'Down there on the right of the gangway. She's still sitting down. At any rate it looks as though she's not coming out for the interval.'

'How long is it since he left Mrs Manning?'

'A year,' said Alerick. And he steered Bridget and Sally out, shuffling their way to the coffee queue.

Theo stood in the foyer with two cups of coffee in his hands; one he gave to Kitty as she advanced, offering her cheek. From his pocket he took a mini bottle of brandy which he unscrewed and poured into their coffees.

'Thank you, darling Theo,' she greeted him. 'How kind. I'm feeling somewhat fragile.'

'You don't look it.' He smiled. 'It suits you.'

She looked down at the unrelieved black. The dress was not inexpensive. 'I've had this for a hundred years,' she said.

'Amazing how it's lasted.'

She tried not to smile. 'I spend nothing on clothes nowadays. I have nothing to spend.' She fiddled with the gold bracelet on her wrist, and he nodded. He had a sympathetic way with him. 'Life isn't a bed of roses, Theo.'

'I'm sure it isn't.' He did hope she wasn't going to say what a long time it was since she'd seen him; or that one discovered who one's friends were once one was a woman alone.

She spared him all that, but paradoxically her doing so unnerved him. Perhaps she had not even noticed. Perhaps she had plenty of new friends.

'I'm in mourning for my marriage,' she said.

'That had not escaped me. I think . . . I think . . .' he said, 'it is a very telling touch.' That was daring of him.

She looked away.

He put out a hand and touched hers, but fleetingly.

'It's the only way I know to fight,' she explained. 'I mean . . . if he's allowed to forget I *exist*!'

He thought it unlikely that could be possible, and said so. She seemed to ignore it.

'The girls are talking to that Alerick MacKinley boy with the beautiful sister and the spotty friend. Those two used to play in a little quartet with Nina and Tattie, do you remember? When they were children. Before the parents moved up to Edinburgh.'

'Um – yes.'

'I know they were never very gifted.'

'Well, I wouldn't go so far as . . .'

'Jethro always said they had no aptitude. He thought it was a complete waste having them taught. But then, he never wanted another musician in the family.'

Theo looked at her quickly to see whether there was any bitterness in the remark, but it seemed there was not.

'I wonder whether the boy still goes to him. He used to think he could be a high flyer one day.'

'Jethro's always been very generous with young talent,' said Theo. Then, 'Isn't your mama here?'

'No. Isn't it extraordinary? She's been down in Brighton

7

for a few days and she hasn't even bothered to come back.'

'Perhaps – in view of his treatment of you.'

'Oh no. Mother's nothing if not tolerant. It's always rather hurt me. She's quite bland about Jethro's behaviour. It's just that she always does what she wants and she wanted to stay down there. She's quite self-centred in her way.'

'At any rate,' said Theo, 'it makes life simpler. A little intelligent selfishness . . .'

'I wouldn't know.' Kitty was haughty. 'It isn't really my style.'

'She's fond of Brighton?'

'She has a little flat down there. Didn't you know? A whim. She scampers down on the train and nobody knows what she gets up to. It's a very tiny flat on a top floor in Lewes Crescent.'

'Maybe she has a lover,' smiled Theo.

'Possibly. I wouldn't put it past her.'

'Remarkable woman.'

A man Theo didn't know came and kissed Kitty's hand. Three women he did fluttered up to embrace her. Graciously she received them and allowed them to know when they were dismissed.

'It's a very peculiar programme. Almost as if he's bending over backwards not to show off what he can really do.'

'Yes, it is an odd choice. But it's difficult to see how the Schumann, for instance, could be improved.'

'I've always loved the Schumann.'

She yawned to disguise something, he was sure. 'The Field's a boring bit of trivia,' she said.

'Yet he brought something to it. A kind of rural innocence.'

She opened her eyes wide. 'Are you saying, Theo, that this is a new, improved Jethro? I don't know that I could forgive you. . . . Oh! There's Bryce Morrison.'

He laughed. 'I wouldn't dare. I'm only saying it's a delicate, sensitive performance . . . so far.'

'Even introverted?'

'Possibly.'

'Hm,' she said. 'I didn't think the audience went overboard.'

'They're not warmed up yet. You wait.'

'It's Jethro who isn't warmed up.'

'Oh well,' Theo said. 'It'll be interesting to see what the critics think.'

'Will it?' she asked. And then, 'He's not happy,' she added.

Theo looked at her, unsure what next.

'Of course you know they're living in Barnes now.'

He nodded, although he was uncertain how much he was supposed to know about Jethro's new life.

'Some people like Barnes,' she said.

He put his head on one side and nodded sagely.

'Do you see him?' she asked sharply.

Confused, he spread his hands with what he hoped was a reassuring gesture. 'Seldom,' he said. 'Very seldom.' In fact, he had been drinking with Jethro only last week and found him sombre over the Californian plonk, not particularly communicative, but he had put that down to the coming recital.

'Here's Arthur,' announced Kitty, as though that were the end of that. 'Hello, darling Arthur. Where's Irene?'

'In the ladies.' Arthur kissed her. 'You're looking very beautiful.'

'Do you know that woman has had the effrontery to come?' Kitty said.

The men glanced at each other.

'Tell me, you two dear men, what is it he sees in her?'

'Always impossible to know what people . . .' mumbled Arthur.

'Ah. Here's Irene.'

The two women kissed.

'Very subtle and sensitive performance,' said Irene.

John Sorensen joined the group, stood by until Kitty caught his eyes, took his hand and pressed it to her cheek. 'Dear John,' she said. The others were introduced. 'Jethro and John sometimes have a duo,' she told them.

'I like it,' he said. 'Jethro is in a very quiet mood. It's nice.'

'Don't congratulate me. It has nothing to do with me, nothing at all.' Kitty unwound a black chiffon scarf from around her neck. 'Whew, it's hot!' She looked languid. 'Here's my golden boy! They let him out to come and hear his father – or maybe it was for my sake. His house master is enormously compassionate.'

9

'I see we have *The Times* here.' John jerked his head discreetly in the direction of the critic, who was standing alone the other side of the foyer.

'When, if not this afternoon?' said Irene.

Antony shook hands with the men and was kissed by Irene.

'We're just saying what a thoughtful performance your papa's treating us to tonight,' said Irene, and the boy, smiling politely, nodded.

'Though it's a good thing we have the Mussorgsky *Pictures* to leaven the second half, perhaps,' she concluded.

'I should think so!' Kitty looked around the foyer. 'Thank God that woman seems to be staying in her seat during the interval.'

'Shows some delicacy, at any rate,' suggested Theo.

'Delicacy!' exploded Kitty.

'Discretion,' amended Arthur.

Tatiana separated herself from the Alerick/Sally/Bridget/Nina group and joined her mother. Theo kissed her first, then the others. John didn't kiss her.

'I think Daddy's gone bananas,' she said. 'This isn't the kind of programme you play for a South Bank Sunday afternoon. And he's playing as if it's in the music room at home, for himself and a few cronies. His following won't like it. I thought they were lukewarm. The *Guardian* looks bored. I'm surprised Roger didn't have something to say about it.'

'You know your father wouldn't take any notice of Roger.'

'Well if he doesn't, he ought to. A good agent ought to be able to have some say if he thinks the pianist's lost his senses.'

'You know perfectly well what Jethro's reaction would be, darling, if Roger started telling him what to play!'

'By the way,' asked Irene, 'is Roger here?'

'Of course he's here.'

'It's just I haven't seen him.'

'I think he's stayed in the auditorium,' said John. 'It occurred to me he might be a little afraid Paula might go round to see Jethro and upset him.'

Kitty laid a hand on John's arm. 'How very tactful of you, John dear. How well put. You're sure you didn't mean he might have been afraid I would?' For once, her eyes were laughing.

'Or both of you together!' roared Arthur.

Irene looked at him coldly. 'I don't think that's at all funny, Arthur,' she said.

The alarm rang and they drifted back, Irene and Kitty walking together.

'You've lost weight,' said Irene.

'Are you surprised?'

'Have you done it purposely?'

Kitty gave her a look. 'No, I haven't, Irene dear. I don't need to. I have lost weight consistently since Jethro left.'

Irene put a hand on her arm.

John walked beside Tatiana. 'I want you' he whispered.

'Sh,' she said.

Paula Kingston sat in her seat throughout the interval. To go out there and mingle with the audience, perhaps even to overhear appraisal or criticism of Jethro's performance, would have been a refinement of torture for her.

She would have preferred not to have come at all, although that would have been unthinkable.

'I don't mind whether you come or not,' Jethro had said. Which was a royal command.

Anyway, twisting the rings on her fingers at home (not yet a wedding ring, thanks to the woman Ekaterina) and imagining something going wrong, would have been even worse. Would she ever become sufficiently relaxed on these occasions to enjoy them? She doubted it. She could not imagine that a time could ever come when she would be able to eat the day of a recital, or sit here in a concert hall without this nausea of fear creeping through her entrails.

'I must say,' Jethro always complained. 'It isn't flattering. What the hell do you think I'm going to do?'

'Nothing. I mean, everything.' She would try to smile convincingly. 'I know you'll be marvellous.'

'How would you know? You're tone deaf.'

'True,' she would say, cheerfully enough. It had never come between them.

She just wanted the whole thing to be over. She looked forward now, during the interval, to the moment when they could walk away together from the artists' door, leaving this place and all these people behind them. Then home, and the comfort of his enclosing arms.

Although God knew what kind of a mood he might be in when it was over. You could never tell. Sometimes he would distance himself even from her after a concert, because he was irreconciled to the performance he had given, convinced it was in no way worthy of him; but however critical he might be of his own final performance, he seemed confident that nobody else would or could have played the work better or even half so well. Except, perhaps, Michelangeli. Or possibly Gilels. He seldom went to other people's recitals, but those two, occasionally Brendel, he would attend, sitting quietly among the audience, escaping people he knew in the interval, silent on the way home, driving at such times, she often felt, 'without due care and attention'. After recitals such as these he would indulge in a burst of concentrated practice, often working until very late at night, which called forth the most appalling hostility from neighbours who seemed quite unmoved that they lived next door to a genius. Once, when he was at the piano at 7 a.m. on a Saturday morning before a Sunday afternoon recital, they called the police.

His anger then would be unrestrained and anything that got in the way, such as herself, would suffer. She realised that Kitty, too, must have suffered. She had aligned herself with an excessively difficult man, but never did she regret their liaison. Never did she relax her quiet antipathy to Ekaterina, whom now she saw out of the corner of her eye, returning to her seat accompanied by her three handsome children. She recognised the woman saying goodbye to her at the end of the row. Irene Heygate. A violinist. She and her husband lived in Kentish Town and were among the Mannings' oldest friends, yet they had been very civilised when Jethro insisted she meet them. She had felt astonishingly awkward, afraid on the one hand of her own aggressive feelings and on the other of being ingratiating; and it had been good that she had measured up to the occasion.

'Good girl,' Jethro had said, patting her bottom as they had climbed into their car somewhere in a dark, narrow street in Covent Garden after a post-performance dinner with the

Heygates. 'A-plus!' It had been an evening off, sitting beside Jethro in the stalls circle listening to Verdi. On her other side Arthur had sat, close enough for her to hear him grinding his teeth. She often wondered how Irene bore it.

She closed her eyes and tried to imagine what he might be feeling now, alone in the Green Room, waiting for the second half. He would be sitting on the floor as he liked best, with his back up hard against the wall. Bits of carpet would cling to his trousers when he stood up. He called it meditating. On one terrible occasion, very soon after he had left his family and come to live with her, she had crept in during the interval to be with him, and been appalled at the passion of his reaction. She had backed out, shaking, and been too upset even to return to her seat. She had stood just outside the doors, listening to the second half then, leaning against the wall for support, wondering whether she had lost him for good.

And yet, when it was all over, on the way home, he had never even referred to it. He appeared to have forgotten it had ever happened. And she – unlike the Kitty woman, it seemed – learned quickly.

Oh God – she thought – if only he would come on. If only he would begin. Once he started to play she always felt immediately better, the confidence pouring back into her veins. Once she heard those first notes, saw the assurance of the concentrated body, the perfect tone swelling from the instrument and felt, telepathically, the rapt attention of his audience, her fears melted away. And then all she could feel was awe that anyone could do this, be this, bring this right here into the clinical hall with its black seating and its bare platform, its stark, empty concrete box up there – and above all, the man to whom she was now so knotted in the bond of love. It wasn't only in concert halls she experienced this sensation of awe, gratitude – even more she felt it in the house, while he was practising. When she worked quietly in her studio, hearing him in the room beyond the kitchen on that great black Steinway which had taken up almost all the space in her own living room and meant half her old furniture had gone to be stored . . . then she was fulfilled. For this she would accept days of semi-silence, dark withdrawn moods and bursts of manic energy.

13

Why did he not come on? Was he not well? Was he capable of real nerves? She thought not, but now as she sat thinking about Jethro she wondered how well even she knew him. She had heard some people in the row just in front of hers saying that they thought the first half had been a bit peculiar, that he had not projected. She supposed she understood what they meant, but not being musically sophisticated, it was difficult for her to judge. It made her angry they should find anything critical to say. But perhaps that was stupid. Jethro always said he didn't mind her ignorance.It meant she didn't say idiotic things afterwards like half the morons who came clambering round the Green Room after the recital – or, even worse, the critics. It was certainly a very gentle programme, but haunting in a way. Her mind had been full of landscape images, woodlands, blue butterflies over downland, night skies. They were the kind of pieces she liked best, really, not too much noise and violence. Those Prokofiev War Sonatas he loved to play left her exhausted, spent, racked, full of nightmare visions of tanks carving their way across corn land, of bells tolling over the steppes for the dead and dying, of skeletons and skulls lying in rutted mud and snow. Jethro teased her about the way such sounds evoked places and pictures for her as if it were all programme music; but she couldn't help it, and this was the only way she had as yet learned to listen.

No doubt the woman Kitty with her music college background listened on a different level. But it hadn't kept Jethro by her side or in her bed.

If he would just come on.

She hoped he was not feeling unwell. He worried about his health, and she never took it very seriously, realising that before a recital he was simply finding something to worry about. Perhaps it was her imagination, but it seemed to her that it was getting worse. He made such a fuss about whether he was going to catch a cold or a virus from somebody that now they seldom went out in case he might be subjected to infection, and with the number of engagements he had nowadays there was always something important coming up. If she had been his wife she might have spoken to Roger Dilke, his agent, about whether he ought to ease up a little, but as yet she had no status. Anyway, Dilke always made her nervous. She blushed with guilt when she saw him although he behaved pleasantly enough and had never, to her knowledge, made any moral judgements. And she doubted whether he could have done much. Jethro was an artist who had to be kept busy. Allow him too much time to think and he could begin to imagine that he was losing his grasp or that the public were falling out of love with him. Dilke no doubt knew what he was doing.

But please, Jethro, come on.

Now her eyes were open and focussed on the platform, smarting a little with the concentration. She ought to have brought her glasses, but vanity had prevented her, in front of all these people who knew him and knew Kitty and would be watching her.

Unlike Kitty, her idea of hell was personal publicity and when the Press had picked up what was happening in Jethro's marriage and descended with whoops of glee and telephoto lenses, she had wilted, retreating for a while to stay with her friend Anne, incognito.

'Kitty's looking peaky,' Irene leaned over and said to Arthur.

He yawned. 'I don't think so. She looks remarkably well to me.'

'There are circles under her eyes.'

'Too many late nights,' said Arthur. 'She's a beautiful woman. Probably much in demand now Jethro's not around.'

'It's going to be dreadful if Kitty and Paul both go round afterwards. What shall we do?'

'We can't cut Paula.'

'I wasn't suggesting we did,' Irene said. 'But it won't be pleasant. Kitty will think we ought to have nothing to do with her but frankly I'm not going to start taking sides. Jethro's just as much one's friend as Kitty. It could be so much easier if Kitty'd give him his divorce quickly and then they could marry and everything'd be above board and official.'

'I don't think that would make it any easier for us.'

'I feel sorry for Paula,' Irene insisted.

'I reckon she can look after herself. She did well enough

before Jethro came along. Presumably.' Arthur crossed his legs, and settled back in this seat.

'Just because she's got a career doesn't mean she's emotionally secure.'

'It's more than Kitty ever had. Thanks to Jethro.'

'Kitty would never have made it as an actress. One has to accept that. She wasn't good enough. She knew it, too. She couldn't really cope with the life. Too highly strung.'

Arthur shrugged, then turned as Jethro strode on to the platform to a flurry of applause, not deafening but substantial. The audience were expectant of the second half.

He stood awkwardly for a moment by the piano, not sitting. He seemed to hang over and then to straighten to his normal stance.

Paula sent him a small prayer across the heads in front of her. It might have made him angry to have her invoking God, but he was not to know.

'What in heaven's name is he going to do now?' demanded Irene.

'I have decided,' he said, in his very soft voice and the audience bent forward to hear him, 'to make a slight change in the second half of my programme . . .'

'He must have been out of his mind!' Arthur and Irene rose from their seats after Jethro's final Scriabin Sonata.

'Yes, it isn't like him to refuse an encore,' said Arthur.

'You know that wasn't what I meant. Changing the Mussorgsky for yet more Scriabin! I mean . . ! The Sixth Sonata, as if that wasn't enough . . . those late preludes, then the Album Leaves and then the Tenth! Of all things! I think he's really pushed his luck this time. What will the Press say? Just tell me that.'

'Why did he do that?' Bridget asked Alerick.

'Don't ask me. I expect he had some good reason.'

'I thought it was potty,' said Sally. 'A little of that late Scriabin goes a long way, but to do that to an audience. . . . And choosing those two sonatas out of all the ones he might have. . . . Even if he were going to play two Scriabin Sonatas and that's odd enough, why *those* two?'

16

They shuffled their way down the gangway.

'Are we going to go round?' asked Sally. 'Or is it a bit difficult to know what to say?'

'I am,' Alerick replied. 'I don't know about you two.'

'I'd love to meet him.' Bridget always 'went round' whether she knew the performer or not. She said they were always so glazed afterwards that they'd never remember whether you were a friend or they'd never met you.

'Honestly,' said Sally, 'I don't quite know what I'm going to say.'

'I wouldn't imagine,' Alerick retorted, 'it's going to make a world-shattering difference to him what you say.'

Kitty and her children joined the queue in the narrow passage backstage, which led to the Green Room.

'Ah . . .' said Theo, sliding in beside her.

'Did you think,' asked Kitty, 'that I wouldn't be brave enough to come round and see my own husband after his recital?'

'I would always think you brave enough for anything, my dear.'

Kitty was silent.

'Did you approve?' he asked.

'Of his changing the Mussorgsky? No. Of course not. I thought it was absolutely extraordinary. I can't imagine what's got into him. I'm only so worried the Press will be very unkind.'

'You couldn't really fault the playing. Only the balance of the programme. I don't know . . .'

'It just wasn't a concert performance,' said Kitty. 'That woman must have had some sinister influence on him and I'm . . . oh . . . Theo . . .' She tugged at his sleeve.

'It is natural she would come round after,' he said gently.

'I don't think it's natural at all.'

'Shall we leave, Mummy?' asked Antony.

'Absolutely not, darling. Nobody's going to push me out and stop me from seeing your father now – certainly not that fat cow.'

'She's in quiet good shape considering her age,' said Nina. 'You can't really call her fat.'

'Do you not think perhaps Antony's right, Ma?' suggested Tatiana.

Kitty put her chin up and turned away her face from her family. To Theo, she said, 'They're taking for ever opening the door.'

Indeed, it was true. People were beginning to get restless, shifting from one leg to another, yawning, leaning against the wall. Up in the main vestibule beyond the auditorium, the door-keepers were sweeping out the last of the audience and soon it would be impossible to escape that way and pick up a parked coat.

'You're tall, Theo,' she said irritably. 'Can you see any sign of Roger?'

'Aye,' he replied. 'He's up at the front of the queue.'

'Well, why's he not opening the door and letting us in? People are getting restive.'

'Do you want me to ask him?'

'If you can get through the crush, yes. But . . .'

Theo began to push, saying 'Excuse me'. People looked at him with curiosity and faint aggression, but he smiled and said, 'I'm so sorry, sorry, just trying . . .'

Paula stood well behind the Mannings in the queue, where the people were thinning out right back in the auditorium where suddenly the lights were switched off. She did so pray that Kitty and Co. would have given their congratulations and passed on and out of the Green Room before she reached it. Thus she was certainly not hurrying. There was nothing she wanted less than a confrontation with so many of his friends present, his and Kitty's friends, at a time when both he and even she herself would be feeling emotionally drained. Not that you could ever be quite sure with Jethro. Reaction could suddenly turn round in reverse and he could be very extrovert, excited, still borne along by his own power, not yet deflated. With Jethro you never knew quite which way the cat would jump.

She couldn't risk being too late into the Green Room or he would think she hadn't come, or had funked coming round now; but she was in no hurry to be among the first.

But now, to her horror, she saw Roger Dilke waving at her from the Green Room door. Waving and smiling tensely, beckoning. She smiled back and shrugged her shoulders, looking, she hoped, sympathetic but non-committal.

18

'Paula,' he called right down the queue. 'Paula – could you come?'

She knew she was flushing from the collar bone upwards as she was forced to make her way up the queue, asking people to excuse her, passing the Heygates and John Sorensen and so many others. Irene put a friendly hand on her shoulder. Arthur said, 'Hello there.' And then she had no alternative but to pass Kitty and her children, Kitty freezing, cutting her, looking away; the girls plainly very uncomfortable and hostile. Only the boy had she never met, and he looked bewildered, as though he had no idea what was going on, which indeed he hadn't. Away at school he had been sheltered from more than the girls, the female part of the family drawing in to protect him from the more overt pains of the family break-up than they were able to side-step themselves.

At last she reached Roger, who seemed to be in frantic consultation with two other men, one of them the bearded man she had seen Kitty talking to ahead in the queue.

Roger Dilke dropped his voice and took her aside so that they could not be heard by the people waiting at the front of the queue.

'The door's locked,' he said.

She stared at him, uncomprehending.

'I don't know what we ought to do. He seems to have locked it.'

'Why?' she asked stupidly.

'I've no idea.' He was harassed to extremity. 'I can't understand it. I've never known him do so before. He always asks to have people kept at bay for a few minutes, so he can mop his face and have a quick wash and a drink, but this has been ten minutes.'

'Have you knocked?'

'Naturally.'

She knocked softly herself. Quietly she called through the door, 'Jethro.' She waited. The people in the van of the queue had stopped talking, and she was aware that everyone must be able to hear her. But there was no answer from within. She turned to Roger. He bit his lip and raised his shoulders. She could see a muscle twitching in his cheek. 'Jethro,' she said again, but by now you could have heard a pin drop along the passage and her voice could be heard clearly. 'The door seems to be locked. It's Paula, darling. Can you unlock the door?'

A man in a dark suit appeared from just behind Roger, Theo, John Sorensen and herself. He had a key, and put it in the lock, but shook his head.

'The key's in the other side,' he said. 'I'll go round the other way.'

Paula felt sick.

Kitty held tightly to Nina's hand, so that her nails dug into the girl's palm. Tatiana looked scared. Then suddenly Kitty burst down the queue, pushing her way through with no ceremony until she was standing beside Theo and the others. She ignored Paula.

'What's the matter?'

'I think he's locked the door by accident and left the key in the lock,' said Theo. 'He's probably just having a quick pee and couldn't hear us . . .'

'Of course he could hear,' said Kitty. 'What the hell's happened?'

For the first time her eyes met Paula's and it was a moment before both women looked away. It was the first occasion, during their few brief and hostile encounters, that there had been any communication between them, any real meeting, however fleeting, since Jethro had left Kitty.

'That man's gone round,' said Paula.

After what seemed to be an eternity the key was turned in the lock the other side of the door. The door opened and the man in the dark suit stood the other side. He shook his head.

Kitty burst through into the empty room.

'He isn't here,' said the man. 'He seems to have gone.'

Chapter Two

John Sorensen walked back with the Mannings to their car. Kitty strode along on her stilettos, jabbing them into Waterloo Bridge like weapons. She walked some paces ahead of the others, who made no attempt to keep up with her. Nobody felt very communicative.

Antony, unsure what all the fuss was about, thought his father might merely have been bored by the prospect of the whole pantomine. In a way he didn't blame him, although that didn't exonerate such behaviour, and he found it an arrogant thing to do, to rush off and leave a queue of friends and family and fans and sycophants standing in a poky passage. It was the kind of thing Father was capable of doing. He, Antony, would never behave like that. In any language it was bad manners, and Antony set a good deal of store by good manners, if good manners were what he took them to be, which was not to discomfort anybody else.

Jethro always seemed to believe that if he put himself out to please other people too much, he diminished his own strength, but Antony, having as a child watched a lot of vigour expended by both his parents in 'preserving their own integrity', and 'not allowing other people to erode their energy,' had come to the conclusion they were burning up more vitality in self-protection than would ever have been spent in giving freely. Antony, amiable, nobody's fool, had already learned to make his way in life by opposing 'head-on' only those things he could not possibly avoid any other way. If really pushed, he would dig his heels in, because, like all the Mannings, he could be obdurate. But he would always weigh up a cause carefully before deciding to take a stance; and in his opinion, it was a lot more trouble to have to explain this little breach of behaviour away afterwards than simply to have stood there in the Green Room for half an hour shaking hands with well-wishers and saying 'Thank you.'

He was, of course, like the rest of the party marching across the bridge after Kitty, quite sure that Jethro, irresponsible and self-indulgent as always, had simply locked the door to give himself time, let himself out by the back, and driven home, with little or no thought for his own family, for Paula, for anyone else at all. There he was probably back at the keyboard with a cup of sweet tea on the floor waiting to be kicked over, frowning and working over the things he'd not been satisfied with tonight, and disregarding the neighbours banging on the wall from next door.

Now, watching his mother's black legs in brisk, angry motion along the pavement, watching John – short and fat, an improbably unromantic figure for a cellist who could make such swooning sounds – padding along between Nina and Tattie, obviously hoping for and expecting a lift, he felt detached from them all, tolerant, but unmoved. They seemed to have little to do with him. Now it slightly shocked him that he could be so detached, he who had idiolised his father, craved scraps of attention thrown down like gristly lumps of meat from the table for the dogs, wept inconsolably at fifteen years old when, after a row which literally shattered glass, Jethro had simply upped and gone.

Looking back, it seemed like another person who had suffered all this, flinched from the idea of another woman in his father's bed, planned ways to kill Paula, been taken back to school at the start of term red-eyed, swollen lidded, avoiding questions of concern from inquisitive boys or 'caring' masters. How he had lurched between a fierce protective feeling for Kitty his mother, an outrage that she should be so insulted, so wasted, and a distate that she seemed to be able to express her hurt so freely to others. He winced, standing by in the street, while she stood talking to her friends or emptied her psyche down the telephone.

Perhaps he had by now used up the store of sympathy and suffering. The well was dry. It felt false to try and whip up emotion where none flowed freely. He no longer minded whether Jethro lived in Loudoun Road or Barnes. He himself seemed to be at home less and less as new activities ate into the school holidays, sending him off climbing in Cumbria or digging in Crete; and the house had never been a tranquil place to live. Too much shouting. Too many telephones. When he was finished with school and, one hoped, Cambridge, he looked forward to a series of bachelor flats, increasing in comfort and quiet style as success came his way. He would like to be a merchant banker. He hated gritty haircord carpets and balding upholstery and cats moulting over everything and, if truth be told, that continual claim for attention made by the piano, all day every day. And Mother bothered far more about her own person than the house, which probably made sense, since she was not often at home.

In his flat he would entertain a series of nubile young women, all intelligent, rich, independent and ardent without being in the least clinging. He might have a spell living in an apartment of faded period charm just off the Etoile and meet women out of Colette. He had it all mapped out and at this moment, battling over Waterloo Bridge into a chill north-easterly, he managed to make it feel much more real than all this carry-on between his mother and father.

As he went, now and for the first time, he spared a thought for Paula. He wondered how she felt tonight. When Nina had pointed her out he had been surprised. For some reason she was not at all what he had expected. Like places when you finally arrive. Now he could not remember what it was she had looked like in his imagination. She was fairer, vaguer, more distracted-looking than any mental picture. She was not dressed in any way you could possibly remember, almost as though she wanted to be forgotten or lost in the crowd. She looked tired. Living with Father, she probably was. He couldn't hate her now. She had looked so scared, turning to catch Kitty's eye; there had been such dark circles under her eyes.

Kitty stopped at the dusty Citroën (it bored Kitty to take the car through the carwash), and fiddled around for the key. John, who was one of those people who had a gift for getting other people to do things they didn't necessarily want to do for his convenience, climbed into the back with Nina and Tattie. He looked like Paddington Bear wedged in between them.

For the briefest of moments, Tatiana dropped her head on his shoulder. Nina noticed, and sighed. John sensed, rather than heard the sigh and nudged her knee companionably. All her life, Nina had been sharing with Tatiana, but never, it seemed, on entirely equal terms. Tattie, the elder by twenty minutes, was a living proof of 'first come, first served'.

'I suppose you want me to drop you off in Highbury?' Kitty asked, scowling over her shoulder. It was entirely out of her way.

'Thanks a lot,' he said.

'Would you rather I drove, Mummy?' asked Nina, whose sense of duty overcame other inclinations, such as enjoying the warm and pressing pleasure of John's loaned thighs.

'No,' said Kitty.

The girls glanced at each other across John in the back and Kitty saw their faces in the mirror.

'You need have no fears,' she said, and jerked away, careering into the traffic and crossing lanes with no warning, in order to dive down into the tunnel under Aldwych. A chorus of hooting followed her, of which she appeared supremely unconscious.

As she came up into Kingsway she suddenly said, quite viciously, 'Silly cow!'

It was normally Jethro's prerogative to drive badly, but tonight she was establishing her right to express herself. In Theobalds Road she ignored a pedestrian crossing, leaving one frightened Arab supporting another who jumped out of her way. A nurse hurrying across with a cloak wrapped round her turned and scowled. She ignored a filter and sat waiting for the lights to change with a pile-up behind her, then overtook in a narrow street, turned left from the right-hand lane, cutting in on an elderly gentleman driving an elderly lady home from the Festival Hall, and shot across the lights several seconds after the amber had turned to red.

Her foot made pugnacious small stabs at the accelerator and when she braked they all shot forward. In the front, Antony, who was the only believer in the family, prayed, and the three in the back held hands tightly. John loosed his right hand and slipped that arm around Tatiana's waist. Nina looked out of the window.

Nobody spoke until they reached Upper Street.

'If she encourages that kind of behaviour, she'll be his undoing,' Kitty spat out, drawing up at the lights with squealing brakes. 'And I shall waste no tears.'

'What makes you sure she does?' asked Tatiana, a little too reasonably.

When John got out in Highbury Hill, Nina spoke to Antony. 'You happy in the death seat or would you rather move back here with us?'

'He can stay where he is,' said Kitty. 'It makes me feel like a chauffeur with everyone in the back.'

Nina put out a hand and pressed Antony's shoulder, and he turned, smiled a little wanly, and said 'I'm OK.'

As Kitty crossed London to take them back from east to west, she sobered down. Perhaps it was because now there was no stranger in the car to impress and she could ease up. Half way down Camden Road she said, 'I'm so bloody tired,' and Nina quietly insisted that she pull in and allow her to take over the rest of the way back to St John's Wood.

'You're a silly old thing,' said Nina, adjusting the mirror, looking in it and pulling out with precision. 'Why do you give John and people like him lifts when it means you have to go half across London to do so. He could perfectly well have gone by tube.'

Tattie gave her a quick look and said nothing. She was well aware of Nina's feelings. But there was nothing she could do about it, and instead she patted her mother's knee as Kitty came and flopped wearily in the back. Kitty said, 'I don't mind John. He's harmless.' It made Tattie smile just a little.

Thus they went home.

As they turned into Loudoun Road a thought suddenly crossed Kitty's mind, a thought that brought a momentary flicker of panic and triumph. But it was quite ill-founded. Jethro had not come home.

After a cheerless cup of tea in the Festival Hall café, Theo went to a favourite wine bar with Arthur and Irene.

'This place makes me feel a hundred and one,' said Irene. 'They're all so disgustingly young and horribly beautiful.'

'You don't feel some of it rubs off?' asked Theo.

They bought a bottle of Sauvignon and sat down among the foliage and youth and chatter to drink it.

'Hm. Not bad at all,' said Theo. 'Unassuming.'

A pianist in braces and a waistcoat was very relaxed at an upright on one of the lower levels, among the tables, offering Bogart nostalgia: 'As Time Goes By'. Theo went and bought him a glass of wine and put it on the piano. The young man looked up, smiled and nodded, continued playing, moving into 'The Way You Look Tonight', 'A Foggy Day', 'Goodnight, my Beautiful'.

Theo came back to the table.

'Well,' said Irene.

'Well,' said Theo and Arthur. They all three raised their glasses.

'A not unpleasant end to a slightly odd afternoon,' said Theo.

'We've just seen a display of unsurpassed . . . what would you call it, Theo?' asked Irene.

'Bad manners? Selfishness?' he suggested.

'Perhaps he really did feel he couldn't face any of us,' Arthur said, slowly.

'Oh lovely!' snorted Irene. 'Great! We're only the friends who've supported him and come trailing into or across London to his wretched concerts since he was a student. We always came, even when we lived in Southend, remember?'

'I suppose it's a strain, when one's been giving one's all . . .'

'Was he, though?'

'I . . . I'm not sure. What do you think, Theo?'

People often deferred to Theo, for a calm opinion.

He was watching the pianist whose sleeves were rolled up and upon whose arms lay the pale fuzz of hair blurring young, smooth, elastic skin. Theo sighed and turned back to his friends.

'I think . . . there was something very odd about Jethro tonight. I don't believe he cared a damn for anyone in that

26

hall, not for us, his old cronies and fellow students, not for his family, nor even his mistress, and certainly not for the great unknown public out there. I think he chose that programme for Jethro Manning and he was playing for Jethro Manning and then he simply went home. To bed, perhaps. And the fair Paula will find him there. I think it wasn't even a rude gesture. No, the more I think about it, the more sure I am we hardly existed for him tonight.'

'You make him sound round the twist.'

'Not at all. It's probably quite a sane way for a great artist to feel, and make no mistake, our Jethro is a great artist. Half the time we all debilitate ourselves pleasing other people. Maybe a man like that, in the final resort, owes it to his public *not* to.'

'I suppose that's a way of looking at it,' said Irene.

'After all, bear in mind the rough ride he's been having recently.'

'Kitty?'

'The first flush of that may be over. Yes, Kitty up to a point. But I was thinking more of the Press.'

'The Press worship the ground the man treads on – normally. Whether they will after tonight rests to be seen.'

'I'm not talking about *The Times* and the other two, my love. I'm talking about the ones *you* don't see – and not the reviews, either. They hounded him when he was breaking up with Kitty, if you remember.'

'That was actually Kitty's fault.'

'Doesn't matter whose fault it was, it must have been wearing. Having the *News of the World* reporter on your doorstep because your wife has been breaking bottles over your head and letting down all your tyres!'

'She didn't!'

'She did.'

'I really find it difficult to believe Kitty could ever behave like that,' said Arthur.

'Do you?' Theo asked Irene, and Irene, grinning, shook her head.

'I don't think Arthur here reads the Popular Press. No,' said Theo, 'quite seriously, I have it on good authority that Kitty actually rang the *People* and gave them an unsolicited story.'

Arthur looked distressed. 'You take my breath away,' he said.

'Hell hath no fury, etc. etc. Think of the Parkinson affair. An outraged lady will go to almost any lengths. Anyway, it was the way those two were used to living. They've always thrived on screaming matches and drama.'

'It would kill me,' said Arthur, sincerely.

Irene patted his hand. 'It may kill Paula in the end. I doubt if she's equipped to cope.'

'Maybe he won't fight with her,' suggested Arthur.

Irene looked indulgent. 'What a dear thing my husband is! But under it all, you know, Kitty'd have laid down her life for Jethro.'

'That may be putting it a little strongly,' Theo smiled gently.

'It's not *that* much of an exaggeration. Everything to do with our splendid Ekaterina and Jethro was larger than life. And Kitty knows no half measures. If she loves you she'd give you the skin off her back . . .'

'I wouldn't want it,' shuddered Arthur.

'I'm trying to say that she is generous to a fault – generous with her love, her sympathy, her time, her talents – and her money.'

'Which is one reason why, despite Jethro's success, they've seemed hard up all the years we've known them.'

Theo looked across and smiled at the pianist, who had stopped and was drinking the wine. A young man abruptly rose from a table of six companions, mixed sexes, carrying his stool under his bottom, and lined himself up beside the pianist who pulled down to the bass end to accommodate him. They started playing around together for a while, experimentally, extemporising, and then they launched into a full-scale impromptu jazz duet.

The bar fell silent for about three minutes. Then people began, more quietly than before, to talk again.

Theo turned back to the table.

'Good, aren't they,' commented Irene.

'I'm enjoying myself,' said Theo.

'And Jethro can go jump in the lake.'

'I hope he hasn't,' said Arthur suddenly.

28

Alerick, Sally and Bridget were sitting eating things with chips in the Film Theatre restaurant.

'I still can't get over it,' said Sally. 'It was an unspeakable thing to do.'

'You're so facile,' snapped Alerick.

'Just believe in normal standards of behaviour.'

'You haven't the remotest idea what it must be like to be a top international artist. The stress, the jetting, and then all this in his private life.'

'Bollocks,' said Sally. 'I know enough about prima donnas, don't I? Anyway, whose fault is it?'

Alerick ignored her. 'I reckon,' he said, 'that he knew he couldn't take a whole load of boring people trying to pretend they understood what he was doing.'

'Did you?'

'Did I what?'

'Understand what he was doing.'

'I think so.'

Sally raised an eyebrow. 'Lucky old you, brother dear.' She picked up a chip delicately in her fingers, dipped it into Alerick's tomato ketchup and ate it. 'I have to say I felt very sorry for Kitty.'

'I'm sorry for Nina and Tattie.' Now Bridget spoke up. Her chin was greasy. 'And Antony. They've had a horrible time for a year with all that in the papers on top of losing their father.'

'They haven't lost him!' said Alerick. 'You talk as though the man's dead!'

Paula simply went home alone.

She was rather surprised to find the car keys, when she had been able to get into the Green Room, on the top of the practice piano, left there with no note from Jethro and no indication what she was meant to do. Also on the piano was the scruffy old notebook in which he often wrote addresses, shopping lists and odd thoughts about his music. She pocketed this, and took the keys.

On the side table stood a dozen bottles of Decanter Red and Decanter White, bought by her from the Wine Society on special offer when they had closed the line. Unopened. Trays of glasses still turned upside down. He hadn't even opened a bottle for a quick swig himself.

Presumably he had walked out and taken a cab home.

She extricated herself from all these people, muttered a word to Roger Dilke, who looked pale and tired, glanced away from Kitty who by now was holding court, and left, finding the car where he always left it in the car park. She had come on after him by tube to the Embankment and walked over Hungerford Bridge, which for some reason she always found a calming experience. It had something to do with the muddy, swirling waters of the Thames below and the certain knowledge that, whatever happened in life, she was not the kind of person to throw herself into that.

She drove home to Barnes in driving rain. Whirr-whirr-whirr went the windscreen wipers.

'You look lousy,' said Nina to Tatiana in the bathroom as she emerged from under the shower, tearing off her bath-cap.

'I feel lousy. I think I've been cooking something up all day. Maybe I've got some virus. Everyone in that place was coughing and spluttering this afternoon. Everyone's got something.'

'Stay at home tomorrow,' suggested Nina.

Tatiana groaned. 'I can't. I'm so busy. It's all very well for you.'

'As it happens I'm working tomorrow. I've got a studio booking first thing.'

'Anything nice?'

'Adaptation. E. M. Forster. I'm playing Jacky in *Howard's End.*'

'Who's Jacky ?'

'You're illiterate. Honestly, you really do look grisly. Hadn't you better take your temperature?'

'I never take my temperature.'

Nina smiled. 'Not exactly Daddy's daughter, are you?'

'Maybe I'm reacting. Stop fussing me. I'm OK.'

Chapter Three

No lights lit inside the house, nor curtains drawn. The garage doors swinging and banging, unbolted presumably from when Jethro had taken the car out earlier. Paula's ginger Persian sat on the steps inside the porch, under the unlit, mock Art-Deco lamp.

Next door, the curtains were drawn, sloppily, chinks of light visible. She could hear studio laughter from their television, her own house silent as the tomb.

She turned the key and opened the door. A circular from a firm touting for antique silver and jewellery fell to the floor. Mechanically, she picked it up and put it on the hall table in the dark, feeling for the light. The hall sprang to life, unlovely thirties staircase with its square, boxed-in bend, incongruously elegant satinwood table Paula had inherited from her grandmother, and some of Paula's own landscapes on the walls.

The cat stalked up the stairs.

For a moment she stood, then walked around the ground floor drawing curtains and turning on lights. The house made no effort to greet her. Instead it was surly, as though it had been brooding like a hostile child, whose parent was late home. 'It's nothing to me whether you've come home,' it seemed to be saying.

Paula had this childish relationship with the house. She felt it disapproved of her and Jethro. It had been left to her by her Aunt Virginia, her mother's sister, and the fabric of the building, bricks and mortar and woodwork, seemed to have absorbed something of Virginia herself, a lady disappointed in marriage when her own husband ran off with a dull girl thirty years his junior, whom he had met when performing a Rattigan play with the local amateur dramatic society. For the remainder of her life, Aunt Virginia had held strong and articulate views about 'other women'. Sometimes, Paula felt she had cheated Aunt Virginia who would now, were she able, revoke her will, take the house back, and throw Paula and her lover out into the street.

Now she went into the kitchen, half hoping to see signs of Jethro in the comforting, familiar havoc he always left behind wherever he had made any contact with food. Cake crumbs under the table, bread crumbs on the butter, milk bottle with the top off, coffee rings on polished surfaces and fat splayed and sprayed all over the cooker, tacky to touch and rancid to the nose. But all was as she had left it five hours before, cheerlessly clean, swept and crumbless.

She felt as though there was a hole where her heart ought to have been. She felt like one of those eerie modern sculptures in parks and public gardens, a woman shape with the centre carved right out and gone. A stone woman to stare at and through, set on a plinth in a lawn surrounded by beds of ericas.

If Jethro were the kind of man to go drinking with the boys he might have been out drinking with the boys, but he was not. He had a few friends, most of whom he neglected shamefully with no excuse other than that he hadn't time to do two things at once and playing the piano was a full-time occupation; yet – and this was something that constantly surprised her – his friends remained loyal, extremely tolerant. He could misuse, even abuse them; he never answered letters, made telephone calls, sent cards or thanked anybody for anything; and still they stood on the sidelines, quietly getting on with their own lives and pleased enough to accept the odd lollipop that came their way if and when he actually bumped into them.

Jethro seemed able to pick up the threads of an ancient friendship as though he had seen the person a week before, and he never had any hesitation in using the people he liked. He would never have used anyone whom he did not. Thus, if he wanted a bed for the night from somebody he had not seen or contacted for five years, he would simply ask for it. As he said, if often saved him a hotel bill.

But she could think of nobody he would consciously have sought out this evening, after a South Bank recital, especially when he had gone to such lengths to avoid meeting any of his friends afterwards.

Paula made herself a pot of tea and allowed it to go cold. She could not escape from the one persistent thought which had hammered into her mind from the moment she had pulled into the drive and realised he was not here. If he had not come to *this* home, he must have gone to the other. The thought of that made her frozen with impotent anger and despair. For the past few weeks she had known they had not really been relating on anything more than the most superficial of levels; eating, sleeping and making love together but hardly talking at all. She had allowed it to happen, partly because she was mature enough, pragmatic enough to know that with Jethro she would only keep him so long as she gave him exactly what he needed when he needed it, and that for some strange reason she couldn't grasp he transparently did not need close contact at the moment: and partly because it was Hobson's Choice. Jethro was and always had been the one who influenced states of mind in their household. It might not have been like that with Ekaterina; but then that, possibly, was why he had left her. Could it be that tonight, after that strange, introverted performance, he had simply turned round and retreated into the past? Had he run away because he could not face her? It was possibly the way he would react to an emotional crisis. He would defend it, deny any question of cowardice, make it sound almost a virtue to be so protective to his own creative energy. Self-conservation was something Jethro talked about with no hint of shame.

He must have gone back to that woman.

Paula was sure that, if he had, Kitty had not known it at the Queen Elizabeth Hall. Not even she could have put up quite so convincing a demonstration of frustration, confusion and concern. Could she? There had been a moment when the two of them, she and his wife, had seemed almost to meet, a contact of eye and heart, or was it mind? Difficult to say. Simultaneously, they had realised (Paula was sure Kitty had realised too) that this was not something to encourage; that naked hatred was far easier to deal with than anything verging upon sympathy, which must be repelled before it had time to take root. Mutual understanding, however scanty, could make for a very messy situation.

No, nothing had been planned between them, Paula was as sure of that as she could be sure of anything. If Jethro had run back to Loudoun Road (loathsome words) he had given his wife no warning and she would arrive home to find . . .

Paula buried her face in her hands. Then, quickly, with a kind of tense vigour, she rose and paraded right round the house, from room to room, as though searching for any sign of him. Upstairs she marched, knowing she would find nothing, into their bedroom, the room in which Aunt Virginia, as recently as three years ago, had lain under her cellular blankets and mauve nylon fitted sheets, alone, deserted in the big bed she had also bequeathed to Paula. Glancing down at it as she drew the curtains, Paula avoided thinking that it looked as though tonight she, too, would be sleeping there alone. She had done so before, many times, but they had been times when Jethro was away on tour, flying home tomorrow or the next day. It had never been for long enough for the other side of the bed to lose his special scent.

Something made her look under his pillow.

His pyjamas had gone. Only a clean white hanky remained, still folded. She held it to her cheek. Now she wept, sitting on the edge of the bed, rocking, her own arms wrapped tightly round herself. But it was a silent weeping. She could not possibly have faced the sound of her own distress. The tears rolled unrestrained. And with half an ear she still heard the television next door, hymns, *Songs of Praise*, Christians with clear faces raised to the cameras in a parish church. The people next door never went to church, she knew. But they seldom turned the television off.

She pulled the wastepaper basket towards her and emptied it on to the bed, scrabbling through the paper and tissues and cotton wool balls soaked with cleansing milk as though to find some clue; and all the while the tears running soundlessly down her cheeks. She had no idea what she was looking for, a letter, some piece of evidence, any kind of communication from Ekaterina, or even from one of his children. Or anyone

34

else? That was an entirely new thought. Was it even possible there could be a third woman involved? She dismissed the idea almost immediately, telling herself that he had no time to see a 'mistress' (and now, entirely subjective in her wracked state, the singular irony of the use of that word never even struck her) in his crowded life. Yet as she demolished that unlikely scenario, the new, uneasy thought sprang up, fully armed – that Jethro had plenty of time, in aircraft, at terminals, on trains. Wherever he moved there were women, admiring, ministering, listening, being instructed, smoothing out the wrinkles of his life. Sometimes even Jethro must have time to kill in foreign cities, between flights.

After all, he had found time to meet her, right here in London, sitting on a seat in the Courtauld Institute staring at a Ben Nicholson, shortly after the photographic session in Loudoun Road. They had both been rather taken aback at being brought face to face again so soon. It seemed like fate, he said grandly, after. She didn't think in such terms. Then he had found time for all that had followed, confronting her aggressively with all the paintings and places and books and even thoughts with which she felt most at home, uprooting them for her, making her see them afresh, blasting anything that smacked of security. Because Jethro was an iconoclast about almost everything except music. In music he had so many sacred cows she hardly knew how to steer a safe path through them without being kicked or butted.

Their first quarrel had been about Saint-Saëns. 'But I know nothing about the wretched man,' she had wailed.

'Then why utter such idiocies,' he had shouted at her, storming out of the room to thunder Chopin études on the piano.

Later he had come suddenly into her study, put his arms around her and said, 'What a waste of a bloody row!' She had looked at him amazed for a moment and then laughed. 'It wasn't my row,' she had said, ill-advisedly, and then it had damn nearly begun again. Since then she had grown wiser, accepting any olive leaf that dropped from the branch.

Some of the friends she had known when first she began to get involved with Jethro had thought she must be mad to fall in love with such a man, and assumed it was merely for the prestige of having a celebrated lover. They were of course entirely wrong, but it was difficult to explain Jethro to anyone who was not able to experience him on the same terms, and that was something she could hardly want or encourage, and so she lost her friends. It was really far simpler. But it meant that now she had very few. And even those were inclined to be astringent with her. They would make unsympathetic shoulders were Jethro now to return to his wife.

The telephone rang and she jumped to answer it at the bedside, drying her eyes with a corner of the duvet cover as though she were visible to Jethro, whom she knew, at once, it would be. She must never let him know she had been crying. He would have walked along the river from the concert hall. He could have reached Tower Bridge or Hammersmith Bridge or any old bridge you liked to mention by now and this would be him ringing to tell her to get the car out and come and collect him. She felt quite ill with relief until she heard Roger Dilke's voice asking whether she had any news of Jethro and then she felt even iller, although in a ghastly way it was almost a relief to talk to someone, even though that someone sounded, if anything, more distraught than herself. Jethro was, he reminded her, playing in Manchester tomorrow night and Hamburg the following week. As he talked she began to feel there was a note of accusation in his voice, as though she personally had mislaid Jethro and could be held responsible. She put an edge in her own. But Roger was too fretful to hear it and after about ten minutes of surmising and guessing and verbal wringing of hands she pointed out that if by any chance Jethro was trying to ring her he wouldn't be able to get through. That dealt with Roger. After she had put down the receiver she realised that she had never asked him whether he had yet telephoned Ekaterina. But she was glad she had not.

She made herself an omelette because she thought food might stabilise her, but was quite unable to eat it. By now new thoughts were parading through her brain, new questions, the most pressing of which was, should she phone Ekaterina herself? Simply demand to speak to him, insist upon an explanation. At any rate Kitty could not, would not want to deny it were he there. She would be exploding with triumph.

To ring her would be to play into her hand. It would be immensely humiliating. In fact the whole idea was untenable, out of the question, she wondered how she could ever had dreamed it up. Unless, of course, he was not there. If he was not there, then Kitty, she supposed, must imagine he was now safely back here in the Barnes house, either with his feet up watching some lunatic television show for mindless viewers (the only kind of thing he would ever watch) or else pounding the guts out of the piano as a reaction to the restraint and strangeness of his afternoon's playing.

But he must be with Kitty.

And if that was who he wanted, where he wanted to be, there was nothing she could do. She would never resort to the tactics of hysteria as Kitty herself had done. It would exhaust her, make her ashamed, drive him further away. No, if he had gone back to Kitty there was only one way to play her own cards, and that was to wait, to lie low, to make him wonder why she was not making any effort to get him back. She must allow Kitty to burn out his whim, this nostalgia trip upon which he was obviously set, while she went to ground; she must wait for them to start to quarrel again, for Kitty to demand the impossible, to throw her tantrums. And Jethro, the vainest man she knew, would find it unbearable that she should accept his loss. He would refuse even to believe in it. Within a week he would be back, hammering at the door, shouting to know why it was she loved him no more.

She would have the lock changed. She would throw his shirts and suits from the window into the rose bed below. She would fling his bow ties upon the thorns, impale his socks. She went to his wardrobe, threw the doors open and stared, trying to assess what had gone, what remained. Most of it was still there. She could not really see what was missing, except, oddly, an old pair of corduroy trousers, a sweater or two, some brown shoes, a few shirts, one rather shapeless suit she had been trying to persuade him to throw away. And of course the outfit in which he had played. Wherever he was now, he would be wearing that, presumably, since he had not left it here.

But surely there had not been time for him to come home, change and pick up these things. He must have gone to the Hall packed and prepared.

Would Kitty, stiff with arrogance, send for the rest of his wardrobe? Would she come herself, or send the girls, or a friend? Or even hire someone? Paula would put nothing past her. One thing was sure. He wouldn't come himself, not until he wanted 'out' of Loudoun Road. He didn't have that kind of courage.

She went to the telephone again, laid her hand upon the receiver, took it away and drove to Loudoun Road instead. Before she left she set the instrument to take recorded messages.

By now it was later than she had realised, but she was not tired at all. A new energy fired her, driving her forward to do battle with him and Kitty. She would tell him that as far as she was concerned she never wished to see him again and that he had twenty-four hours to collect all his chattels before she gave them to Oxfam. She would tell him that he was giving Roger Dilke nervous convulsions but that as far as she herself was concerned she didn't care a damn whether he went to Manchester or Hamburg or what or where, that she was having her locks changed and if ever she caught him on her property again she would dial 999.

By the time she was on Westway she discovered she was talking to herself.

Loudoun Road was full of cars and she was unable to find a place to park near the house, so she had to walk some way along the pavement before she came to it. Kitty's car was outside, with its residents' parking permit in the windscreen. Quietly she walked past it. Yet her heart was beating as though she had been running.

She stopped at the gate and looked up the steps to the porch. The house was unlit except for one upstairs room. She stood with her hand on the gate.

'They're up there together,' she thought. 'He's with her now. The great reconciliation.'

She felt Aunt Virginia close to her shoulder and shrugged her off, although she could not bring herself to climb the steps.

For some little time she stood there watching the house with its dead windows, only the muted light behind the drawn curtains in the bedroom. Then a car came hurtling at speed down the road past her, engine roaring, no silencer, radio blaring and window open. As it passed, the curtain upstairs was drawn aside for a moment and it was possible to see right into the lighted room. At the window, holding the curtain, stood Nina. Not Kitty. Nina looked back over her shoulder and seemed to be saying something to somebody. Tatiana came to the window. Paula moved quickly behind a bush of speckled laurel until the curtain had been closed again and the two girls were back in the room.

Now another light illuminated the kitchen downstairs and she saw Kitty in a dressing gown move into the brightness, take an electric kettle, fill it at the sink and plug it in. She stood by it, waiting for the water to boil before making a pot of tea. She held the pot in her hand. It struck Paula that she looked beyond tiredness. Her shoulders seemed to sag and, believing herself unseen, her back slumped, forming what Aunt Virginia had always called a 'widow's hump'. The dressing gown was a dark colour, severe in cut, shabby, and in a moment of vision Paula understood that it must be one of Jethro's old, cast-off garments. It was tied at the waist with a length of gold chain.

Kitty made her tea and sat at a table to drink it. For quite some time Paula watched her thus, until at last she crept out from the screen of laurel and up across the patch of waterlogged grass in front of the house. If anybody came to a window again they would be able to see her, but she minded not at all now. Danger fortified her as alcohol might have done. Stepping on to the flower bed beneath the kitchen window she cracked a fallen twig and for a moment or two she froze. She thought Kitty raised her head for a second – but perhaps she was wrong. Her medium heels sank deep into the soil, well watered not only by days of continual rain, but also by Ekaterina's lavatory cistern overflow which had for months spouted a jet of water into the flower bed from the first floor unless the last person to pull the plug pushed down the ball valve with a sharp, authoritative shove. Antony always did so, but was not here often.

Shivering, she stood and watched Kitty, who wrapped her hands around her mug and seemed lost in reverie. It occurred to Paula uncomfortably that she did look human, even vulnerable. The kitchen was not clean. There were dishes stacked high on the draining board and a tall binette seemed to be overflowing, the lid propped up with paper refuse, a discarded Weetabix packet sticking drunkenly out, next to an orange juice carton. On the wall behind the table at which Kitty sat was a notice board of cork, to which a variety of family memoranda – playbills, addresses, timetables and notes to the milkman – were pinned with big-headed coloured tin-tacks. From one such poster Jethro's face stared moodily out from under the raised piano lid. It gave Paula a very strange feeling to see it thus, for that particular picture had, as it happened, been taken by her.

It was one Kitty had commissioned her to come in and take at a time when she, Kitty, was scolding that it was high time he had some new publicity stills done. Paula had met her at a reception given by the Tourist Board of some South American State, and Kitty had pounced upon her with trusting enthusiasm over a glass of nasty, acid, cheap champagne. She could still recall the solid lump lodged somewhere in her gullet as she had lain in bed that night, alone in the house so recently vacated by Aunt Virginia, now interred under a mound of nemesia which, having been her favourite flower, Paula had faithfully planted above her remains although, in fact, she found them rather tiresome little plants.

Kitty had fallen upon Paula, who was happy to be rescued because she was being pursued by a very self-confident Nigerian with a shining hot face, who was pressing her to leave the reception with him in favour of the National Film Theatre.

'What a blissful little man!' Kitty had said, as she steered her away over to Jethro. 'Have I torn you away?'

'Not really.'

'They can be a bit overwhelming,' Kitty had suggested.

'A bit,' Paula had said faintly.

It was irony now, standing heel-deep in squelching flowerbed, that had it not been for Jethro – who had now met her, quiet and apparently brooding about some recital just past or some recital imminent, and been informed by his wife that this was the *marvellous* photographer she had just discovered, and who was going to take a new set of pictures of him at home, at the piano – they might even have been

40

friends. Kitty had been dressed entirely in a scarlet, fringed shawl, with peacock blue stockings and scarlet high-heeled sandals, and Paula had thought she seemed rather fun, although possibly in small doses. Paula had listened, apparently attentively, to everything Kitty had said, smiling with her warm, gentle, brown eyes, and had thought her very '*sympathique*'. Kitty had told Jethro so afterwards in bed. What a joke! Now she called them spaniel's eyes. And of course she had never known that most of Paula's concentration had in fact been fixed upon the bubbles of steel in her chest and a determination not to throw up on the bronze and gold sculptured carpet or be caught by the Nigerian again.

And so Paula, telephoned and reminded by Kitty, had come to the house to photograph Jethro. Kitty, having made the arrangement, forgot and went out. Jethro continued practising while the door bell rang and it was not until Nina had come home, slamming her car door and the garden gate and running up the steps, that she had been found, waiting patiently in the seat in the porch.

Poor Kitty. When she came home to find the photographer up to her ears in lights and wires she asked her to stay to supper. Nina cooked the meal, of course. Kitty seldom cooked and when she did people remembered the occasion with slight bewilderment.

'She came like a viper into our midst,' Kitty told everyone after. 'I opened the very doors of my home to her . . .'

Of course Paula had never meant it to happen, though. One didn't do that kind of thing. Aunt Virginia's niece most certainly didn't. She had never done it before.

Carefully, now, she stepped her way out of the mud, levering her heels out with suction, leaving Kitty still sitting at the kitchen table.

For a little while she sat in the car, acutely unhappy, confused and frightened. It looked as though Jethro was not there after all. Which left open still the question, with all its alarming potential. If not in Loudoun Road, where was he?

Slowly she drove away. Somewhere in the Paddington area she stopped, went into a call-box and lifted the receiver. To her surprise, in this cubicle whose floor was stuck with saturated paper and which stank of stale urine, the instrument had not been vandalised. She dialled, heard Kitty's voice answer, put in her coin. The pips continued and continued . . . and then cut off. With only one more ten-pence piece left in her purse, she began again. This time Kitty's voice came over fast, desperate, before the pips began.

'Jethro?'

There was just time for the one word. The pips pipped relentlessly until Paula hung up.

She imagined Kitty returning to the table and the cold tea. And now she knew Jethro was not there she drove home, having tried unsuccessfully to get the operator so that she could reverse the charge to her own number and see if he had come home. Her two futile calls to Kitty seemed to have been too much for the telephone and now it was dead.

She considered all manner of accidents. She wanted to ask someone when, at what point, one telephoned the police without making a total fool of oneself. She wanted a person to consult, to share this with, but one didn't telephone one's lapsed friends at (she stared at the car clock) one o'clock in the morning to ask what one ought to do if one's lover didn't come home to bed.

At one point she wanted Kitty. She wanted to be able to talk to Kitty and discuss what, together, they could or should do. It occurred to her now, and gave her no comfort, that if she thought she knew Jethro and the workings of his mind, Kitty knew them better. She felt immeasurably lonely and helpless. She could only pray that Jethro had come home.

She smiled at her own histrionic fears. She laughed away her waking nightmares. She spoke sternly to her alarmist self for stirring up such melodrama. Of course Jethro had come home. He would be irritable at her absence – or quite unaware of it in a fever of quiet concentration at the keyboard, oblivious to the neighbours' thumping.

She would probably hear the piano as she pulled into the drive. But she did not. For Jethro was not home.

Dismally she went to the phone to see if the answering machine had a message for her. Perhaps to say he had gone to Glasgow on impulse and wanted her to come for him because he had neither cash nor credit cards. She didn't stop to ask herself why Glasgow or how Glasgow. Anything seemed possible.

The machine had indeed recorded a message. The obscenity of it coming then, when she was so ill-prepared for such an invasion, the insinuating sickness of the unknown voice the other end, sent her huddling into the big chair in which, sometimes, she and Jethro cuddled of an evening if he felt so inclined, which he did less often now.

In the morning she woke, still in the chair, and dressed, the mud from Kitty's flower bed on the heels of her boots, to hear the dustcart grinding and clanking its way up the residential road, an orange monster. Mad dustmen flung the contents of her bin about the drive, scattering used Kleenex and dead tea bags to the wind, knocking the bin back on to the concrete pad after so that the lid rolled away right down the patio.

Monday morning. But this morning she had no heart to go out with rubber gloves and pick up the pieces as was her habit.

She merely went to the telephone, rang the company from whom she had rented the answering machine, and told them to take it away. She was told that the rental agreement had X months to run. She said she didn't care. She would pay them to take it away.

And then she telephoned the police.

Chapter Four

Kitty took herself up to bed very disconsolate and found she had forgotten to switch on her electric blanket. She huddled in bed wearing a sweater and rubbed her cold feet together. After all this time she was still unused to sleeping alone, but she had allowed no-one to come between the sheets and her own stubborn, tenacious insistence that this parting from Jethro was no more than his temporary aberration. One day he would leave that smug cow and come home. It was to underwrite her conviction that she had taken herself off to the Queen Elizabeth Hall today, with her (his) family in tow, to make her protest, albeit under cover of unshakeable loyalty.

And now she was smarting from humiliation yet again, although she was damned if she would let anyone know it. Not only had Jethro, presumably forewarned of her presence in the audience, rebuffed her cruelly by running away, but everyone had seen it. He had, in effect, cut her in that most public of all ways and places, and who could be to blame but his mistress, who must, she had now decided, have been party to the whole ridiculous episode. For a moment she had thought . . . been confused and misled by the other woman's act at the door of the Green Room . . . but she had to remember, she was dealing with somebody very devious. No doubt she had told Jethro during the interval that Kitty was in the audience. She would have convinced him that Kitty had come to make a scene and arranged for him to slip away; but if she had, something seemed to have misfired, for according to Roger he had not gone home at all. Roger's telephone call now had been the final unkind postscript to a beastly evening.

That Roger saw fit to blame her, Kitty, had wounded and left her smarting under a sense of injustice. It seemed she was to be insulted at every turn, misinterpreted and misused.

Tonight Roger had gone too far, raising his voice at her down the telephone, so tense and accusatory, suggesting it was she who had sent Jethro away 'on the run'. He had called her a 'liability'! He had dug up a lot of things from the past that anyone decent would have left buried. If he'd had the slightest shred of sensitivity he could have seen how she had taken herself in hand since those early days when she had been (perhaps) a little beyond herself, overwrought. But who would have been anything else? Only a vegetable. Her father, Nikolai, had always said, 'You're the race-horse breed, my darling, not like these English carthorses.' Considering her fine mettle, she had surprised herself by her control, by the way she allowed her intelligence to check her. She had been proud of herself tonight. But then, Roger had never liked her. She had always been aware of that.

So Jethro hadn't gone back to that creature in Barnes after all. That was the gist of it. He must have had enough. Perhaps things had not gone quite the way he had intended, and now where was he? In some hotel bedroom sleeping it off? Sitting in his car scowling at the river, mulling over tonight's performance before going home. Home? Which home? She turned her ear away from the pillow, alert for any sound in the lock downstairs. For as far as she knew he still had his front door key to this house. When he had returned it, she had posted it back to him in a registered envelope.

She lay listening right into the small hours of the morning, waiting for the sound of a car drawing up outside, for the slam of a car door, for the click of the garden gate, for the key in the lock. And at about six o'clock, one hour before Antony's alarm was set to wake him for his return to school, she fell asleep.

Antony brought her coffee and a bowl of muesli on a tray, drew the curtains and sat on the end of her bed while she adjusted herself to the cold morning light and the sound of the commuters dodging down Loudoun Road to escape the Finchley Road. He threw her a cushion from the chair and watched as she settled it behind her back. He poured her coffee from the pot and it smelled delicious. He took the pot away again for safety and placed it upon her dressing table, a walnut piece of faded elegance and considerable age, now generously stained with rings from mugs and glasses. Despite these, he placed it carefully upon the folded magazine section of the *Sunday Times*.

'This is luxury,' said Kitty.

He smiled at her.

'I wish I could keep you here.'

'You've got the girls,' he said.

'They don't spoil me.'

'They do. In their way. You're just used to them.'

She poured the milk and scattered sugar on her muesli.

'I've sugared it already,' he told her.

'What time have you got to be back?'

'For the last period before lunch.'

She wrinkled her nose.

He ran her bath.

And an hour later they were on the road, making for Godalming, fighting their way through traffic congestion. Westway, reduced to one lane by road works, was a long slow crawling queue, but Antony quietly kept his tension to himself, looking down at the network of damp streets below them and over at the windows of the high-rise blocks of flats whose inmates had this to look at every day and listen to all night.

'God!' he said. 'How lucky we are.'

She glanced at him.

'If one had to live there . . .' He waved a hand to their right. Soberly, he considered the possibility, allowing his imagination to create a new morning for himself. He conjured up a stained and stenching lift, thick with graffiti, shuddering its way down to street level and a greasy, litter-infested forecourt. A school full of hostile, indifferent children and beaten, soured teachers. Kitty was unable to make the jump of imagination. Unlike her son, whose conscience involved him in a number of social projects instigated by the Church and contacts made at school, she found it impossible, really, to conceive a way of life very different from her own.

'Give them cake!' Jethro had sometimes mocked. But he

46

was hardly better himself, finding it difficult to relate to or even believe in people who were musically uneducated, or even appreciative but naïve. Until he had fallen in love with Paula, that is. If fall in love was what he had done. He found it quite hard to allow for vast millions whose lives ran along perfectly smoothly untouched by the world of music, musicians, concerts and recording. When reminded of the fact, he supposed they must exist, but the concept held no reality for him, in much the same way that yachtsmen find it inconceivable there might be those who would not want a boat if they could have one, or animal lovers can credit animal haters, or those who are numerate can tolerate those who become confused and sick at the sight of a column of figures.

Now Kitty circumvented Shepherd's Bush and Hammersmith at last, knocking nobody off his bicycle, and then they were driving across Barnes Common. As they passed the road which led to Paula's road she wavered, stopped, then suddenly and shriekingly reversed, causing the drivers behind her to sound their horns and swear. She turned right and right again and drove slowly past the house. Antony was silent. He was now aware where his father lived; this kind of exercise distressed and irritated him, but he knew better than to try and control his mother.

'There!' she said.

'Roger rang this morning before you woke,' Antony told her.

'So he said. I rang him while you were getting your things together. Apparently your father never went back to that woman last night and if he gets no news by lunch-time he wants me to ring around a few people. Of course, Jethro may go straight up to Manchester. He's playing there tonight, it seems. But I'd have thought he'll want to spend the morning with his own piano, knowing him.'

Antony wanted to say something like, 'I always think the house seems strange without the big Steinway,' but he held back. It was something best left unsaid, although they were both, presumably, thinking the same thing.

All the way out along the Esher by-pass Kitty talked to Antony of his father. And herself. She spoke of them together, romanticising a good deal and telling him stories he

47

already knew. He reckoned she knew he knew it all, but that it was in some way necessary for her to repeat herself, that the act of articulating events past gave her a kind of hold on them, security of a sort. Perhaps a hold, too, still, upon his father. So he listened, or appeared to listen, permitting her plenty of space, allowing his own mind to wander, to wool-gather, to make plans for the week ahead.

He enjoyed school now. He had enjoyed it before, but not in the same way, for it was only since he had been a Specialist that he had begun to acquire some relish for the work itself. Now, post O-level, there seemed to be a purpose in it all, and the masters had his attention in a way which gratified them and was reflected in his reports. He liked too, the new freedoms. It was pleasant to be able to arrange his timetable around the fewer, more intensive commitments of A-level work, and he responded intelligently to the more liberal challenge of life as a First Year Specialist. He appreciated the fact that it had been possible to come home for his father's recital and to stay over until this morning, instead of having to rush back on Sunday night.

'How well do you remember the Twickenham house?' she was asking.

He replied, uncertain of what had gone before. He had missed the past three minutes or so. 'Oh, quite well, really.'

'You remember the little music room at the bottom of the garden?'

'Yes, of course.'

'It may have been the first mistake ever leaving that house,' she went on. 'Daddy used to take himself off to a bench in Marble Hill Park and stare for hours at the river when he was struggling with something new. I think he found it nourishing. The quiet. Things were never quite the same after we moved.'

She fell silent for a while and he allowed her to dream of Jethro, sitting on a bench in Marble Hill Park, scowling and throwing pebbles into the river. Jethro sitting alone and silent in the pub down by the waterside, looking into his pint.

'Sometimes the road used to flood at high tide,' she said.

'I remember.'

She laughed. 'Once he came back from one of his walks and found the water up and he just took off his sock and shoes and his trousers too and waded along in his underpants.'

'He could have rolled up his trousers,' said Antony.

'But this made more of an impression . . .'

Antony remembered with discomfort some of the occasions his father had 'made an impression'. There was the shaming afternoon when Nina had been practising her violin. She had been learning for about six months. Antony could recall it all, very clearly. It had made a deep impression upon him, and for a while after he had been loathe to go out of the front door for fear he might meet somebody who had seen it.

Jethro had burst into the bedroom where Nina had been practising and shouted, 'How long have you been learning that infernal instrument of torture, then?'

'Since November, Daddy,' she had answered, putting it down a shade anxiously.

'And how much do I pay for your lessons?'

'I'm not sure.'

He had called Kitty, who didn't seem to know either.

'I don't mind spending money,' he had said, 'but I do mind swilling it away. I could do better than that and I've never had a lesson in my life.'

'You couldn't, Daddy,' Nina had said, reviving. 'You don't understand. It's very difficult. You couldn't play it at all.'

'What d'you bet me?' He had snatched the violin and taking it out into the street outside he had thrown down on to the pavement a flat cap he had once bought in Norfolk. He tore it off the antlers of a stag in the hall as he passed. The thing was, he had put up an almost creditable performance, and with Nina beside him, wringing her hands and crying 'Don't Daddy, don't,' he had soon collected a small circle of friends and neighbours and afternoon strollers around him. Kitty had watched, in helpless laughter, from an upper window. An American tourist had actually put some silver in the cap.

'Do you remember the time when he took Nina's violin, and . . .' Kitty began.

'Yes,' said Antony

'We had some very happy times.'

He smiled at his mother with some tenderness, considered putting a hand over hers, which rested on the gear lever, but decided against.

For himself he had not enjoyed the Twickenham days enormously. Jethro had always seemed to be quarrelling with their neighbours and writing angry letters to people. Clearly Kitty had a vision of a rather different man.

'And there was the time he put a clothes line up across the road and made me play tennis with him right there in the street, because we couldn't get a court.'

'I thought it was to stop the traffic using our street,' said Antony.

'It may have been.' She was vague.

And soon, this way, they were at Charterhouse.

'I'm sure he's all right,' said Antony as he kissed his mother goodbye. 'I expect they'd had a row. You know Father.'

Kitty nodded curtly. She did not, as it happened, like the thought of Jethro quarrelling with Paula. It implied an intimacy as close as making love, as was her own prerogative.

'I expect he's back in Barnes by now.'

'Possibly.'

He watched her drive away. He felt affection and some measure of regret, regret that the adult world should be so incompetent when it came to happiness; but these empathetic feelings were soon dissolved as he hurried into his House to drop his night bag and pick up the work he must take into the history period, the last of the morning. By lunchtime he had quite forgotten the world he had left behind. Reality, for Antony, was where he was and what he was doing, and his sense of well-being or otherwise had to be ordered, at this stage in his life, by his own goals and achievements. He was extremely thankful he had not been sent to a London day school as had been mooted when he left Arnold House Preparatory School at the far end of Loudoun Road. It would have left him far too exposed to his home.

Before Kitty's car was quite out of sight he turned and went into his House. A little of the family superstition had rubbed off on him, against his better judgement, and he usually avoided hazards of fortune were he able, stepping on the outside of ladders and never letting a glass ring out. Jethro never forgot to count to twenty-seven before actually walking on the platform. Nina never turned a mattress on a Friday. Kitty never turned a mattress any day – she left it to others.

Natalia had always insisted dire things could happen if one watched anybody right out of sight. Natalia was Kitty's mother. Most people smiled when they thought of Natalia.

Tattie said all superstition was nonsense, indeed, immoral. She might well be right. But Tattie was a free spirit.

At this moment, Tattie, running a small temperature and flushed for that reason and others, was lying on the balding leopard rug before the open fire in Loudoun Road, watching the landscape made by the burning logs which Kitty still used in a smokeless zone regardless of authority. She had not gone into work after all. Nina had persuaded her.

John Sorensen was lying beside her, stroking the inside of her arm with his cellist's fingers. He stopped for a moment and she shifted position, like an irritated cat. 'Go on,' she said.

He laughed and stretched out his own arm over the rug, so that she settled comfortably within it; and he drew her close now, with her head on his well-upholstered chest. Upon him, she, too, rose and fell with his breathing.

'You are like a comfy old chair,' she told him sometimes. 'You absolutely spoil one for anyone else. Angular and exquisite young men, no hips and bums and pigeon-chested – ugh. How could I settle for anything like that? Not after you, so squashy and gorgeous and sexy. It just shows, looks are nothing.'

She nibbled his generous neck. He stroked her hair, separating strands of it.

'You'll catch my horrible disease,' she scolded. 'You ought not to have stayed. It's terribly irresponsible of you with your booking on Thursday. You'll just about be at the worst by then.'

'Nonsense,' he said. 'I don't catch things.'

'Father'd be gargling with whisky by now! That's his antidote. But then, you know what an awful old hypochondriac he is. He's always convinced all the bugs in the atmosphere are making a bee-line straight for him.'

'More to bother about than the odd snuffle,' said John, stroking the underside of her breast. 'You're not slimming, are you?'

51

'Am I too skinny for you?'

'Well, you can't afford to lose any.'

'We can't be two fat people cuddling together.'

'Why not?'

'I've often wondered,' she said, 'how a pianist would cope if he sneezed all over the keyboard in the middle of the cadenza.'

'But they never do, do they? Any more than my nose runs into my shirt front when I'm playing.'

'How do you explain that? It must happen sometimes.'

'Concentration.'

'You think concentration can actually stop you sneezing?'

'Certainly. Really busy people don't get ill, anyway.'

'What an arrogant thing to say! I'm busy!'

He laughed. 'Busy, but not presumably indispensable. When Nina rang, nobody insisted you came into Floral Street. They didn't say the place'd fall down without you.'

'They're too nice. Hey – do you suppose I've gone down with this from worry about Father?'

'Are you worried about him?'

'Well, it was a very funny way to behave.'

'Jethro's all right. Though I half wondered,' he said, 'whether I'd find him sitting on my doorstep when I got home last night.'

She raised herself on one elbow. 'Why would he do that?' she asked.

'It has been known.'

'When?'

'Oh – from time to time.'

'Just come to you? Simply arrived?'

'Mm-hm.'

'To stay?'

'For the odd night.'

'Having walked out on Paula?'

'Walked out's a heavy way of putting it. He always goes back.'

'Everything my father does is heavy. You know that. Do they row a lot?'

'Jethro rows with everybody, doesn't he?'

'Not with you.'

52

'Oh no. He says I'm just foam rubber. But I wouldn't have thought she gave much value back. She'd soak up anger like a sponge herself. Maybe she and I are a bit alike.'

'You! You're not serious!'

'Well, she's a funny sort of a girl for him to have got tied up with but people's sexual partners are a constant surprise. That kind of female would have infuriated him, I'd have thought.'

'But might suit you?' She moved away from his enclosing arm.

'Only in a certain mood,' he said. 'Not as a fixture.'

She rose and pulled on her skirt. Unperturbed, he lay and looked at her. 'I've ruffled your feathers,' he acknowledged.

'Yes,' she said, shortly.

'No woman,' he reflected, 'can ever accept that one might, from time to time, be capable of thinking another even mildly attractive.'

'Not that woman.' She made a face at herself in the looking glass above the fireplace, then turned and put a foot in his rotund stomach. 'What a silly little man you can be. Or is it not silliness at all? Is it maliciousness?'

'I'm not malicious. I couldn't be bothered to be. I simply forget, sometimes, what a child you are. You give this illusion of maturity – and then . . .'

'I'm a hell of a lot more mature than Mother.'

'True,' he acceded. 'That's not saying very much.'

She sneezed. 'But to expect me to find anything redeeming about Paula Kingston is going too far. Stupid, destructive bitch.'

He wrinkled his nose. 'Your lovely face is quite twisted, darling,' he said. 'It spoils you. Don't. I withdraw it. There is no mood in which I could be suited by Paula. Paula would quickly pall. Does that satisfy you?'

She shrugged and left the room. Later, she came back with a mug of tomato soup and knelt on the floor, handing it to him. He supped, while she held it.

'This is not Heinz,' he said.

'No, it's Nina's. It's made with spices and red wine.'

'Mm.'

'What an amazingly indolent man you are,' she said, wonderingly, and the way she said it, it seemed to be a compliment. When he had finished, she threw him his trousers and his sweater. 'I think you ought to be out of here before Kitty comes back. She won't want to find you littering up the place.'

'OK,' he said, amiably, getting dressed. After which, he opened his arms and asked, 'Are we friends again?'

She walked into them and laid her head on his chest once more. 'How could we be anything else,' she said, very softly, so he had to bend his head to hear. 'I love you, twit.'

'Mm?' he asked.

'It's not the kind of thing I repeat.' And now she extricated herself and, holding his hand, took him to the front door. There they kissed, just inside the closed door. Then Tatiana grabbed her own coat and they left the house together.

Kitty controlled her urge to stop at Paula's house on the return journey, and demand to see Jethro whom she, personally, was sure would by now be back at his piano before leaving for Manchester and another performance. She thought it most probable that Antony was right, that he and Paula had quarrelled, perhaps before the recital, and that he had punished her by storming off to a hotel bed. Were that the case, she would have expected his performance on Sunday to have thundered, been towering rather than meditative, but with Jethro one never knew how he would react.

A lassitude had descended upon her, now she had parted with her son. She had whipped herself up for the challenge of Jethro's recital, for any confrontation that might occur in the Green Room after it, but now the anti-climax of last night had played her out and she felt spent. Feeling her vitality to be her trump card, she had enough wit not to open herself to Jethro's critical eye when least able to compare favourably with his mistress. Natalia always said, 'Never allow anybody who matters to see you on an off day.' Kitty was today on an off day.

She would certainly have preferred Theo not to have been sitting in her Loudoun Road drawing room when she came home to fling herself down upon the sofa.

He was sitting in the big wing chair beside the grate, in

which the remains of a fire still smouldered.

'Who let you in?' she asked ungraciously, throwing a log upon the ash and kicking it. She picked up an empty mug, dirty with the remains of tomato soup, from the rug and put it on the mantelpiece.

'I did. You shouldn't leave your keys under the bay-tree tub. Any self-respecting burglar would think of it.'

'You take advantage of your grey hairs and my tolerance,' she said. 'Do you make a habit of breaking in and entering?'

'Not me,' he smiled, shaking his head. 'Whereas . . .'

'It would serve you right if I called the law.'

She kicked off her shoes and plumped up the sofa cushions beneath her head.

'However,' he said, 'as it happens . . .'

'I didn't want company,' she complained. 'I wanted to be alone. I'm worried about Jethro and I want to be allowed to worry in peace.'

'It was because of Jethro . . .'

'What's that you're trying to hide so ineffectually?' she demanded, pointing to something pink hidden rather badly beneath a cushion.

He brought out the day's *Financial Times*. She looked enquiring. 'Not nice?'

He simply handed it over and she read aloud.

'I imagine many among the audience in the Queen Elizabeth Hall at Sunday afternoon's recital by Jethro Manning will have been as astonished as I was by his apparent disregard for the conventions of concert planning. His last-minute substitution of late and difficult Scriabin for Mussorgsky's "Pictures at an Exhibition" put a bizarre seal on a recital programme which had already teetered on the verge of incomprehensibility.

'The first half was composed entirely of miniatures – Schumann's *Waldscenen*, three Field Nocturnes and three of Grieg's Lyric Pieces. Predictably, the result was a succession of exquisitely beautiful, delicately shaded watercolours. Mr Manning's pianistic control was remarkable in the enigmatic Schumann set, but both here and in the Field there was little tonal projection, the waywardness of the music inducing a kind of muted introspection in his playing.

'After the concentrated gloom of Scriabin's Sixth Sonata the vivid pictorialism of the Mussorgsky would have been a welcome contrast. However, Mr Manning chose instead to offer a further selection of late Scriabin. This was music of ever more esoteric appeal – the Opus 74 Preludes, Opus 65 Studies, and finally the Tenth Sonata. In these Mr Manning's mastery of the keyboard and of a seemingly endless range of pianissimos was never in doubt, but by the end of the afternoon one felt baffled by this display of wilful eccentricity from one of the leading virtuosos of our time.'

Kitty handed the paper back to Theo. 'All critics should be hung, drawn and quartered,' she said.

He read the review again, very slowly, to himself. 'One does have to admit, though . . .' he began.

'One doesn't have to admit anything.'

'But you yourself . . .'

'Jethro is a great artist.'

'They're not actually saying he isn't. Look, Kitty, you know perfectly well . . .'

'Do go and make me a cup of tea,' she said.

He obliged.

As he bent by the sofa to give it to her she sighed. 'I can't bring myself to ring that woman and find out if he's gone back to Barnes yet,' she pondered.

'I don't think he has.'

She raised an eyebrow.

'I think he's gone further afield.'

'Where?'

He shook his head. 'If I knew . . .'

'D'you think he's left her?' she asked. She had propped herself up on one elbow to drink the tea. 'You've made this far too strong,' she said.

He smiled. 'I wouldn't count on anything like that.'

'But something must have happened.' She tossed her head restlessly on the cushions, flopping back. 'I hate not knowing. Almost anything is all right if one knows.'

'Not *every*thing, surely?' He was sober.

'Are you trying to frighten me?'

'No.'

'Jethro's not the kind to do himself any damage.'

'I didn't say he had.'

'I wish Antony were here,' she said, suddenly. 'He's my favourite.'

'Nonsense, my dear. You're far too sensible to have favourites.'

'He's far too nice to be Jethro's son,' she said. 'Yet he is.'

'Maybe he's a changeling,' suggested Theo lightly.

For some inexplicable reason she burst into tears. Theo had never seen her cry. Few people had. It made her very angry now. Theo gave her his handkerchief.

'I hate Jethro!' she cried.

Theo waited patiently.

'I hate him. I detest his name. I wish I'd never met him.'

'Kitty. Is there anyone he might have gone to?'

She stopped crying. 'A woman?' she asked. 'Is that what you're saying?'

'Not necessarily. Just anyone.'

'Why couldn't he just have come back here? To me and the girls. This is his home. He knows that.'

'He's playing in Manchester tonight, isn't he?'

'How do you expect me to know about his engagements? I'm the last person to hear anything nowadays. Ask Paula.'

'I'm sure Dilke said he was.'

'Then Roger'll have the hotel.' Suddenly she was all relief. 'He's obviously gone up there. He'll have gone last night. He'll be practising in the hall. Where is it – Free Trade Hall?'

'Presumably.'

'Then that's the explanation. He always acts on impulse. He just drove straight up after the recital.'

'Not in his car.'

'Why not?'

'He left the keys for Paula on the Green Room piano, and she drove herself home, apparently.'

'But surely they've each got a car?'

'It seems not in action. He was using hers last night because his battery was dead. But she needed it for her work this morning so – very considerate for Jethro – he left it for her.'

'How do you know all this?'

'Dilke.'

For a moment she was silent. It disorientated her to consider domestic arrangements between Jethro and Paula. Then she said, 'So he'd have caught a train up north. It makes no difference.'

'Only he didn't.'

'Oh God!'

He looked at her, questioningly.

'Are you saying he's had an accident?' She began to rise from the sofa.

'No, no. Rest assured. That is, not as far as I know. And I would be the first to hear. You see Kitty, Jethro stole my car. Damn and blast his eyes.'

Chapter Five

Paula, who would have preferred to have stayed at home in case there should be any message from or about Jethro, was forced out of Aunt Virginia's nest by the vicissitudes of her profession for most of Monday.

She felt leaden with misery, stupid from lack of sleep and jittery with anxiety. Her limbs were stiff as posts from sitting up in the chair all night and her eyes felt blanketed, her throat raw. But there was no way she could stay by the telephone. Throughout the morning she was committed to taking pictures of the interior of a newly opened wine bar in Petersham; and for the afternoon she had a booking to take production stills during a rehearsal at a small Hampstead theatre. The two engagements were badly planned, in a sense, and meant she had to traverse London from the one to the other, but she had originally organised them so that she could end up in Hampstead where she was supping with a female friend. With Jethro booked in Manchester it had made sense to visit Anne in her Fitzjohn's Avenue flat, but now of course nobody even knew whether Jethro would be in Manchester at all. She was convinced he would. There was no way she could imagine his behaving in an unprofessional way. Last night he had been rude to his friends, and that was one thing, but those who knew him well understood he allowed nothing to come between himself and his performance; indeed, it was said by some that since leaving Kitty he seemed to be pushing himself even harder than ever. And that surprised those who had sometimes murmured that Kitty was the driving force, pressuring her husband into ever more concerts, ever more tours.

Some said she would kill him one day. Many people loved Kitty, but those who didn't, loathed her.

The Petersham engagement was frustrating from the start in that when she arrived, booked for ten-thirty, the place was still locked and there was no sign of life. Dark green cotton blinds decorated with gold champagne magnums were pulled down over the windows and the door too, although it was possible to see, by peering through cracks between the blinds and squatting down to peep through the letter-box, that there was a dim light on in the room within. She rattled the door handle, at first diffidently, after a while irritably. Then she went back to sit in the car with all her equipment, put her head back on the neck rest and, with her eyes closed, considered.

Wherever Jethro had gone, he had gone without the car. He had left the keys for her on the Green Room piano, remembering, presumably, that she would be needing the car on Monday, that her schedule depended upon mobility. This gesture of consideration moved her. It brought him close. She huddled into the driving seat. She ached for the man. Had he left her? Dully she blamed herself, although unclear for what. Living with him, had she changed, become less desirable, less lovable, less satisfying as friend and mistress? Did she bore him? She considered that possibility quite seriously, having slender confidence in her own entertainment value after one such as Kitty. It was true that recently he did seem to have retreated somewhat from her, but she had felt instinctively that it would, at such a time of pressures, be unwise to invade his space. Worries had beset him, with all this unpleasant business about him and Kitty in the gutter press. It amazed her that they should be so interested in the love life of a concert pianist, but Jethro had always been one with a catholic public image, particularly since the *Master Classes* when viewing figures had shown a surprising statistic among people who would not normally go to concerts. Some genius quality in the man attracted people of every kind to him. He professed not to be able to understand his charisma. And there had been that sour profile in one of the more reputable Sundays. He had insisted he didn't care a shit, but it had stung, she knew. Had he needed, then, something from her she had been unable to give? In giving him space, had she made a grave mistake?

The prospect of having to meet the two young men who ran the wine bar seemed daunting, let alone setting up her lighting and camera and producing something scintillating to enhance their image and celebrate their opening. She had met them only briefly on her introductory visit, while the shop was still being fitted, and even on such a cursory introduction she had recognised that they did not relate to her – nor she to them. Like many of their kind they possibly accepted women with more defined edges than herself, directive motherly women less tuned to masculine men. Whereas Paula, with her wide mouth and vague eyes, her air of having mislaid something a strong chap might be able to find for her, found that homosexuals frequently were on their guard against her.

Outside, the rain was now streaming down the car windows, and her breath had steamed up the inside so that she could see nothing. I could stay here – she thought – and never get out. Cocooned against brute actuality. Oh Jethro – where are you? Come back soon or in your absence I could dissolve and disappear, a vanishing reflection in a pool.

It had often seemed to her that she owed her existence to other people's awareness of her. She found the idea restful at times. At others it disturbed her. But with Jethro she had begun to feel substantial. Sometimes he would pinch her and make her squeal and then shout, 'You're here, you're here!' He used to say that he liked to pin her down like a butterfly. 'Rape, rape!' he would growl as he tethered her on Aunt Virginia's soft-piled, silky Chinese carpet until she was shaking with laughter, her eyes watering.

If Jethro never came back to her she would shrivel quietly and fade away and drop from the branch of life. She would die. She knew she would. Kitty would fly through pain and disaster, a Valkyrie bearing her hero away at the end. It was all right for Kitty. She was a survivor. Paula doubted whether she herself was.

She recalled the occasion when, returning from a demanding tour of Central Europe, some mechanical fault had meant that his aircraft sat on the hot tarmac at Bucharest for five hours, and then he had returned to find Heathrow on strike and himself diverted to Gatwick. Home at last he had discovered her in bed, sweaty and fretty with some peculiar,

61

low-key virus. When Paula was ill she never fought it, as Kitty would have done; instead she crawled away like a sick animal. Everything about her lost lustre.

She had left a note in the hall and taken herself off to the spare bedroom, so that there was no risk of her infecting him before his pending engagement in Hull at the end of the week. When she heard the door slam and his feet pace lightly up the stairs she had called out from behind the closed bedroom door, telling him what to take from the freezer. But he had burst in, sat on the bed, stroked her sticky hand and put a thermometer in her mouth, silencing her while he gave a blow-by-blow account of the journey home. He made her nearly choke with limp laughter, but pressed his finger upon her lips and shook his head, looking sternly at his watch until three minutes was up.

'I never did trust these three minutes,' he said, shaking it down.

'Am I dying?' she had asked, husky and hardly audible, but allowing her eyes to smile for him.

He had answered by opening the small zip bag he had flung on to the chair in the corner and bringing out a pair of scarlet, totally transparent knickers, very minimal, a black appliqué heart modestly veiling the crutch.

Weakly she had begun to giggle when he had pulled back the bedclothes, removed her warm brushed nylon nightie, put it in the wastepaper basket and slipped her legs through the briefs, pulling them over her thighs and standing back to examine them seriously.

'Mm,' he had said.

She had folded her arms behind her tangled, dandelion clock of a head and lain stretched out, smiled, then sighed and relaxed down into the pillow. He ruffled her hair and teased it into tiny plaits until she made small screams. Then he had brought the dressing-table mirror from across the room and held it above her; but she shielded her eyes with her arm and began to laugh, turning on to one hip and hiding the heart with a raised knee which quietly he removed.

He replaced the looking glass on the dressing table and took off his shoes.

Later she said, 'It can be quite nice being ill. Really.'

'Let's stay here tonight,' he had suggested.

'Why?'

'I don't know. Makes a change.'

'But its a single bed.'

'Makes it seem illicit,' he said. 'Gives me a frisson.'

'But we are illicit,' she had pointed out.

He didn't seem to be listening. 'At any rate, one doesn't feel the presence of dear Virginia here,' he said.

She pondered that while he was downstairs getting their supper, which he brought up on a tray and ate, sitting on the bed beside her. While he was in the kitchen she had taken the red transparency and put it in a drawer in their own room, together with all the other knickers he had brought her back from other tours. There were virginal white briefs from New York embroidered with pale blue tennis rackets, and a purple lace G-string from Paris. There were cream pure silk cami-knickers from Rome and black chiffon from Hamburg. But her favourite of all were from Carlisle – thick wincyette bloomers in an evil salmon pink, hot and heavy, mid-thigh caught with elastic. Jethro had buried his face in them and they had both laughed until Paula had hiccups.

In the drawer still lay two of Aunt Virginia's pot-pourri bags, scenting the treasures. She took them out and held them in the palm of her hand, closing her fingers over them until Jethro called that the fish fingers were getting cold.

Now, in Petersham, it seemed to have stopped raining. She wiped the steam from the car windows with her hand and through the hole she made looked at the telephone box down the road, a red wet shape looming. She went to put a call through to Roger Dilke's office.

All three of his lines were engaged. She stood, chilled in body and spirit, and tried repeatedly until she was able to get through.

The voice the other end belonged to Caroline, Roger's partner's secretary. Roger, she said, was in a meeting. Could she help?

Paula asked for Roger's own secretary, Tamsin. Tamsin, it seemed, was hurrying to Heathrow this morning with some tickets for Diana Casimir, the world-famous contralto on her way to Melbourne direct from her house in Great Missenden.

There had been problems surrounding La Casimir, whose teenage daughter had attacked the singer's twenty-three-year-old lover with a carving knife in the night and La Casimir had been distraught at the prospect of leaving the house. Normally speaking, of course, Mr Dilke himself would have gone to the airport to see her safely into her flight, but today, with all this business of Mr Manning, things were somewhat disrupted.

'But you said he's in a meeting,' insisted Paula.

There was a moment's pause on the line before Caroline said, 'I'll just see whether he's available for a moment.'

Paula waited, shivering. After what seemed to be a long time she heard Roger's voice.

'Yes? Have you any news?' he asked.

'No. Nothing. That's why I'm ringing you. I got on to the police.'

'I know. They've been on to me.'

The pips began to bleep and Paula searched desperately in her purse, found a ten pence and said, 'I'm calling from a box in Petersham. I haven't any more coins – could you call me back at this number if I run out . . .' And she gave him the number.

'Perhaps it was premature,' she suggested. 'Ringing the police.'

'I don't think so. There's rather a lot at stake.'

'Jethro would be very angry. That's what's been worrying me.'

'It is nothing,' said Roger coldly, 'to how angry I am with Jethro. And I doubt how much that's worrying him.'

'There must be an explanation we haven't thought of.'

'It will have to be a good one. If he lets them down in Manchester . . .'

'He won't.'

'You sound very certain.'

'Jethro's far too professional. It's unthinkable.'

'So what's your explanation?'

There was a hesitation before she had to admit, 'I haven't one. Maybe . . . maybe he just needed to be alone.'

'Hardly flattering.'

'I don't mind.'

64

'You seem extraordinarily forgiving, Paula, Or is this an act?'

'It's an act,' she admitted.

There was a pause. Then she added, 'Possibly we're worrying quite unnecessarily. He'll roll up after he's done Manchester. I'm sure he will.'

'If I were free I'd run up there myself this afternoon and make sure everything's all right, but Jethro isn't my only client you know.'

'Not the only one, but surely the most important?'

'That is not actually so.' Roger sounded icy. 'Perhaps you'd like to have a glance at our list of clients some time? Diana Casimir carries equal weight with anyone.'

'Yes, but you're packing her off to Melbourne today.'

'You seem to know all about our business, but there are others, although frankly I don't have the time today . . .'

The pips began again. 'Please ring back,' shouted Paula, and waited. She was faintly surprised when he did.

'What I'm trying to say,' she began quickly, 'is that one shouldn't assume great dramas simply because Jethro's gone away for a night.'

'Does he make a habit of it?'

'Well . . . not exactly, but . . .'

'Has he ever?'

'Well yes, but . . .'

'But what? I am very pressed, Paula.'

'In his own way he's quite considerate. I mean, he's always telephoned me from wherever he is and told me not to have hysterics.'

'Are you prone to hysterics?'

'Not at all! That's Kitty's prerogative. It's just his way of talking.'

'So you'd have expected him to have rung you by now?'

'Oh yes.'

'In the morning?'

'Any old time. He's done it at three in the morning on one occasion. He said he couldn't sleep without me and he was coming home for breakfast.'

'And might I ask where he'd been – where he was speaking from?'

65

'No,' said Paula.

Roger sighed. 'If I am to be honest,' he said, 'I would not be so concerned were it not that Jethro has been worrying me a little recently.'

'Has he?' she asked. She felt chilled.

'Haven't you? Been worried?'

'A bit. Possibly,' she admitted.

'He's been depressed.'

'He sometimes is depressed. I've learned not to take too much notice.'

'I have found it very difficult to know what's going on in his mind,' said Roger. He seemed to be feeling his way. 'He's been – inattentive. And Theo says . . .'

'What does Theo say?'

'He's been fussing about his hands. Complaining about some tingling sensation. Has he said anything to you?'

'Once or twice. But he's always been edgy about his hands.'

'Has it occurred to you to ring the place he was staying – when he rang you at three?' he enquired.

'I'm sorry,' she said. 'I can't do that.'

'Not even to establish everything's all right?'

'Sorry.'

'I see.'

'You probably know most of his friends. You may know more than I do.'

'You're very different from Kitty Manning,' he commented.

'I thought you realised that. Why especially?'

'She would ring anyone, anywhere, to find out he was OK and on his way to Manchester.'

'She might well, Why don't you ring her?'

'I have done. She's taken the boy down to Godalming, but I've left a list of possible numbers with Tatiana who's home sick, and she's been doing some telephoning. When Kitty gets back, she'll ring people too. It's a tedious business and very time-consuming. Meanwhile, I just have to wait until I hear something from Manchester and I can only pray it's reassuring news.'

'I think you're fussing,' she said, suddenly. 'Maybe you should take a holiday.' And she put down the receiver.

'Rude bitch,' Roger said to Caroline, as he went back to his own office. His partner, Philip Foster, was sitting in his stockinged feet smoking a pipe, his wet shoes propped up and drying before the open fire which was a pleasant and homely indulgence in the offices of Allen, Marvell and Dilke. He was reading his morning's correspondence through a cloud of smoke, the scent of which disguised his socks.

The office, a ground floor room in a double-fronted red-brick Victorian house in Ferncroft Avenue, NW3, was familial in its ambiance, cosy and informal, in no way suggestive of the passage of great people and famous names, not at all the kind of place the concert-going public might imagine. The house had once belonged to Charles Marvell, an old friend of Philip Foster's youth – and of Theo Bristol's, as well. He had left it to the firm, in the absence of any family.

Roger, a younger man than the others, had come in later, after Charles's death, at Philip's suggestion. Nobody knew or bothered much to enquire why Philip's own name was not joined with Allen (long since deceased), Marvell and Dilke. Roger and Philip today virtually ran the business, each with a young and lovely secretary drawn from the more promising sixth forms, while the accountant, Guy Knight, looked after the money-bags. A bright boy from a north-country grammar school, he always claimed he was there to add a bit of grit and nobody argued with him. It amused him to cling to the last vestige of his Bradford accent. And they all rubbed along very happily together.

Behind the house, in a large Hampstead garden secluded behind privet, there was a tennis court upon which the girls played during summer lunch-hours. In the winter they took hockey sticks on the heath and terrified anybody who came within ball distance. They were very jolly young women, as well as being beautiful. They thought Philip was sweet and could never be convinced otherwise, however loudly he shouted at them.

Roger seldom raised his voice, but today he did. Sitting down at the enormous desk which dominated the far side of the room, in a generous leather chair without one caster, he said, 'I dislike big artists excessively and everything and everybody that surrounds them.'

67

Philip looked up, putting his national-health spectacles on the end of his nose. 'But we surround them. Don't we?'

Roger sighed. 'I dislike their women. I dislike daughters who try to knife step-lovers, and I dislike hysterical wives, but at this moment I dislike mistresses more than any of them.'

'Paula Kingston?'

'Her. Yes, her.'

'Tiresome woman,' said Philip, returning to his papers.

'I wish,' said Roger, 'we could take only those artists who possess neither wives, mothers nor daughters.'

'Seconded.'

Caroline came in with coffee.

'I wonder if I ought to put off Vellaccio tonight and run up to Manchester,' pondered Roger.

'I wouldn't have thought so,' mumbled Philip. 'I'm sure it's not necessary. He'll turn up.'

'I wish I were so sure.' Roger paused. 'I suppose you wouldn't care to have a trip north?'

'You suppose right. Ugh. This one's got the sugar!'

Walking back to the car, Paula fell on the slippery pavement. A passing man in overalls picked her up and when he took her elbow she felt a tingle of comfort. He turned through noble gates into one of the Petersham grand houses, a Georgian pile of presence with an impressive portico. There were a number of them along this road and she wondered who would live in such places today, with the traffic oozing past, expelling fumes into the gracious swagged and tasselled curtains. As she turned the corner a squirrel shot across the road and was narrowly missed by a car. When she turned her face to the wine bar again she saw that the blinds had been pulled up at the windows and a bright light shone out into the gloomy street. She opened her car door, took out her photographic equipment, and crossed the road.

There was no doubt she felt very rattled. Talking to Roger Dilke had done her no good at all, and it worried her being out, away from the house today. There was no way Jethro could get in touch with her. Dislike Dilke as she did, she would have to telephone him again, because this would be the

68

only link with Jethro all day and all evening. Unless she rang Kitty. And that was unthinkable.

'I'm a pacific man by temperament,' said Theo, sitting in Roger's office while Roger sat, dialling Manchester numbers with the wrong end of his felt-tip pen. 'Why does Jethro have to make me angry?'

'Other people's feelings are not and never have been of the faintest interest to Jethro.' Roger put his finger on the plunger and began to dial again. 'This is nonsense. How can the hotel be unobtainable?' He held the instrument away from his ear.

'It gives me indigestion,' said Theo. 'Being angry.'

Roger slammed down the receiver, then picked it up again.

'There are times,' he muttered, 'when I wonder why I do this.'

'Let the girl get them,' suggested Theo. 'Why keep a dog and do your own barking?'

'Because quite honestly I feel too rattled to do anything useful with what's left of the afternoon. He's successfully managed to waste the best part of a day for me. Him – and Diana.'

'Ah! Diana! Do you think you're going to be able to keep the Press out of that one?'

'I'm doing my best, but nothing would ever surprise me. The daughter's quite capable of giving an interview to the *Sun*. Attention-getting. That's all it is.'

'Isn't that a little unfair?'

Roger shook his head and grinned. 'She's not her mother's daughter for nothing.'

Theo sighed. 'This love-hate relationship one has with musicians . . .'

'Love?' asked Roger. 'Since when love?'

'I think I used to feel a rough kind of affection for my clients, don't you know? In the days when I used to be involved with agenting.'

'You're just suffering from a nostalgic glow. You've forgotten. Performers are all the same. Either they need their egos bolstered up all the time to keep them going, or they're larger than life and crush everything else living in sight.'

69

'I suppose it would be different if one represented writers. Quiet, civilised-thinking sort of people.'

'Don't you believe it,' smiled Roger. 'People only want to write because they're self-engrossed. There's nothing to choose between them. Playrights, novelists, actors, singers, pianists. They're children, the whole lot of them.'

'You'll feel better tomorrow,' said Theo.

'And you? Will you? What about your car?'

'I suppose it depends on the state it comes back in,' mused Theo. 'Though it has been damned inconvenient.'

'You're a tolerant old bugger,' said Roger. 'Too tolerant, I think.'

'Oh no,' said Theo quietly. 'I've just got a long memory. Jethro has his redeeming side.'

Roger glanced at him, ignorant of what he could mean.

But Theo remembered. He remembered the time, long ago when he had taken to his bed for some months with a curious, unexplained bout of depression, never powerful enough to push him over the edge, yet sufficiently disturbing to bring about a crippling inertia. Friends had lost patience after a while, especially since Theo had refused to taken any advice, the most freely given of all bedside gifts. Only Jethro had come without advice, bearing, not grapes or sympathy, both of which turned Theo's stomach, nor trying to persuade him to get up and get dressed, but merely his own person. He seemed to have been content to lower his lean, stringy form down into the cane chair in Theo's bedroom and simply sit, more or less waiting for Theo to speak should he want to. Sometimes neither had spoken for a full hour. Jethro picked up any book that happened to be lying around, and frequently brought a child's comic which he would look through seriously and leave behind, lying on the chair, when he left. Once he was alone, Theo would get out of bed and take the *Beano* back to bed with him, whereas he flinched away from any book. It seemed to him, then, that Jethro was his only friend and afterwards, back in the world he had temporarily left, he marvelled at the perception of the man.

'Truly,' said Theo. 'You do him an injustice.'

Roger dialled the operator, who kept him waiting.

'What's the fair Paula really like?' enquired Theo, mildly bored.

70

'Peculiar,' said Roger. 'Hullo . . . hulloo . . .?'

'I'd have given him money if he'd asked for it,' said Theo. 'God knows I've done that often enough. But the car's a bloody nuisance, What sort of peculiar?'

'You shouldn't give him money,' said Roger. 'If I have to lend Jethro something every now and again out of the kitty, that's one thing, all part of the hazard of managing him; you're another matter. Oh – I think something's happening . . .'

'Lend?' Theo laughed very loudly. 'I don't lend. Certainly not to Jethro. If I feel so inclined – I give. Withhold or give.'

Roger held up a warning finger. His number was ringing.

'I suppose you can dock it the next . . .'

'Hullo,' said Roger. 'Reception, please.'

He drummed his fingers on the desk. Theo thumbed through a bound set of *Music and Musicians*.

'Could you tell me whether Mr Jethro Manning has registered at the hotel yet, please? Manning. Yes. For tonight. No, the booking was made by us, Allen Marvell and Dilke, Concert Agents. Yes, the reservation was made by us at least six weeks ago and my secretary confirmed it in writing.'

He waited, frowning. Caroline slipped in and put a folder of letters on the desk, before him, for him to sign. He never looked up at her.

'Ah – you've found it. Now could you tell me whether he has yet arrived at the hotel and registered?' Another pause. 'No? I see. Thank you.'

Roger put down the telephone. He took out a large hanky and blew his nose. 'If I weep don't think ill of me,' he said.

'Would he have arrived yet?' asked Theo.

'Yes.'

Theo had the feeling he was contributing nothing, and rose to go. However, Caroline came back with two chipped mugs of tea, so he glanced at Roger.

'Feel free,' said Roger.

'Four sugars,' said Theo. 'Suddenly I feel very old.' He sat down again and put the mug by his feet. 'Were it not that Jethro is rather special I would say it is simpler not to have friends. A little love, perhaps, from time to time, but friendship demands so much more.'

71

Roger stared through him. He was not listening.

'I am genuinely anxious about the dear man, you see,' he went on. 'I daresay you think I'm a sentimental old fool. Senile.'

'I should pick your friends more carefully were I you,' said Roger.

Theo sighed, deeply. 'He climbed in through my lavatory window, you know. He helped himself to my car keys and seventy-five pounds in cash from the wallet in my suede jacket hanging up in the wardrobe. I'm surprised he didn't take the jacket too. The car was out in the road with a flat tyre – do you know that – and he must have changed the wheel in the road. That was why I'd taken a cab to the South Bank. Flat tyre.'

'It surprises me,' said Roger drily, 'that he left a note. If he didn't want to be traced.'

'It was his way of doing things. "Taken your jallopy",' it said.

The telephone rang. The clock on the wall said four-thirty.

Theo could hear what the person the other end was saying. Quite distinctly. The voice was male, raised and anxious.

'Hello. This is The Hallé Concerts Society. I'm speaking from the Hall and we've got the tuner here, but Mr Manning hasn't arrived yet. Do you know what train he was catching or was he driving up?'

'He's . . . er . . . driving up,' said Roger faintly.

'It's half-past four. After.'

Roger took a gulp from his mug. 'Traffic, perhaps?'

'He's not contacted you or anything?'

'No. I'd hoped he . . .'

'Hoped?' The voice the other end sounded concerned.

'Well, maybe . . .'

'I've been on to the hotel where you said he was staying and he's not checked in there.'

'Can we give it a little . . . before we begin to . . .' Roger's voice began to sound strangled.

'We are getting a bit concerned. I know Mr Manning's familiar with the Hall and the height of the platform here, but naturally the tuner wants time to adjust anything he feels is necessary and we don't want to cut it too fine, do we?'

'I'm sure he's on his way.'

Someone laughed the other end. 'He'd better be,' they said. It was a joke.

'Ha-ha,' said Roger.

'If he's in any trouble you'd have thought he could have stopped off at a service area on the motorway and rung us – or you.'

'Yes indeed. Look. May I ring you back if I've heard nothing in an hour?'

'That's pushing it,' said the man in Manchester. 'We must open the doors at seven for seven-thirty. Some of the public arrive as early as half-past six.'

'OK,' said Roger, bravely. 'I'll be back to you in just forty-five minutes. Right?'

'Right,' said the voice doubtfully.

Roger stared across his desk at Theo. 'And now tell me what I do?' he asked.

Theo took out his hip flask.

From Petersham, mid-morning, an embarrassed Paula had rung the police and asked them to disregard her request for a search to be made for Jethro, so sure was she now that he would have gone straight up to Manchester. It disconcerted her that she now spoke to someone who seemed not to know about her early call, and that she was asked to give all the particulars again. Was Jethro thought to be at risk in any way, asked the officer to whom she spoke?

'At risk?'

'Yes, madam. Do you have any reason to suppose the gentleman to be under any kind of threat?'

'What kind of threat?'

'Kidnapping?' suggested the policeman.

'Good heavens, no. But he's a concert pianist. He just disappeared after his recital on the South Bank yesterday. It's not the kind of thing he would do.'

'I can quite see that, madam, but unless you had any substantial fears for his safety, we would not normally instigate a search at this point.'

'When would you?'

'The gentleman is in sound health?'

'Yes.'

'Not suffering from any depression or anything?'

'No. He's under pressure.'

'Aren't we all, madam!' said the officer sympathetically. 'I would suggest, then, that if he hasn't contacted you within a week – or been in touch with anybody else with whom you have contact . . .'

'A week!'

'Say six days, perhaps . . .'

'I don't believe you!'

'In the case of a small child, of course . . . or a very old person . . .'

'He's not a child. And he's not senile. He's a famous artist and he's been under considerable strain . . .'

'Maybe he decided to take a little break, madam.'

Paula drew in her breath.

He went on, 'Sometimes, you know, perhaps after some little marital disagreement, a husband or a wife or, if I may say, a friend, might go away for a night and we really could not and would not set up a search in such a case.'

'We didn't have a row,' she said.

'Ah,' said the policeman. He sounded comforting, understanding. 'I'm sure your "friend" will be in touch with you soon. Do you think' – he coughed – 'that he could have gone to stay with another friend, perhaps?'

She rang off. The conservation had unnerved her, although before she had made it she had been quite convinced that Jethro was quietly practising in the Free Trade Hall. It seemed much the most likely explanation that he had gone off without a thought for anyone but himself, his mind full of music. She wondered at herself for being so hysterical as to suppose he would have gone back to Kitty. He never mentioned Kitty. To the best of her knowledge he never gave her a thought, although occasionally he saw one of the girls. If one chose to share one's life with an artist, especially one of Jethro's calibre, one had to be prepared for a few small eccentricities.

She almost laughed with relief, talking herself into good sound sense, decided not to be intimidated by his temperament and, at a quarter to five, during a tea-break in the theatre, she made a telephone call to the Hallé Concerts Society in Manchester. She was going to ask if someone could get a message to Jethro Manning requesting him to telephone home after the performance tonight. Just that. She would not even refer to last night or the fright he had given her. She would be warm but undemanding when he rang back, as he liked her best, ask about the recital, say the bed felt cold without him. She would explain to Anne and hurry home to be in Barnes for the call. Her heart beat with decision, the relief of making the bridge, as she put the coins into the box, coins she had collected from the actors, whom she had told merely that her 'chap' was up north playing the piano. Certainly she was a little scared. The telephone stank of tobacco and stale breath and that turned her stomach somewhat: many people had, in their time, defaced the code-board behind it.

But the other end they told her that Jethro Manning had not arrived for his practice period, that he had not checked into his hotel and that they were waiting to hear from his agent within the next half hour. The woman to whom Paula spoke sounded distinctly harassed. She said that the tuner had been waiting for some time. Had she herself any light to throw upon things?

Alarmed, Paula showed her confusion. The woman in Manchester picked up vibrations fast enough and questioned Paula quickly about Jethro's movements during the day.

'I don't know,' admitted Paula. 'I thought he'd be with you by now.'

'What time did he leave?' asked the Hallé woman.

'I . . . I'm not sure.'

'Forgive me – I thought you – er – shared the same address.' It was tactfully put.

'Yes, but . . . he left last night you see.'

'Last night. But surely he had a South Bank recital yesterday?'

Then Paula fell apart. She needed to tell someone.

'You mean you never saw him again after he left the platform?'

'No. Yes. I mean I didn't. Nobody did.' Paula was trembling. One of the cast, passing the telephone, put a hand on her shoulder.

'He just walked out of the Green Room reception?'

'Yes. Well no. He never went to it. I mean, he wasn't there. He'd locked the door. When the man went round the other way he'd gone. He'd left me the car key and just gone. You see, he knew I needed the . . .'

'But why didn't Mr Dilke tell us this?'

'I don't know,' said Paula miserably.

'But it's extraordinary. I can't understand his not alerting us.'

'I think we all assumed he just wanted to be alone and had gone straight up north on the evening train.'

'But apparently Mr Dilke informed us that he was driving up.'

'I can't understand how that could be. He didn't have the car.'

There was a silence the other end.

'Does he often act so unpredictably?' asked the woman.

'Well . . . not really. A bit. Sometimes. He's a bit of a law unto himself.'

'I see.'

'You know what I mean.'

'I'm not sure I do.'

'But presumably you know Jethro?' asked Paula rather wildly.

'Not personally.' Another pause. 'Professionally. He's never done anything at all like this before.'

'I'm sure he'll still turn up.'

'He is leaving it,' said the Hallé lady, 'a little on the late side.' She was not warm. 'Do you suppose his wife would be able to help us rather more?'

'I can't see why she should,' protested Paula. 'They *are* separated.'

'Nevertheless, perhaps one should make contact with Mrs Manning. And I had better telephone Mr Dilke now. If you will excuse me, it would be better if I clear this line and lose no further time in trying to find out what has happened.'

'But . . .' began Paula.

'We do have an audience to consider, you know. And the Hall is fully booked. A recital by Mr Manning is something of an event. If you'll please forgive me now . . .'

And she hung up on Paula, who felt so upset by the whole

76

exchange that she had to put her head between her knees. A kind actor found her and brought her another cup of tea. To her humiliation she threw it up on the scuffed foyer carpet. The assistant stage manager put all her gear into her car which, she found, had a parking ticket on it.

She drove round the corner into the main flow of evening traffic and down the hill to Anne's flat, where Anne gave her a brandy and soda and sat down on a bean-bag to listen. The flat seemed to be full of exhausting young with yellow egg-white hair and black painted fingernails eating take-away kebabs. Two of them were Anne's children, quite unrecognisable from eighteen months ago when Paula had last seen them.

'They grow up so fast,' said Anne lovingly.

'Is that what it is?' asked Paula, wan. Unsteadily, she began to rise from the other bean-bag, where she had been put by Anne, since the young were sitting on all the chairs. 'I think perhaps I ought to go home, actually.'

'Nonsense,' said Anne. 'You look done in. I think you should stay the night.'

'I couldn't possibly. I must get back . . .'

'Why?'

'The telephone . . .'

'Better you stay here and ring the hotel when he gets back from the Hall, love. We'll tuck you up in Lynnie's bed.'

Paula looked around the throng with a mixture of alarm and awe to see which might be Lynnie.

'I'm going to the party,' said a girl with jet-black, lavatory-brush hair streaked grass green.

'But when you come home . . .'

'I shan't come home.' Lynnie took a mohair sweater off one of the chairs and put it round Paula's shoulders. 'You're shivering,' she said. 'You look awful!'

'Lynnie's going to be a nurse,' Anne told her when all the young people had gone off to the grumble and rumble of motor bikes, roaring down Fitzjohn's Avenue.

Paula felt she would be surprised at nothing today. And after a quiet supper of Greek lemon soup, trout and pine-apple slices zipped up with Kirsch, she gratefully allowed herself to be propelled towards Lynnie's bed.

'Jethro!' she suddenly remembered, padding about in one of

77

Anne's nighties and her own bare feet.

Anne gave her a sideways look. 'I rang the hotel when you were in the bath, I'm afraid. He never turned up.'

'Oh my God!' Paula sagged on to the kitchen stool and crumpled. Anne put an arm around her, led her back to bed, produced a sleeping pill and put a glass of water beside her.

'I never take things,' said Paula.

'Then it ought to knock you out all right,' Anne said. And it did.

When she awoke in the morning it took a little while before she realised where she was. There was an unfamiliar sound which, in time, she realised came from outside, a clop-clop, clattering up the hill. She drew aside the purple corduroy curtains and saw a procession of cavalry, one man to three horses, astride in the centre. Quietly, sitting straight in khaki, they rode, taking two or three minutes to pass. The officer who took up the rear looked up at her, standing there in Anne's nightie by the drawn curtain, and smiled. She raised a hand in greeting. The communication gave her a strange sense of warmth, of life.

For the Hallé Concerts Society management it was difficult to know what to do, since although Jethro had not turned up by six o'clock, they still had received no proper cancellation. In London, Roger quivered with tension and fury, snapping at Theo but refusing to let him leave the desk-side, while they, in Manchester, conferred a little grimly together. There was an air almost of wartime emergency as they discussed strategy, whether or not to ask the local radio stations to put out an announcement, but by the time they could be sure he was not honouring his booking it was already too late. However, once early concert-goers were arriving, the booking office tape announcing the recital had been changed to one explaining that, owing to unforeseen circumstances, Jethro Manning would be unable to play this evening, and that money would be refunded at the box office the following morning, or by postal application. As by this hour the banks were already closed and it was too late to arrange for a sufficient float to cover the reimbursing of ticket-holders, there was no alternative.

'Concert Cancelled' flashes were hastily pasted over the posters at the Free Trade Hall, and an announcement set up in the arcade outside the main doors leading into the stalls foyer. And shortly after six-thirty a small contingent of Hallé officials – the commissionaires, doormen, the two booking-office ladies, the deputy general manager and the general manager himself were all standing out in the arcade, explaining and apologising to the public as they arrived. The air of disaster was somehow miraculously overlaid with a kind of northern good humour smacking of philosophy, but every-one agreed that one emergency of this nature was enough for a concert manager's life-time.

The public, as they surged off the buses, out of the car-parks and along the arcade, seemed slow to grasp what had happened. One old lady became greatly distressed and was inconsolable. It seemed she had come down from Penrith by hired car specially for the occasion, which happened to be her eightieth birthday, booking herself overnight at the Midland Hotel. A belligerent young woman with a pudding basin haircut and a rucksack became positively abusive to the deputy general manager, who protested with controlled civility that he could not conjure Jethro Manning out of the air. But for the most part, people behaved as British people normally will at such times of frustration, delay and dis-appointment, as they do at times of strikes and technical problems with aircraft, with dogged stoicism. They looked at the cancellation flashes on the posters, read the notices, listened to the announcements, asked a few questions of each other and went their way, bewildered but unbowed.

Within the cool quiet of the empty auditorium the piano, positioned in the centre of the platform, was slowly and majestically descending to the basement by means of the piano lift. Above it, now, the platform slid back into place as though nothing had happened.

At seven-fifty the staff retired behind the closed doors and shuttered up. The bars had never opened, so that the bar staff went home, with everyone else except the general manager and his deputy who stayed awhile in the hall manager's office to shake their heads over the infamy of Manning and Dilke, and look glumly into the one glass of Scotch with which each allowed the other to console him. They discussed the possibility that Jethro might have had an accident en route, which silenced them for a moment as though they might have been speaking ill of the dead, but then they dismissed that probability, sighed and rose to collect their coats.

'Should we telephone Dilke once more before we leave, do you suppose?' asked the deputy general manager.

'Why?' asked the general manager.

'Why indeed?' said the deputy.

'Tomorrow,' they agreed.

They left and the rain fell on the silent hall. Blown in from the street, splashed up as the buses passed, it began to soak and peel away the 'Cancelled' notices pasted over the posters from which Jethro's brooding, craggy face stared out. And up and down the arcade prowled two cats, one after the other, well into the night.

Chapter Six

Kitty went to visit her mother, Natalia. At times of great anxiety she usually did.

Natalia lived in a Victorian block of flats just off Baker Street, in a nest of pale pink. Pink, she affirmed, gave one a helping hand. All the lampshades were pink and so was the hair rinse which lent sheen to the luxuriant, satiny coils she twisted around her head and from which fronds escaped to curl about the earrings. She wore Jean Patou's "Joy", partly because it was so expensive and she never forgot what it was like to have been very poor for part of her emigré life, partly because it was redolent of roses, and partly because she thought the name so life-enhancing. She drank iced Tavel Rosé right through the year with her *déjeuner* and pink champagne occasionally for fun although her palate was quite discriminating. Having put a fraught childhood firmly behind her, she was dedicated to the sweet and innocent pleasures of life and these had included, in her expansive and unrestrictive morality, the taking of charming lovers when appropriate, both before and after her late and beloved husband's death. It had been a marriage of intense sympathy and companionship; she knew that Nikolai would never have intended her to mourn. She made her lovers very happy and wished them well when she parted from them, which was seldom by their choice, but she had a genius for the new challenge, the adventure, the voyage of exploration, and held strong views about promiscuity which she considered to be the having of more than one lover at a time, although one husband and one lover was in order.

Family portraits of a few pretty women with lovely shoulders, and handsome men in uniform, hung from her shell-pink walls. Above her bed hung icons of some magnificence, the intensity of their colours contrasting strangely with the rest of the boudoir which Kitty always said was a bit reminiscent of a French bordello. This made Natalia giggle a good deal. She loved her treasures and took care of them, although never insuring because, as she said, their price was above rubies. They had a history, these few pictures and pieces of French furniture, brought as they had been across the border from the country estate near Smolensk when Natalia's mother, two aunts, the English governess and a senile chef escaped with the little Natalia and her big brother Mikhail. Mikhail had died of scarlet fever during the journey to Paris, but Natalia, showing then the life-force which continued to support her through life, survived the disease and many others, as well as the loss of Kitty's own twin at their birth. She had assimilated all experience of life and never lost her gaity. She lacked the Russian capacity for pain and pride which Kitty seemed to have in her blood.

Her sofas and chairs were now upholstered in cream velvet, with rose scatter cushions; she said cream didn't show the hairs of her two, perpetually moulting, King Charles spaniels. She was mistaken. People who visited her always brushed the chairs carefully with their hands before sitting down – especially Kitty, who preferred nowadays to wear black, of which, of course, Natalia strongly disapproved.

She took a little time to answer the door to her daughter today, and when she came she was flushed, her hair escaping prettily from its coils and pink pearly combs.

'Whatever have you been up to, Mama?' demanded Kitty.

Natalia twinkled. 'Look! Watch!' she cried, tiptoeing out of the hall through the double doors of the living room, doubling back and darting into her bedroom.

Kitty followed her, but the room seemed to be empty.

'Where are you?' she asked.

There was a muffled whisper from the closet. 'Sh! I'm playing hide and seek with the dogs.'

'They don't seem very interested,' said Kitty. 'They're both lying on the sofa looking extraordinarily inert.'

Natalia emerged, wreathed in smiles. 'They were loving it before you came.'

'I'll go away again if you like,' said Kitty, now following Natalia back into the drawing room where the dogs were sitting, immovable as Staffordshire pieces, eyes bulging with little show of interest.

'Madeira, darling?' she asked, pouring each of them a sizeable glass.

'Mama,' said Kitty, taking hers. 'Jethro's run away.'

Natalia hesitated before she asked, 'He's come home?'

'Didn't you hear what I said?' Kitty spoke crossly. 'I said he's run away.'

'But . . . from whom, Kitty, my love?'

'How do you mean? Well, from that woman, I suppose.'

'That's what I thought you meant.'

'But not to come home. It's not like that. He's run away from everyone and everything. He's disappeared. Or someone's abducted him.'

Natalia's eyes opened wide and she clutched the arms of her chair as she sat. 'Oh my God!' she said. 'Our precious Jethro. Those devils.'

'I didn't mean that bit very seriously, Mama. But he's gone.'

'The Soviets!' One of the dogs slid down from the sofa and jumped up on to her knee. His mistress acknowledged him.

'Oh, Mother!'

Natalia was trembling and Kitty moved the little table which was perilously near her elbow before the bottles wobbled off. 'Those fiends.'

'I'm sure it isn't anything political.'

'You don't understand anything,' said Natalia. 'Uncle Evgeny. Have you forgotten?'

'No. But it was possible to see why they might "eliminate" Uncle Evgeny. He was playing a very complex and sophisticated game and once they were on to him it was only matter of time. He knew that. He always knew what he was doing. Jethro never knows what he's doing.'

Natalia turned her head to looked at the photograph of Uncle Evgeny, silver framed and standing on the upright Bechstein at the other side of the room.

'He was a brave man,' she said simply, turning back. They both fell silent for a moment out of respect to Uncle Evgeny until Natalia, at length, reflected, 'I still don't believe he's dead, you know.'

'I'm sure he's not dead. I never said he was.'

'I didn't know you were so certain. I always felt you had begun to accept . . .'

'I'm talking about Jethro, Mama.'

'Of course.' Natalia collected herself with a small shake. 'Poor Jethro. Poor darling Jethro.'

'Not necessarily. If he's simply torturing us all with anxiety while he's waltzed off after some eighteen-year-old student . . .'

'I think you had better tell me exactly what has happened, sweetheart.'

So Kitty told her mother, who sat absently stroking the silky fur of the spaniel as she listened.

At length she said, 'If I had never told him to make himself known to Larisa Petrovna he would never have met Misha or felt so strongly about those wretched manuscripts.'

'If, if, if. . . . You must stop this, Mama. You couldn't have known Jethro would get himself so involved. He's so unpredictable. Another time he'd be capable of being quite ruthless and keeping himself brutally apart from other people's ideals or suffering.' She put out a hand and laid it on Natalia's. 'With Jethro one never knows which way the cat will jump. For myself, I've become adjusted to that. I can cope. I met him young and married when I could mould myself to him . . .'

'*You* mould yourself to *him*!' Natalia rippled with laughter, and Kitty removed her hand, offended. 'Kitty darling, my sweetheart! You never moulded yourself to anyone, least of all Jethro. I've never seen people struggle so hard to keep their own sovereignty within a marriage.'

'You kept yours,' said Kitty.

'Ah.' Natalia went quiet. 'That was . . . rather a special case.' She fondled the dog's ear, bent to pick up a comb lying on the floor by the chair and began to comb the fur. The dog looked at her with large, mournful eyes. 'How Nikolai loved the dogs,' she murmured, abstractedly.

'How one misses him,' said Kitty. 'Still. It's the only point on which I feel any sympathy for "that Paula" – that she lost her father.'

'It was our delight,' said Natalia after reflection, 'to give each other delight. We never felt constrained to assert ourselves. It was very effortless. We were so lucky.'

Kitty looked into her mother's eyes. 'You weren't lucky,' she said. 'You were clever. And so maybe I can allow you to be smug.'

'What are we going to do about Jethro?' asked Natalia suddenly. 'What is that agent man doing? What are the police doing?'

Kitty explained that as yet the police were uncommitted to a search and that Roger Dilke was impotent.

'I'm certain it's nothing to do with the Soviets this time, Mother, although we know they don't like him and won't let him back in. Whatever this is, he planned it.'

'Did he leave a note?'

'You make it sound like suicide. No, but he left that woman his car keys so she could get home. He left them on the Green Room piano. I saw her pick them up. I don't know, you see, how he will have gone wherever he has gone.' She paused and lifted her chin. 'Of course, I naturally thought he might have left her and come home. I half expected to find him there, when we got back from the concert.'

Natalia sighed. 'You'd have him back – any time – wouldn't you?'

Kitty looked away, out of the window to the grubby sash one veiled in net, over the street.

'What a silly question, Mother.' Then she whisked round. 'And so would you if you were me.'

Natalia smiled and now Kitty relaxed sufficiently to give the ghost of a smile, too.

'Oh yes,' she replied. 'Naturally. I've never made any pretence about it. I've always adored Jethro.'

'Not sufficiently to come to his recital with us!' Kitty retorted.

'But darling! I was in Brighton for the weekend.'

'Could you not have come back to London yesterday instead of today?'

'I don't like Sunday trains,' she said amiably.

85

But Kitty was cross. 'It wasn't anything to do with that, Mother, and you know it.'

Natalia's eyes widened. The brows were gently shaded in pink.

'What was it, then?' she asked, all innocence.

'You didn't want to come with me.'

'Possibly,' she conceded.

'I embarrass you.'

'On such occasions. It is possible.' She puckered her face sweetly, put the dog on the floor, and poured each of them another Madeira.

Paula rang Roger's flat at eight-thirty a.m. He came to the telephone from his bath, loins wrapped in a small thick white towel, dripping all over the carpet, leaving footprints in the pile and Caroline in the bath. He had never felt any fondness for Paula.

'I was planning to telephone you when I got to the office,' he told her.

'But I'm not at home. I stayed with Anne in Hampstead and we, that is she, rang the hotel last night but he hadn't ever checked in. Did he never turn up at the Hall?'

'No.' Roger sat on the bed and dried his toes.

'What on earth are we going to do?'

He was silent.

'Roger?'

'If and when I meet Jethro again I shall suggest he finds himself a new agent. That is what I shall do. You, of course, are free to do what you want.'

'That's rather a stupid thing to say.' She blushed as she spoke. She had always been a little nervous of Jethro's agent. 'Have you given him a thought?' She surprised herself by her own belligerence.'

'Too many.'

'I can't believe this conversation. Have you just written him off? I thought he was supposed to be your golden boy.'

'I do have other clients.'

'So you say – constantly.'

'It is true.'

The effort of trying to keep her voice steady and low was bringing her out in a slight sweat, heat rising from her neck. Anne sat quietly at the breakfast table her coffee mug between her hands, watching her friend as the storm gathered. It was all the more alarming because Paula was normally so diffuse. To see her sharpening, becoming focussed for the attack, was distressing to Anne, who feared she would be unable to hold her position with any conviction if Roger really took up the offensive. Anne had met him once, at the Wigmore Hall, and the briefest of interchanges had given her an impression of a controlled bitterness, an arctic tension, and some command of language. Paula, pink and flustering, falling over her words in anger, would be no match for him.

'You don't care about the man,' she fumed. 'Only the pianist.'

He said nothing.

'Are you still there?'

'I am.'

'He could be dead for all we know,' shouted Paula.

Now Roger laid the receiver down on the bedside table and padded back into the bathroom to pull the plug out on Caroline. 'Can't lie there all day, sweetie,' he hissed. He brought back the talcum powder and, putting his feet up on the bed, he powdered them. He could hear what Paula was saying quite well, but nothing seemed to call for an answer until she said, catching Anne's eye and droping her voice, 'Is anyone going to inform the police about this now? Seriously?'

'I think they might take us seriously now. Yes. If you like I'll ring them as soon as I've dried myself and got some clothes on.'

'Did I get you out of your bath?'

He ignored that and continued. 'They may start moving. Concert artists don't normally go making bookings and then fail to honour them. I'll be surprised if they don't take this seriously.'

'Could he have been abducted?'

'The thought hadn't occurred to me. I don't honestly think we need to worry about that.' Now the temperature had dropped he spoke almost kindly. 'By whom, for example?'

'Where's the bathrobe?' called Caroline from the bathroom.

'In the washing machine,' he shouted back, putting his hand over the receiver.

'Is there someone there?' asked Paula.

'Only my partner's secretary,' he said, coolly.

'Oh . . .' she floundered.

'She lives with me.'

Paula reddened, out of sight. It was mad, really that it should embarrass her. Jethro lived with her.

'You were saying?'

'You remember the last Moscow trip?' She collected herself yet again. 'When he got involved with the dissident musicologist? He always says he cooked his goose with the Russians by bringing that man's article on Shostakovitch back to the West, and the banned manuscript.'

'Yes, it was a silly thing to do.'

'It was a matter of principle,' she retorted.

'I'm not sure that an international artist can afford to have too many principles. It may be very difficult, indeed impossible, to get him a visa again, and that's very bad news.' He realised, suddenly, that he was still speaking as Jethro's agent, and the thought silenced him for a moment. She, too, had noticed.

'Still – that's his problem,' he said.

'It's possible the Russians don't know it was Jethro who got the piece out.'

'They seem to know most things.'

'How frightening!'

Roger had a picture of her wide lips trembling, her eyes slightly swimmy. He thought Kitty infinitely preferable. Caroline, having joined him, sat on to the bed too.

'Frustrating, more than frightening. One would have hoped that Jethro could have kept his head screwed on better. Known where his interests lay. He should have been more wary after the business of the woman.'

'What woman?'

'Didn't Jethro mention her?'

'Mention who?'

Anne came and sat beside Paula.

'It's nothing of any importance. Jethro handled that OK, thank God. They simply sent a woman to his hotel room. You know the way they do these things. Accidentally on purpose. It happens all the time.'

'He never told me.'

'I suppose he didn't think it of any significance. He dealt with her quite properly and showed her the door.'

'Did she knock?'

'I expect she had a pass key. Apologised. Wrong room. You know the kind of thing.'

'Not really,' said Paula faintly. 'But I . . . I hadn't realised they were actually trying to incriminate him. Roger! I'm scared.'

'I don't think the KGB have drugged Jethro and popped him in a sack. He's not important enough to them. Look – would you mind very much if I get dressed. I'm cold.'

'I'm sorry,' said Paula.

'That's OK. I'll get on to the police in the next half hour. But I can't answer for what they'll do about it – not yet.'

'I'm very grateful.' Paula was humble now. 'I'm terribly sorry. Ringing you in your bath.'

'Right,' he said. And put down the receiver his end.

'Poor woman,' said Caroline.

'Is he going to ring you back?' asked Anne.

'I don't know.' Paula returned to the table and slumped over the coffee Anne had just replenished.

'You'd better hang on here for a bit.'

'But you've got to get to work.'

'Doesn't matter. You can stay and collect yourself, wait for him to ring. Ring him back at his office if you're brave . . .'

Paula smiled, barely. 'I'm afraid I nearly went to pieces. He makes me nervous any time, but now . . .'

Anne rose. 'Lynnie'll probably be back mid-morning. She'll look after you.'

The thought of Lynnie and her friends were enough to get Paula moving. She and Anne left the flat together, in different directions.

Paula called, unannounced, upon Arthur and Irene in Kentish Town. They welcomed her kindly, nervously avoiding any intimation of patronage. Arthur took her coat and hung it up in the hall as though they expected her to stay, for which she was grateful.

'Irene's off to rehearsal soon,' he said, 'but I'm spending the morning at home with some papers, so let me get you a coffee.'

'I mustn't keep you,' she said, mechanically.

'No problem.' Arthur was too hearty.

'About Jethro . . .' she began.

'Don't worry. It didn't matter,' boomed Arthur. For a small man he made a lot of noise. 'Nobody minded. Must be hell having to shake all those hands. Meant to give him a ring yesterday.'

He clattered round in the kitchen, filling kettles, slapping down mugs, rattling spoons. It all seemed to go through Paula's head.

'He wouldn't have thanked you,' shouted Irene. 'He was shooting off to Liverpool. Have you forgotten?'

'Manchester!' yelled Arthur.

'Only he didn't come home, you see . . .'

Arthur was standing at the kitchen door. He looked embarrassed. It was one thing being pleasant to Paula, but if he was going to be asked to take part in someone's emotional mess . . .

'Well of course . . .' began Irene.

'No. He didn't go there either. I thought he might have, but he didn't. I don't know where he's gone, that's the point. Nobody does. Not me. Nor Roger Dilke. Nor . . . Kitty.' It felt curious to be using that name, which normally she avoided, to throw it in casually as though there were no taboo.

'But didn't he have this booking last night up north? Presumably he's there.'

'That's the thing,' said Paula. 'He isn't.'

Arthur brought the coffee through and set it down.

'He never turned up, you see. I've spoken to Roger this morning. I rang him at his home. He thinks Jethro's just gone out of his mind and stood them up – the Hallé people – but Jethro'd never do a thing like that.' Her voice now had an edge of hysteria in it. 'Whatever Jethro would do, he wouldn't ever do that. He'll do unpredictable things sometimes, but not when it comes to his career.'

'Who's promoting the concert – I mean – who was promoting it?' asked Arthur.

Paula looked bewildered. 'I don't . . . I don't know. I don't know much about all that side.'

'They're not going to be pleased. Woof!' Arthur sat down heavily.

'Don't you want your coffee?' asked Irene.

Paula picked up the mug, hovered, and put it down again.

Arthur said, 'Jethro's always suited himself.'

Irene rounded on him. 'What a ridiculous thing to say. Jethro's a performer, an international concert artist. His whole life has been geared to keeping commitments and honouring professional engagements. A man like that doesn't suddenly go berserk and let a whole audience in Manchester roll up to hear him and just not turn up.'

'Jethro could.'

'Balls,' said Irene.

'There was that time he refused to play in Norwich because the piano hadn't been tuned.'

'That was quite different. Anyway, it was King's Lynn.'

'Why was it different? It was still letting his audience down. It let us down. We'd driven miles across the beastly fens.'

'Any first-rate musician takes the state of the instrument seriously.'

'I remember thinking at the time he could whistle for me to come and hear him again.'

'I don't suppose that sent him into a decline.' She turned to Paula. 'You ought to drink that. Do you good.' She rose. 'I must be off.'

'I'm afraid I seem to have gone off coffee,' said Paula in a small voice. 'I don't feel – not desperately well.' She looked around, panicking.

'Would you like something stronger? Whisky?'

Paula clutched her stomach and shook her head.

'Lots of people like me make up an audience.' Arthur was raising his voice. 'If he gets people really fed up with this primadonna lark – if he gets a reputation for being the kind of soloist who does this sort of thing often, people won't come and hear him. Someone ought to tell him.'

'They put up with more than you think they do to hear Jethro. It's quite an operation getting tickets.'

'He's not here to tell,' whispered Paula.

'There's a limit.'

'Please . . .' said Paula.

Irene picked up her coat from a chair and began to put it on. She turned to Paula. 'So what've you done?' she asked.

'Done?' Paula felt stupid.

'You've informed the police presumably?'

Probably she had no intention of making Paula feel under attack.

'The police won't do anything as early as this,' interrupted Arthur.

'Of course they would.' Irene was brisk, dressed now for the outdoors. 'They're not entirely irresponsible.'

'Anybody has a perfect right to go away for a little and not tell his family or' – he glanced at Paula '– his friends – where he's gone. It may be selfish, but it's not illegal. Or even fattening!'

Nobody laughed.

'I could go anywhere – tomorrow – and not tell you,' he added.

'Not if you were booked at the Free Trade Hall, Manchester.'

'That'd be entirely between me and the Free Trade Hall and nothing to do with you. And the promoter of course. By the way, who did she say the promoter was?'

'She didn't.'

'Well there's certainly a breach of contract with someone, and somebody must be liable.'

'I would suppose that Roger Dilke's problem.'

'Then presumably if Jethro walks off, Roger fetches the law down on him.'

Paula rose and began to fumble for her coat among the others.

'Ultimately, yes.'

'But obviously he's not just walked off. Something's happened to him.'

'Such as . . .?'

'An accident?'

'An accident would have been reported.'

'Would he have had any identification on him? Was he driving?'

They both looked at Paula.

'I'm going to be late,' said Irene. 'People like Jethro don't go round with nothing to say who they are,' she went on. 'He'd have had papers, music, hotel confirmation. Since he's always nipping off all over the world he most likely carries his passport on his person. If he'd been involved in a motorway pile-up and the car and the man weren't a complete write-off . . .'

Paula was afraid she might be sick.

'. . . he'd have been on to Dilke. And Kitty.'

'Oughtn't we to ring Kitty?'

Paula struggled into her coat.

'Could anyone have had a personal grudge against him?' Irene asked Arthur.

'Not of the positively murderous kind! Plenty of people don't like him, but . . .'

Now Paula stood, robed, at the door.

'Don't go,' said Irene, calling through.

Arthur followed Paula down the staircase of the Victorian conversion where the Heygates had their flat. His slippers flapped, flip, flap. Paula took no notice, hurrying down. He caught her arm and she shook if off. She was so rough that he lost balance and fell against the stair rail, losing his slipper.

'Go away, you useless little man,' she said. 'Go back to your wife. Leave me alone!'

'What's she doing?' called Irene from above. 'She's not got to go just because I'm running off to rehearsal. You could make her some tea.'

Paula crossed the street to her car to find a female warden just at the point of tucking a slip of paper veiled in plastic under her windscreen wiper.

She snatched it, tore it into two and flung it on to the ground.

'Oh no, you don't!' She confronted the warden, who stood firm in dark nylon legs and stout shoes. A policeman on the school crossing down the road stopped talking to the lollipop lady to whom he had been chatting since the kids went into school fifteen minutes earlier, and began to walk heavily up the street towards Paula.

In the police station they gave her strong sweet tea and listened to her, keeping her car in the forecourt until she had composed herself. The two halves of the parking ticket had been put back in her purse by the policeman, who was very patient as she told him all about Jethro and after a little time on the telephone told her that it did seem a formal statement had now been made by a Mr Roger Dilke of Allen, Marvell and Dilke, and a description circulated. In view of Jethro's notoriety and his failing to keep his booking in Manchester, the wheels would be being set in motion sooner than was normal in such cases.

'I hadn't realised so many people just disappeared,' said Paula, dry-eyed, red-rimmed and chastened.

'Oh yes, miss. Although I don't think we can quite yet say your friend has disappeared. Let's just say, he may have found things got a bit on top of him and decided to take a break.'

Paula began to laugh. And laugh. They gave her more tea and asked if she wanted to see a doctor but she shook her head and laughed more. Then she went into the ladies and stayed there for sometime until a policewoman came and knocked on the door. In Kentish Town they were prepared for most things.

'I'm all right,' said Paula, emerging. 'Just a little sick. It must have been all that tea.'

Later, parked safely in the Outer Circle, Regent's Park, opposite the Mosque, about twelve-thirty, Paula sat in the car and read the first edition of the *Standard*. She read the paragraph again and again and then went to sit by the children's boating pond. The seat was saturated from recent rain and the grass, ill-drained there near Hanover Gate, lay half under water. She put the newspaper under her bottom. Above her, the London gulls wheeled and screamed.

She wondered whether Jethro were dead. And if so, how she would live. How she would now pick up the threads of her life, the threads he had so remorselessly broken, and begin again. She felt so listless that she hardly even noticed when it began to drizzle again and the rain flurried across the surface of the pond in eddies, skimming over in the wind, wetting her coat and hair, wild hair and face. People hurried past, umbrellas raised, looking out for puddles. Nobody looked at her.

Her father had used to bring her here when she was a little girl. He had sat on a seat like this reading his paper and waving across the water at her as she had paddled her boat round and round the pond until her allotted time was up. She put her hand down, now, on the wet seat and felt about, almost expecting to be able to feel his bulk, Daddy in his old grey-green suit with the baggy trousers. In the absence of a mother, he and she had spent so much time together. She wondered how she had endured his death and then wondered – perhaps she had not. Perhaps that, when she had been only sixteen, had really been the end of her. Until Jethro had come and filled her. She closed her eyes.

> 'In storm and calm give us to see
> The path of peace which leads to Thee.'

She and Daddy had used to go to church, but after he died she seemed to have lost the heart for it. Now, occasionally, snatches of hymns or the liturgy came back to her, gently chiding. A sense of loss swept over her at such times and yet, behind the reproach, there was always the hint of promise that she could, if she would, find her way back through the maze. And the maze itself, like the maze at Hampton Court (another of Daddy's and her stamping grounds) had become broken down, balding, moth-eaten, full of dead wood, enabling her to peep between the cracks. Now her head was filled with the sound, not of rain upon the boating pond, not of the steady rumble of traffic along Park Road and taxis circling the circle, looking for somewhere to park and snooze and eat mid-day sandwiches, but of the fountains at Hampton Court, the sunny sound of light on water, the silence of noise-less fish, the patter of footsteps along the terraces, the faces peering from the dim cool of the state apartments out through windows of mellow glass. And the chapel.

She could not allow herself to believe now that Jethro, too, had left her. She opened her eyes and rose, because there comes a time when one must rise, when there is no point in staying, and even if there is no point in rising, it gives one something to do.

Walking beside the lake towards the bridge she thought nothing of how wet she was becoming. Then she retraced her footsteps back to the car and drove very fast to Kitty's house.

Tatiana opened the door. She was wearing a chrome-yellow tracksuit and her hair was drawn back into a long, thick pigtail down her back.

Paula stood, drenched, on the step. Tattie made no move. 'Yes?' she said.

Paula looked behind into the hall. She had not been inside this house since those early days when she had been the bright young photographer and the Mannings well-disposed clients. Kitty had been hospitable, as she normally was to people who had some reason to come to the house. There had been no shadow over them. They had sat at the back in the paved garden and drunk from long tall glasses and talked about the St John's Wood songbirds. Kitty had seen a blue butterfly and they had all pored together through the pages of Nina's butterfly book to identify it. Paula had been caught up, entranced by the ménage. The Mannings had seemed to come from space, giving a definition to things which, for many years, since her father's death, had seemed to Paula formless, illusory. It was this old business of needing other people to give shape and substance to her own existential experience, first Daddy, and now people like Jethro and Kitty, who could focus their own light upon her own cloudy perception and say, Look – here it is! This is the song thrush. This is the tench gliding under the green water – listen, feel, smell, look at reality and take it right into yourself so that you may give it out again. Listen to the notes spilling out from the piano, the fruit of one man's vision and another man's understanding. Communication. Light. The Word. This is happiness. This is pain.

And so, to some extent, Paula had been nourished by Kitty's own nervous life-force, as well as Jethro's weight, his smouldering fire, his responsive quick-silver dashes of illumination, by the whole fascinating spectrum that went to make up the man and the music.

They talked, these Manning women, all the time. They talked of insects clinging to a leaf, of the toad measuring his leap up each one of the kitchen steps on a hot day. They talked of love and other people's imperfections. They were often malicious and frequently funny. Paula sometimes had wondered what they said of her. They talked, too, of Russia, of Poland, and politics. They laughed at Roger Dilke no end. They argued about Messiaen, and whether Venice was in peril and whether one could ever tire of perfection and whether one would recognise it if one stumbled across it. They poured scorn on the Church of England and used the word 'middle class' as a term of abuse.

When Jethro had had enough of their talking he would walk away to his piano.

It had all been very strange for Paula. Had she not fallen in love with Jethro, she might have lost her heart to Kitty. As things worked out, the frankness between them was short-lived.

And now here she was. February and a half-closed front door, only a shaft of hall ahead and a sliver of staircase, carpeted in lavender blue which showed every mark and was seldom brushed. Someone had spilt a glass of red plonk on it durng a post-concert party. A black and white tiled floor littered with boots and shopping and correspondence.

'May I come in?' asked Paula.

Tattie hesitated for a moment, then sneezed. She opened the door wider. She was about to concede that Paula ought to come in out of the rain when Nina came down the stairs. The two girls looked at each other. Together Paula could see which was which, although apart, without a basis for comparison, it was more difficult. Nina's eyes were set a little further apart. Tattie's brow was perhaps a little heavier, the mouth more sultry. They wore their hair differently, Nina's loose and layered, softer.

'What ought I to do?' asked Tattie of her sister. She was in the habit of deferring domestically. Nina had been born the second, but it was accepted that Nina made the family decisions.

'Does Kitty know she's here?' asked Nina.

'No. Where is Kitty?'

'Upstairs on the telephone to Theo Bristol. There's something in the evening paper.'

Paula held out the sodden *Standard* and gravely Nina took it. 'I've seen it,' she said, handing it over to Tatiana. 'You'd better.'

Tattie read the paragraph standing there at the still open door while Paula looked around her at the enemy camp. It was strange how familiar it seemed, as though she had never been away. She gave herself a small emotional shake and said,

'I'm sorry. I know it's awkward. But I thought I ought to speak to your mother.'

'Why?' asked Tattie.

'What do you want to say to her?' asked Nina.

'I've not got a bomb in my bag, you know,' said Paula. She moved right into the hall and Tattie, catching Nina's eye, closed the front door.

'Is it about our father?' asked Nina.

'Of course it's about your father,' snapped Paula. 'Why else would I come here?' There was a pause and then she added, 'It seemed to me we should talk.' She felt an absurd desire to say something like, 'We're all in this together.'

'I'm on my way to the Beeb,' Nina told Tattie.

'I thought you weren't working today.'

'There's a read-through this afternoon. I've left a shepherd's pie for you to heat up.'

'What ought I to . . .?'

'You'd better take her through, I suppose.'

And Nina left.

'He was happy until he met you,' said Tatiana, walking down the hall towards the music room, which overlooked the garden at the back. So often Paula had walked along that narrow passage with the garden door ahead. She half expected Jethro to come out of the music room and greet her. It was disorientating.

Paula stood, uncertainly, by the deep gold damask chair, while Tatiana took a basket of shopping from it.

'You had better sit down,' said the girl, and left her.

The Mannings still called this room 'The Music Room' although there was now a curious, ungainly gap where the big

98

black Steinway had once stood. The space, not really assimilated by the room, appeared to accuse Paula even more overtly than the girls had done. An antique card table, littered with papers and tiles, stood like a gauche guest in the centre of the space. Two embarrassed hard chairs, like guards, on either side of it.

Paula pictured the Steinway in her own living room, behind the folding doors. It had never seemed entirely at home there, the great black concert grand, where Paula had sacrificed Aunt Virginia's 'dining end' to accommodate it. It seemed to have come down in the world. Paula had sold Aunt Virginia's pretty little rosewood Bluthner to house it. Aunt Virginia had kept flowers upon it and some of the notes didn't play. Perhaps, thought Paula wildly, the Steinway pined for Loudoun Road, detesting the Barnes house but too well-bred to say so.

In the grate a dead fire accused Paula, too. Ash spilled out on to the hearth. She had taken some pictures of Jethro standing in front of this fireplace, then all leaping flames, a forbidden log fire in a smokeless zone on a chilly May day soon after she had first met the Mannings. John Sorensen had arrived, bringing expensive strawberries from St John's Wood High Street, and they had eaten them, improbably, in front of a roaring fire, straight from the punnet. Paula had a vague feeling that he was in some way sexually connected with one of the girls, but was unsure which. There seemed to be a line of special communication connecting the three of them and when he had gone they both spoke of him almost as a brother – or was it an old love – laughing at how unusual it was for J.S., as they called him, to put his hand in his pocket and bring anything.

'Usually he's rooting round in our fridge,' said Tattie.

'John's the kind of person who comes to a bottle party with a can of Harp lager,' said Nina.

'Poor man's living below the poverty margin, I dare say,' Jethro had said, unexpectedly. 'After all, he's only a first-class cellist. If he was a Westminster City dustman he could eat strawberries three meals a day right out of season.'

'Don't be silly, Father,' said Nina. 'You try living on a dustman's wages.'

'I don't have to,' Jethro had said, putting his arm around

99

Kitty, who had been standing there in a pair of disgusting old jeans and a thin tee shirt. 'I've got a rich wife. John, poor chap, has not.'

He had allowed his hand to stray over Kitty's not very full bosom and settle over one breast. Paula had looked away. She remembered it well.

They were all here, now, the ghosts of them, filling Jethro's room in Jethro's house. Paula sat, looking at the pictures Jethro had looked at, sitting in the chair he had sat in, her shoes on the carpet he had worn away. There was the specially scuffed place where the piano no longer stood. This was his room, his and his wife's room, and it seemed as though he had never left it. Paula sat, inert, motionless, waiting for him to come in and pour her a drink.

There was a tread outside, a creak in the floor boards, and Ekaterina entered.

Chapter Seven

There were deep, dark circles under Kitty's eyes, so deep and dark that they looked almost theatrical in the thin face. The black cashmere sweater dress, belted in snakeskin, the tall black boots, all served to emphasise the height, the narrowness of her, the fine bones. She stood for a moment as though she were waiting, expecting some kind of response from Paula, an ovation, perhaps, for her entrance. Her eyes, tired and yet in an odd way glittering, seemed to appraise her visitor and assess the excuse for such a visit, and Paula, involuntarily, struggled out of the low cavernous chair to rise to her feet. In retrospect, it annoyed her that she had done so. Was she here to justify herself?

Kitty brought into the room a perfume which Paula recognised and which recalled the past in a blurred yet emphatic way. She had never overtly recognised it before and yet now she knew that it had always been there, back in those days when she had come to this house an innocent. Kitty's scent. Pervading Jethro's home.

Kitty was indeed appraising the younger woman, who rose so awkwardly from her chair, crumpled like a piece of used tissue paper. Paula looked frightened. She might have slept in her clothes and never combed the fluff of fair hair. Her eyebrows were colourless, pale, which gave her face a formlessness. She wore a bright, patchwork jacket which killed any colour in her cheeks. There were hairs of some animal upon her skirt.

Neither woman held out a hand.

'I wondered whether you had heard anything?' asked Paula.

101

Kitty shook her head.

'I – I spoke to Mr Dilke earlier. At his flat.' As she said it, she was irritated with herself for not calling him Roger.

'He told me.'

Kitty crossed the room and opened the window slightly, although it was February, and cold. She was diluting the essence of Paula, who wore no perfume and yet, to Kitty's finely tuned nostrils, brought her own aroma with her. It seemed to Kitty that Paula's presence filled the room.

She sat on the window seat and crossed her knees. Paula hated her. She wanted to leave.

'How did you think Jethro played?' asked Kitty.

Paula blinked. This was not what she expected. It seemed that Kitty was expecting an answer. Paula was quite unprepared.

'I'm not qualified to say. I'm not all that musical. I think you know that,' she added, with a hint of belligerence.

'But what about the programme? Didn't you think it was a little odd?'

'I thought it was very nice,' said Paula. And blushed.

'Did he talk about the programme before?' persisted Kitty. 'Did you discuss it?'

Paula shook her head.

'He always used to play through his programme to me when he was planning it,' Kitty said.

'I wouldn't want to interfere.'

'I would.' And Kitty smiled for the first time, so that Paula was unsure whether to smile back or not. She felt extremely unsafe.

Then she decided it was perhaps time to say what it was she had come to say. 'Do you think anything awful's happened to him?' She reddened again and was alarmed that there was a prickling behind her eyes. Quickly, she looked away.

'I don't think so,' said Kitty slowly, rising and beginning to walk about the room. 'I've had my bad moments, of course. Nightmare visions. One is bound to. But I keep them under control.'

'Accident,' said Paula, pale. 'Walking under a long vehicle.'

'And kidnapping. Terrorist hitch-hiker on the motorway, heart attack, the lot.'

102

'But we'd have heard,' said Paula.

'Those things don't happen to Jethro. Or they don't happen when you expect them. Things never do. Life isn't like that. It's the unexpected that happens.' Her eyes were dreadfully penetrating and Paula flinched.

'You don't think he could have . . .'

'No. I'm quite sure he couldn't have,' said Kitty. 'He's not suicide material. We had a friend who killed herself. I know how he feels about it.'

It occurred to Paula how many things about Jethro Kitty knew and understood.

'But you see,' Kitty went on, 'whenever Jethro's done anything dreadful I've never had any warning. He doesn't send out signals first. Like leaving me for you.'

Paula winced. Kitty appeared to notice not at all.

'You see,' she went on, 'that was about the most unspeakable thing he could do to me. And yet he just upped and went.'

'It was a bit different,' said Paula.

'In what way? Worse, you mean?'

Standing by the fireplace, Kitty picked up a small bronze eagle. For a moment Paula almost wondered whether she was going to hurl it across the room at her. But the fear was unfounded. Kitty was under control, and yet Paula, timid in the face of such explosive violence as she had, at times, met from Jethro's wife, experienced a tremor of alert. Her senses sharpened.

Kitty put the eagle back on the mantelpiece, and the moment was past. Her eyes were gentian blue, set in deep shadow. Paula tried to read the right meaning into them in order to arm herself against whatever swerve of direction this meeting might take.

Looking at her, Kitty thought, 'She has gone to pieces. Heaven preserve *me* from going to pieces.'

Kitty underestimated Paula. She had not gone to pieces. She relied upon her own, less focused courage, and if she were opaque to Kitty's brilliant clarity, it gave her a kind of advantage; where Kitty's presence was formidable, Paula possessed, in comparison, a kind of elusive, shifting mystery.

Paula's pale blue-grey eyes, like the possibility of a fine day through a sea fret, swam about the room, finding everywhere familiar yet hostile material objects. As a photographer, she was always aware of 'things' around her, of patterns of living, of objects illuminating and seeming to mirror or even extend her perception of their owner. This room was pervaded with a union from which she shrank.

'He needed to,' said Paula bravely. 'He needed me so much he had no alternative.'

'He doesn't seem to need you now,' Kitty rapped.

'Nor you, it seems,' suggested Paula softly. She settled a little more easily into her chair, still ready for escape, but not so palpably poised for flight.

Kitty paused. Then, 'You were not the first, you know,' she said.

'Then there must have been something wrong with his marriage.'

'Nonsense. We gave each other everything we needed, except novelty. Jethro needs novelty from time to time because he is an extremely vain man.'

'Surely his professional success is enough for his vanity?'

'Unless you understand nothing at all about my husband, you will know that is not so. Adulation of such a kind means nothing to him. He's contemptuous of it.'

'Contemptuous of his public?'

'I didn't say that. Jethro respects his public and to suggest otherwise is to wrong him. But he has no time for hysteria and he shrinks from being the cause of it. He plays the piano because he *must* play the piano, for himself. Because there is such interpretative understanding and musical depth there – technical brilliance and sheer power – he can project to his audience like no pianist I know. But he didn't on Sunday. He didn't even try. He played entirely for the inner man. That's way I asked what you thought. I wanted to see whether you had a meagre little glimpse into the man you have so callously and stupidly appropriated, and it was exactly as I thought – you have not.'

Paula felt beads of alarm rising on her forehead. Kitty was going to demand a fight and she must now, unwillingly, put on her armour.

'Jethro's vanity has nothing to do with his music,' Kitty continued. 'It has to do with his hunter-killer instincts. It's no

104

more than the same boring old masculine urge to demonstrate that he can still make a pretty female lie down and open her legs for him.'

'You are being unnecessarily vulgar,' said Paula, surprising herself.

'Am I?' asked Kitty. Suddenly she laughed. 'Yes. I'm quite often vulgar.'

'Jethro disliked it in you,' said Paula. She aimed the arrow with precision and watched for the wound to open, but Kitty's defences had been programmed before she came into the room and the dark blue eyes sought Paula's, forced them back into confrontation as she said,

'What a very unpleasant little person you are. I wonder when Jethro first recognised it.'

Paula touched the chain and pendant around her neck. Last birthday she had been hurt by Jethro, who had irritably thrust a cheque at her and said he had wasted the past twenty-four hours trying to think what to buy for her birthday and still couldn't come up with an idea. 'You had better get yourself something,' he had said. She had tried to give him the money back, saying a little tearfully that it was the thought that counted; but in the end there had been a small atmosphere, to dispel which she had taken the cheque and bought this piece of jewellery. She had never felt it had come from Jethro.

'I came here because I thought it was possible we might be able to help each other,' she said. 'It was not me who began this. I don't want to come into your house and be rude to you. But I don't like the way you talk.'

'Did I invite you?' asked Kitty.

'No.' Paula flushed. It began at her neck and rose. It drew attention to a coarseness of the skin at the throat, which gave Kitty satisfaction. 'But surely you can see it took some nerve?'

Kitty was silent.

'Do you think I wanted to come here?' Paula demanded, with a sudden explosion of resentment. She indicated the breadth of the room with her hand. Her eyes began to react at the thought of her own courage. There was a hint of a glint.

When Kitty said 'Yes', Paula was surprised. 'Yes I do,' said Kitty. 'I think that now you've lost Jethro you've come back

105

here because this is where you first found him. I think you've come for comfort.'

'Comfort!' Paula's eyes grew round and her voice rose. Kitty, well in control of the dialogue, thought she looked excessively stupid. She gathered strength.

'This house. You almost lived here when you first met us. You were in love with the house and all of us in it. You used to come here and settle in like a cat finding a good cushion. I used to think you were a little stray, and I suppose you really were a kind of emotional waif, so I fed you. In every way. You sat here, cat on a cushion' – Kitty indicated the chair in which Paula was now sitting, she was enjoying the metaphor – 'watching us, watching the girls, the people who came here, listening to the talk, listening to Jethro practising, admiring me' – Paula opened her mouth – 'and gradually settling in. You settled in so well we almost stopped noticing you. You became part of the furniture. Oh yes, you're the kind who can become so absorbed into the general atmosphere, not contributing particularly but just being there, that one fails to see you slinking around, little alley cat pretending to be domesticated. One felt protective to you.' Kitty laughed. 'That's rich! Enjoyed feeding you. I remember jokes about "fattening you up" and I always knew we were talking about more than food and drink although, God knows, you were happy enough to sit at my table. You used to go on about Nina's cooking. At one time we used to laugh when you'd gone and say you had a crush on Nina! Although Theo always said it was me you were mad about.'

'You're crazy,' said Paula. 'It's you that's mad.' She rose from her chair. 'You're inventing all this. You do invent things. You used to urge me to come. You kept open house. You collected people.'

'You grew obsessive about the house and everyone in it and the life that surrounded it. You – from your boring suburban little life and your narrow horizons – where was it you lived – Cheam? Your job had taken you out of that enough to get a glimpse of another world and that was sufficient to set you wondering how to acquire some of it for yourself. At first you thought you could just attach yourself, like a limpet, like a leech, and grow into our life style until you belonged. But that

106

wasn't enough. And so you decided, at last, to *take* the very heart of it for yourself. To steal it, sneak it away. You thought, once you'd done that, appropriated the great beating heart for yourself, it would sustain you, that it would beat for you, you'd grow around it as we had done. You thought you'd flourish and expand and we would wither and shrivel and die. You thought Jethro would transform you into someone like me.'

'You are absolutely out of your mind,' said Paula. And she turned away towards the door because so much of it was true that she could in no way bear to look at Kitty any more.

'Sit down,' said Kitty. 'I haven't finished.'

'I prefer to go.'

'Since you opted to come, you'll hear me out,' said Kitty, moving forward suddenly and pushing her back in the chair. 'You'll go when I throw you out.'

Paula fell back in surprise and made an effort to rise again, but Kitty stood over her.

'But you see,' she persisted, 'you were wrong. Jethro and I were so welded together, so much part of each other, that in tearing him away . . .'

'This is ridiculous,' shouted Paula suddenly. 'I never tore him away. He came. He came of his own free will.'

Kitty leaned over her, a hand on either arm of the chair, hemming her in. '. . . in tearing him away,' she hissed, 'you left half behind. More than half. The vital half. If you harmed anybody, it was him you harmed. And you gained nothing, because he could no longer function without me. And his home. You took him away from his source. You did your best to destroy him. What we don't know is whether you've succeeded.'

'If you and he were so welded together – or one big heart, beating in unison – how come he kept being unfaithful to you?' Paula's own heart felt uncomfortably hectic under her breast. Involuntarily she put her hand to it, and Kitty saw.

'Are you all right?' she asked.

Paula looked up at her and burst into tears. 'Is *he* all right?' she wept. 'That's what matters, surely? Isn't it? Why are you worrying about me. You don't give a damn about me.'

The telephone rang. Somewhere else in the house someone answered it.

Kitty gave Paula a brandy with some soda splashed in the glass and herself only a soda.

'I love him,' Paula sobbed. 'I didn't want to take somebody else's husband. It just happened. He loved me. We never wanted all this destruction.'

Kitty went to sit down herself, and drank a little of her soda.

'I'm sorry to disillusion you,' she said, 'but Jethro didn't love you. He simply wanted to sleep with you and get some sort of revenge on me.'

'What for?' wailed Paula. 'Why should he want revenge? What had you done?'

'Our life was a loving battle-ground,' said Kitty. 'Surely you knew that? He thrived on conflict. It got the adrenalin going. I understood that very early on.'

'We never quarrelled.'

'Oh dear,' said Kitty. 'I'm not surprised he's left you!'

'He hasn't left me.' Paula's voice quivered. 'You keep saying "left" me. We don't know what he's done.'

Of course, it was true. They didn't quarrel. When he felt aggressive Jethro bullied her and when he had finished feeling aggressive he consoled her. It was never a two-way perform-ance. The instant she began to see that he was becoming angry she was always far too frightened to fight back. She looked at Kitty through her tears.

'And if I hadn't thrown him out,' said Kitty, 'he'd be here today.'

'Thrown him out?' Paula keened, incredulous.

'Do stop crying,' said Kitty. 'It doesn't make things any easier.'

Paula shuddered herself to silence and searched for a hand-kerchief. Kitty was silent and gradually the shaking subsided.

'Yes,' said Kitty. 'I told him to go. I packed his bags for him. I left his cases in the hall and locked the bedroom door. He climbed up over the conservatory at the back and in through the window. You were meant to be meeting him that evening. At a public house in Paddington. But he stayed with me. Presumably you waited.'

'How did you know? He didn't tell you?'

'One of those dreadful little letters you wrote him. I found it in his jacket pocket. I burned it with the rose prunings in the garden.'

'You went through his pockets?'

'Of course,' said Kitty.

'I couldn't live with a man that way. Without any trust. Spying on him.'

'At any rate I knew more about his plans than you. Now he's gone and you have no idea where or to whom.'

Paula, slumped back in the chair, stiffened slightly. 'You think he's gone *to* someone?'

'Who's the current distraction?'

'Just because Jethro left you for me, you assume he's left me for someone else. You can't imagine any other way of life, just rows and infidelities and great emotional reconciliations and false promises. Well, it isn't like that. He doesn't run after other women. I trust him.'

Kitty smiled.

'Anyway,' said Paula. 'When it came to it, you didn't throw him out.'

'Yes I did.' Kitty was haughty.

'No. You say he came back over the conservatory.'

'That just shows he didn't really want to go.'

'It shows that Jethro didn't like being pushed around. It shows that Jethro intended to go on his own terms, when and how *he* decided and not because Ekaterina had once more packed his bags and locked the bedroom door. It's in character.'

Even Kitty found it difficult to answer that. She didn't like the 'once more'. It showed Jethro had been talking.

'You'd been locking the bedroom door a little too often, had you not?' pursued Paula with a note of triumph, sensing she had made a kill.

Kitty shrugged. 'I don't see why a woman has to . . .' Then quite suddenly she added, with surprising candour, 'I can see why he might have wanted to sleep with you. It is and always has been beyond my comprehension why he would want to leave everything he valued and *live* with you.'

'Maybe he valued me.'

Kitty ignored this. 'Throw in his lot with a tedious little photographer in Barnes. It makes no sense.'

'I gave him peace,' replied Paula simply.

109

'And has he given *you* peace?'

Paula almost smiled. 'I'm not a performer so it doesn't matter. No, of course he hasn't. But I don't have to be on top form on a particular date willy-nilly, even if my partner has just laid me low with temperament.'

'Take more than that to lay Jethro flat,' said Kitty crisply. 'He thrives on it. A little contretemps never debilitated him – he found an occasional fracas positively stimulating.'

'That's not what he told me. And it wasn't occasional.'

Kitty gave her a furious look. If there was one thing which maddened her more than almost anything, it was having to come to terms with the fact Jethro must have talked to Paula. She minded that more than the thought of physical intercourse – she refused to think of what he did to Paula or with Paula as 'making love'.

'I tell you,' she snapped. 'He will tire of you and your insufferable, claustrophobic blandness. He's tired already. That's why he's gone.'

'He hasn't come back to you.'

'He will. He only left home to punish me.'

'Ah. But what for?'

'He can be very childish.'

'He left home because he had begun to hate you.'

'Hate,' said Kitty, 'is the closest thing to love. As we all know.'

Paula sighed. 'I'm out of my depth,' she said.

The door opened and Tatiana came in. 'Who was that on the phone?' asked Kitty.

'John.'

'He's a good soul,' said Kitty, assuming he must have rung to enquire about her well-being. 'Friends are something at a time like this.'

'Nina left a shepherd's pie in the oven. You'd better have something to eat.'

They walked together out of the room, leaving Paula stranded, standing on the carpet. It was the second time within the same morning that those she was with had ceased to notice her existence. She was unsure what to do. She put the empty glass on the mantelpiece in case it should be knocked over and then picked it up again and made a move over towards the drinks. Unused to morning drinking, it seemed, suddenly, a good idea to fill her glass. She looked dimly at the array of bottles, mostly aperitifs with names she didn't know.

Tatiana was back at the door. 'I shouldn't,' she said. 'You were never much good at holding it and this is the last time to try.'

Paula put her glass down on the tray and realised, in a daze, that her hand shook very slightly as she did so.

'Mother says you'd better come and eat with us,' said Tattie. 'Come along.'

And Paula followed, mute, at the girls's heels, to the kitchen, where Kitty was sitting at the table with her eyes closed and her hands locked.

'Sit down,' commanded Tatiana.

Kitty opened her eyes and watched Paula pull out her chair with some hesitation. Tattie put plates in front of her father's two women. It was thus that Paula Kingston found herself back at Ekaterina Manning's table again.

Chapter Eight

'It's difficult to express' said Paula over the coffee. 'I've been trying to get my own thoughts into some kind of order about just what it has been. For some weeks. Perhaps even months. He's been – distant.'

She dropped her head. It was not something she wanted to tell them, these Mannings. It was an admission she was ashamed to make.

'Of course he was' said Kitty. 'He was always distant before a recital. Any artist has to be. It's a matter of self preservation.'

'Then I don't see how he could have survived with you. I'm easier to distance from than you would be.'

'I have lived with artists all my life,' said Kitty. It was not strictly true.

'Nevertheless, you're a presence it is difficult to overlook. I can disappear more easily.' She spoke without rancour now. 'I always felt that must have been one of the things he found relaxing about me.'

Kitty hesitated, then said, simply, 'Maybe.'

Paula was surprised.

Kitty stared at her with those deep, marine-blue eyes.

'Did you ask him what was troubling him?'

'No.'

'I would have.'

It was Paula's turn to smile. 'I expect you would.'

Kitty asked, 'Have you access to his diary?'

'Access? It's on the desk. But you know what he's like. Half the engagements don't ever go in the diary. He leaves bits of paper around. I've always found it terrifying. One day you suddenly see a note saying 'Hamburg – next Tuesday' pinned on the kitchen notice board. I suppose I ought to look through the diary.'

'I think it's most peculiar you haven't done so yet,' said Kitty, and Paula shrank a little.

'I suppose . . . yes, it is silly,' she said rather humbly. 'I kept the social diary.'

'Social diary?'

'The one with dinners and things. With our friends.'

'Surely the two were inevitably connected?'

'Well, yes.'

'If you didn't check with Jethro before accepting or arranging things you must have got into something of a muddle.'

'I did sometimes. I have to admit. Mostly I just asked him. Word of mouth.'

'Dangerous,' said Kitty.

'Mm. There was one terrible occasion with the Heygates . . .'

'The Heygates?'

'We were going to the theatre with the Heygates,' said Paula, a little defiantly.

'Were you?'

'They were civil to me, you know. They're civilised people. They didn't seem to think I had leprosy.'

'It makes me feel distinctly peculiar,' Kitty said, frowning, 'the way I have to sit and listen to you talking like this about my husband, about doing things together, especially with our friends . . .'

'Still?'

'Yes, still. Indeed, still.'

'Perhaps,' said Paula mistily, 'we both have rather peculiar feelings.'

Drivng back to Barnes, Paula felt quite unwell. All she wanted was to be able to get into bed and recover from the day, and so when she pulled into her drive and found Alerick sitting in the porch she was less than pleased.

113

He looked at her coldly. 'He seems to be out,' he said, not rising.

She fiddled for the front-door keys at the bottom of her bag and in the end turned the entire contents out on to the step. He watched her without moving.

'I do have a lesson at five.' He looked at his watch to make his point.

She pushed money, credit cards, make-up and shreds of Kleenex back into the bag and opened the door. 'You had better come in,' she said. The cat came rushing out angrily and disappeared down the garden.

'My hands are frozen,' he said. 'They're quite useless after sitting out there for an hour. They feel like fish fingers.'

'You've been there so long?' She took him into the kitchen and put the kettle on. 'I'll make you a cup of tea.'

Then she went back into the hall and picked up the day's post on the mat, five for Jethro and two for herself. The bills always came to her. It was, after all, her property. She put the letters on the hall table, examining the postmarks carefully on Jethro's mail and wondering whether to open it. If she had hoped for a letter from him, she was disappointed. Then she listened to the tape on the answering machine, which she had set up to record again despite the obscene calls, and listened to Alerick's plaintive voice leaving his message for Jethro.

'That's me,' he called from the kitchen. 'When I couldn't raise him at the door I went down the road to the call box just in case he wasn't answering. You know what he's like.'

She found he had made the tea himself. He gave her one of Aunt Virginia's rose cups.

'I wish he didn't do this so often,' he said. 'I know he's got a lot on his mind but I don't actually enjoy trailing over to Barnes and finding he's forgotten. It's a horrible waste of time and a hell of a long way to come now. Couldn't you keep a diary for him? Kitty used to.'

(Alerick had a bed-sitter in West Hampstead and had been put out in many ways when Jethro left Loudoun Road. Apart from the convenience of the address, and liking the aura in Kitty's attractively mad establishment, and never knowing who you were going to meet, it gave him an excuse to see Tattie, for whom he had lusted from puberty.)

114

'I'm awfully sorry,' she said. 'But I'm afraid he's gone away.'

Alerick looked incredulous.

'Away,' she repeated, irritably. It seemed to her that this invasion of her privacy was the final straw after a hard day.

'He told me he'd be back in the morning. It's after six. You could have rung me if he was staying up there. I could have been practising. Even I don't have time on my hands.'

'I didn't know his plans.'

He gulped his tea. 'Oh well. How was Manchester?'

She drank hers slowly, playing for time. 'I haven't spoken to him.'

'He always rang Kitty after a concert.' He stared at Paula with resentment he made no attempt to hide, and she was silent.

'There's rather a horrible smell in here,' he said. 'I think it's cat's piss.'

She sighed, rose, looked for a source and found it. She took a bowl of soapy water and the cat-deodorising spray.

'You'll never get rid of the smell,' he said. 'The Edinburgh house stinks of it. My parents don't notice any more, but I do when I go back now. I can't stick dirty animals. I'd have a dirty animal put down. You just can't live with it.'

'It wasn't the cat's fault. He got shut in. I was away all night and yesterday I was working away from home. I forgot to put out any fresh cat litter.'

'You ought to have a cat hatch,' he said.

'I suppose I ought.'

He looked at his watch. 'When do you suppose he's going to turn up? I mean, what time were you expecting him?'

There was nothing in the world she wanted so little as to have to explain to Alerick.

She explained. It might make him go away.

'You're telling me Jethro just never turned up for his engagement at the Free Trade Hall?'

She nodded.

'But Jethro wouldn't do a thing like that.'

'He has done.'

'But we must get on to his agent.'

She sighed. 'I've been in almost hourly touch with Mr

Dilke. He's no wiser than I am.'

'What about Kitty? I must ring Kitty.'

'I've just come from Kitty. I've been having lunch with her and Tatiana.'

'Good God!' said Alerick. 'Tattie was there?'

'There's not much point in your sitting here, Alerick. I'm very tired. I've got a busy day tomorrow and I think I really must ask you to go.'

'Will you let me know when you hear anything? If you hear anything,' he added.

'I expect Jethro will ring you to arrange the next lesson when he gets home,' she said, with simulated confidence.

'You think so?' She thought he looked very young. And nervous.

'I'll keep you in touch,' she said, suddenly kinder. 'I'm sure there will be some explanation we haven't thought of.'

'You don't think something awful has happened to him?'

She shook her head. She wished she convinced herself.

'But it's not like Jethro to do this with a professional engagement.'

She felt so tired.

'I'll tell you the moment I know anything,' she said.

'Sometimes people who've been under a lot of pressure . . .' he began.

'Jethro's very used to pressure,' she said. 'Anyone in his position has to learn to accommodate pressure. It's built into the life.'

'Yes, but – in his case . . .'

She frowned.

'You and Kitty. Everything breaking up around him.'

'Everything has *not* broken up. He decided to change his life-style and his home and I think you have to ask yourself why. Has it not occurred to you that it couldn't have been a very stable home life in Loudoun Road if he wanted to leave it? He and I are very happy, you know. I give him a background he can work in. I give him some degree of calm, at least, some stability.'

'Stability! You can't be serious! His stability was all there, with the people who knew and understood him. OK, he and Kitty fought, but they were a pair. They meant something.

You thought of those two hyphenated – Kitty-'n-Jethro Manning.'

'Yes,' said Paula. 'And why was it never Jethro-'n-Kitty? That's what I never understood. A man like that. His stature. Who's Kitty Manning I'd like to know?'

'You know very well who Kitty Manning is,' he said quietly, and he knew, although she said nothing, that she had heard. 'Surely you can see all the conflicts and the guilt and all the heaviness that could destroy an artist like him.'

'I don't believe that at all. Artists *aren't* sensitive, not that way. They aren't destroyed – they destroy others. They're more self-preserving than you think. And Jethro didn't feel guilty.' She spoke with assurance, yet realising as she spoke that she had little real idea what went on in the caverns of Jethro's mind about his wife. He too often behaved as though she were something of a music-hall joke, but that meant nothing at all because when Jethro laughed it was usually at something he could be finding too painful or alarming or frightening to acknowledge with anything except hilarity.

'I was only wondering,' said Alerick, 'whether you thought he could have lost his memory.'

'He couldn't have done that.'

'Why not? People do sometimes.'

'He knew he was going. He must have made plans.'

Alerick buried his head in his hands.

'Please,' she said, 'please go. I really do have to be alone.'

He didn't move, but continued to sit there, and when he did finally speak his voice was only just under control.

'If Jethro has gone and killed himself I shall hate you with a hatred it frightens me to contemplate.'

'Jethro hasn't killed himself,' she said harshly. 'Stop fantasising.'

'I find you chilling. There's about as much warm blood in you as a refrigeration plant.'

'You're so childish,' she said wearily. 'So superficial.'

'That's not what Jethro thinks.'

'Jethro says it's about time you grew up.'

For a moment she wondered whether he was going to hit her. She waited. She didn't care. If only she could feel something, if she could draw upon some reservoir of anger so that

117

she might respond in the way this young man now needed her to respond. She felt such pity for him, almost an embarrassment that, with this dead weight of exhaustion paralysing her, she could not allow him the release of battle, that she could not react to his fury with suitable and becoming outrage.

'Why did you desecrate everything the Mannings had together,' he demanded, 'if the man means nothing to you?'

Gently she put a hand upon his shoulder. Any anger of hers seemed to have burned itself out. He twitched it off, more petulantly than furiously.

'He means everything to me,' she said, but as she spoke the words she heard them flat in her own ears and she knew how they would sound in his. There seemed to be no way she could put conviction into the statement he was facing her with, forcing her to make for his own satisfaction.

'You're not much of an actress,' he said bitterly. 'You can't even sound as though you really care – just for the sake of decency.'

She sighed. No, she was nothing of an actress. She wanted to say she left the acting to Kitty, but she couldn't even bring herself to say that. She could simulate nothing, nor could she reveal the depth of her disquiet, the pain that paralysed.

'I'm sorry,' she said, taking him by the elbow and prising him away from his place. 'I must insist.'

He allowed himself to be steered towards the door and went silently now, until they reached the porch, when he turned and said, 'If anything has happened to that man, you will be responsible and you will have lost the world one of its most distinguished artists.'

He looked so young. Clichés dropped from his lips like November leaves. There was an enemy and his life was comparatively simple. His energy fed his unhappiness and anxiety and transmuted them into something positive, unlike her own. He would now be able to go back to his sister, Sally, or whoever of his peers he sought, and share the drama of the moment, thus buffering himself and them against shock. She could not. She could only crawl away, alone, and hope for sleep.

'Very probably,' she said. And closed the door.

*   *   *

118

When Paula flew out, Arthur and Irene had not known what to make of it, but Irene was already late for rehearsal so they had no time to talk which, for them, was a deprivation. However, when Arthur came to collect Irene from the Opera House that night after the performance they made up for it. They crawled down Endell Street in the Covent Garden traffic home-bound queue and then right through the network of one-way narrow streets into Bloomsbury and back towards Kentish Town.

'Well,' said Irene, 'considering her behaviour I think that was very forgiving of you.'

'I felt I ought to. It was only over the road to the police station. Just to check she was OK. It sounded as though they were being fairly tolerant, and by that time she'd gone off.'

'I don't think she had any right to speak to you like that. What an odd young woman she is.'

'Mm,' mumbled Arthur, slipping the clutch. 'Funny bird.'

'It isn't as though we've ever been anything but pleasant to her.'

'Damned awkward situation, though. Don't like getting tied up in other people's love lives. Very uncomfortable business. Never get any thanks.'

'When you think of the way we've fallen over backwards never to let her feel an outsider. Considering we're Kitty's friends . . .'

'Must admit, sometimes I've wondered how Kitty would feel. Of course, we're Jethro's friends, too. Tricky. Don't know what to do for the best. Don't like being forced to take sides.'

'Maybe we ought to have had the courage of our convictions,' mused Irene. 'Maybe we ought never to have accepted the Paula woman at all.'

'Still, when Jethro wanted to bring her round . . .'

'Might have been better had we said we couldn't condone it.'

'Can't really say a thing like that. Not to Jethro. Damned awkward.'

'It was pretty insensitive of Jethro to put us in the predicament.'

Arthur laughed, his small face screwing up like a kidney

119

bean. 'Since when has Jethro been sensitive?' he asked.

'It was you who said we had to compromise in life,' accused Irene.

Arthur looked astonished, wounded. 'Hang about . . .' he complained.

'All along I said Kitty was the one I cared about.'

'Actually you said we must never allow their break-up to alienate us from Jethro. You said this was a time for pragmatism.'

'I'm sure I never said anything of the kind.'

'I remember clearly. At the time I thought it odd. But I suppose you've always had this "thing" about Jethro, and women can all convince themselves any action is right if they go on long enough.'

'Thing about Jethro!' she muttered 'What a fool you are, Arthur. How little you know about anything.'

He smiled at the traffic lights ahead of him.

'I simply feel one has a responsibility to one's oldest friends,' she said.

'I'll tell you something,' said Arthur – and paused. She turned to stare at his profile. 'I've always had a feeling we chase the Mannings.'

'What the hell are you talking about?'

'Well – haven't we? Always. I mean . . . would they ever have kept up with us if we hadn't kept up with them?'

'You know damn well nothing ever comes from them. Their social life's so disorganised . . .'

'I didn't know they had one!' he laughed.

'People like them always mean to get around to things. Surely it's up to those who care . . .'

'To see they don't forget us?' He grinned, now.

'What are you saying?' She showed her offence.

'Only that I don't honestly think either Jethro or Kitty would lose sleep if they never saw or heard from us again. We're hangers-on, Irene, my love. Hangers-on,' he repeated. He was rather pleased with his own scrupulous honesty. 'They've always had more to give us than we've had to give them.'

Now she was silent.

After a while, he said, 'It's not so terrible. There are plenty

120

of others like us. Moths around the flame.'

'I don't like to see myself that way,' said Irene, sombre now. 'Not at all.'

'But you can't pretend one doesn't enjoy having famous, bizarre friends.'

'You're really saying I couldn't bear to let Jethro go. And that's why I was kind to the Paula woman – so as not to lose touch with him.'

'There may have been a slight element of that,' said Arthur.

'*He* brought her to meet *us*,' she said, with more spirit.

'Because you pressed him,' he added, gently.

'Well,' she said, after some thought. 'I can't say I think she likes us very much.'

'But do we really like her?' he asked.

'Not desperately.' She sighed.

'I can't think what Jethro sees in her,' he said, companionably.

'Frankly,' said Irene over the telephone to Kitty when they got home, 'neither Arthur nor I can think what the hell Jethro sees in her.'

'I have sometimes wondered,' said Kitty with sudden and unprovoked acidity, even malice, 'what he saw in a number of his friends.'

Irene was decidedly muted as she and Arthur undressed and went to bed, so muted that eventually he asked her what the matter could be.

'Kitty,' she said.

'Poor old Kitty!' he mumbled, tying up his pyjama bottoms cord.

'Kitty's a bit of a bitch,' said Irene, pulling back the bedspread and climbing into bed. 'Frankly I sometimes wonder what Jethro saw in her.'

Chapter Nine

In the morning Paula was sick. She leaned over the lavatory pan and painfully delivered herself of a stream of thin green bile, after which she made herself a pot of tea and threw up the first cup almost immediately. She sat upon a chair in the kitchen with a hand on her stomach, looking at the day's itinerary in the diary which lay on the table. Two engagements sprang up from the page – one written in her own square, almost childish hand – and one in Jethro's black, heavy scrawl. It was not often that he noted his commitments in the diary, but here it was, a recording session in a West London studio for eleven o'clock this morning.

She crawled to the telephone upstairs and flopped down on the bed, resting the instrument on the pillow and mis-dialling the number the first time. When she got through to him, Roger Dilke told her drily that he had already cancelled the appointment and everything else within the week. 'I cancelled Cardiff for Saturday,' he said. 'We couldn't possibly risk another Manchester.'

'Cardiff?'

There was a moment's hesitation, denoting irritation before he replied, 'Yes, Cardiff.'

'I'm not sure I knew about Cardiff.'

'I see,' he said.

'Was he going to play the same things there?' she asked.

'You don't seem to know a lot about his . . . No. He was going to play the Mozart C Minor.'

'Isn't it rather a long time ahead to cancel,' she suggested mildly. 'After all, he might be back by then.'

'Equally he might not,' he said. 'I felt I had to give them reasonable time to find a replacement.'

'Them?'

(God – he thought – the woman's a moron. In fact he said as much to Philip Foster, putting his hand over the receiver. Philip sat puffing away and shrugged.)

'The Royal Philharmonic Orchestra,' he explained slowly and deliberately. Philip chuckled and wagged a finger at him.

'Oh yes, the orchestra,' she said.

'I've been on the phone to them this morning.'

'Goodness,' she said. 'That's early.'

He sighed. 'It doesn't seem early to me. Philip and I have been here since half-past eight this morning. We're not having the easiest time at the moment, you know. And one doesn't want to let the promoters down.'

'The promoters?'

She sounded so vague, he thought he could scream. 'The orchestra are the promotors,' he explained. 'For – the – Cardiff – concerto. At – the – St David's – Hall. Cardiff.'

Philip was nearly collapsing with laughter.

'Oh I see. Well yes, I suppose it's only fair.'

'Now if you'll forgive me,' he said.

'Poor Jethro.'

'I'm a shade pressed . . .'

'Are you going to cancel all his engagements from now on?'

'No,' he said, levelly. 'Nothing so dramatic. We'll play it by ear . . .'

'Ah! So you're not going to leave him!'

He bit his lip. 'Give me a ring if you hear anything,' he said. 'Meanwhile, of course, if I . . .' And he rang off.

'I'm glad you're capable of laughing,' he said to Philip, scowling.

'Have to,' replied his partner. 'Got to keep sane.'

'Sanity and Jethro Manning,' said Roger, 'have nothing to say to each other. Where in heaven's name did he pick up that woman?'

'She took his photographs. Had you forgotten?'

Roger glanced up at the wall where a picture of Jethro glowered down upon him. 'It might be a good idea to remove that for the time being,' he said. 'For my health.'

Paula went to look at the kitchen notice board and found Cardiff under the last week's milk order.

She also looked in her diary to see exactly how late her period was and found she had been due two Fridays before Jethro's South Bank Recital. She had not worried at all at first because stress and anxiety did sometimes delay her cycle, but now it seemed significant.

She went into the hall and found the post had been, bringing five identical circulars for a cut-price wine shop, a letter from her second cousin in Montreal, three mini-cab numbers and a letter for Jethro. Tentatively, she opened it. It was from a music club in East Anglia. She remembered that Jethro, who played at only the most prestigious of the music clubs around the country these days, and those infrequently now he was so much in demand internationally, had given a recital there the week before his South Bank venue, a run-through for the same programme. It was from the honorary secretary. He wrote expressing concern, hoping that Jethro had arrived home safely and suffered no ill effects. He said the committee wished to be included in his good wishes and concern. He said that despite everything the audience had been most appreciative and it had been a memorable evening. That they would all be thinking of him on Sunday, when he would be playing at the Queen Elizabeth Hall and that one or two of their members were actually coming up to London to hear the recital for a second time. The letter was dated the Thursday before the Queen Elizabeth Hall concert, but with a second-class stamp had taken it's time to wander to Barnes.

Paula put it down, confused. What did it mean? She could not make it out. If they had only been more explicit. She toyed with the idea of telephoning the honorary secretary, who seemed to be a retired Wing Commander, to find out what he meant, but put the letter down on the hall table, procrastinating until she felt better. Alternatively, should she ring Roger and read it to him? He would know what to do.

In the lavatory she tried to be sick again but her empty stomach protested. She telephoned the surgery to make an appointment, found it impossible to get one under three days, but booked a time for good measure although by now she knew she must be pregnant and did not need a medical man to

124

tell her so. Finding an orange, for whose sharp sweetness she suddenly felt an unaccountable yearning, she took it back to bed with her, together with a clipboard and a felt-tip pen, to make some notes about her own job later in the morning, photographing the new extension to a cosmetics factory in Slough.

She lay on Jethro's side of the bed as she had done all night. She had wondered whether it might serve to make him seem closer, but that was all illusion. His imprint and his scent had already gone as, frighteningly, even the memory of his face was clouding. During the night she had gone downstairs to find one of the South Bank programmes and brought it upstairs that she might have his likeness under the pillow. From time to time she had turned on the light to look at it. Yet all these ploys and ruses only stretched the length and distance of whatever miles, whatever misunderstandings, lay between the two of them. She felt more alone than she had ever felt before, even after Daddy's death. It was almost as though her life with Jethro had never been, had been a waking dream. Was it the visit to Kitty and his family which had done this? Had their reality wiped out, obliterated her own?

Fear took her bowels and knotted them. Spasms of panic brought beads of unseasonable damp to her skin and although the day outside was clammy cold she threw the duvet off to the floor.

Wednesday. The third day.

She was beginning to doubt whether Jethro was going to come home. Until now, on Sunday night, on Monday and even yesterday, in the midst of all his family, she had been convinced, somewhere deep and pure where the fear could not pollute, that he would, in his own good time, return. There were many ways in which he would do it, and she had rehearsed them all. He might ring, or write with a brief explanatory note, no words wasted, to say why he had gone, where he was, and when he planned to come home. He might get in touch with Roger Dilke, by-passing herself and Kitty and the girls – he was capable of it if sufficiently obsessed with whatever had drawn or driven him away – and he would see no reason why either woman should take offence, for he

125

would expect them to assume that his professional misdemeanour far outweighed the domestic betrayal. Alternatively, he could simply walk through the door. That was the most likely. Saunter into the kitchen, grab a drink, look conspiratorial, sheepish, or scowl to pre-empt any attack. Until now all these permutations had seemed feasible, even probable, and she had gone about the house in a perpetual state of readiness, jumping at every creak in the floorboards, stumbling across obstacles to every ring on the telephone, staring out of the window at the postman as he climbed the steps of the house next door.

She raised herself and reached out for the telephone. Then lay back. Getting out of bed she padded downstairs again, took the letter from the table in the hall, and got back under the duvet, sat up and dialled the number on the letter heading. Her heart began to accelerate. She wondered what the Wing Commander would be like. He sounded approachable. But the number rang and rang and rang.

She put the telephone on Jethro's side of the bed.

Now, this morning, she was suddenly certain that he was not coming back. This baby she was so sure she was carrying, she and the baby, would both have to fend for themselves without a father, without a man. In a bleak world, she would have to be mother and father, supplying all needs, shouldering all burdens, comforting and providing and instructing and above all loving, in the absence of the other. She felt like a Thomas Hardy heroine, desolate, deserted, carrying her child across the heath, holding its little, shuddering body, racked with infant coughing, against her.

She could not, with her own paternal background, envisage the thought of a childhood without a father. To her, parent meant the masculine, the quiet, kind authority, the directive animus, the wisdom and the answer to all sensible questions. How could she manage without a father for her baby? Yet was Jethro, could he ever be, such a parent? A fleeting image crossed her mind's eye, of a baby crying, a pram in the garden, the baby beating the side of the black pram with tiny fists of fury to the accompaniment of an unrelentingly brilliant Liszt study pouring in cascades through the open window, shafts of piercing sound. Of Jethro, impatient, bursting

126

through the door and shouting that she must keep the damn child quiet. Of Jethro, despairing, head in a score, refusing to chastise a rebellious adolescent, dropping notes into the sticky palm of an amoral fifteen-year-old to keep him quiet in the hope he might go away, preferably to an all-night party and leave the house, briefly, a fit place to work in.

Jethro was not coming very well out of all this.

As she dwelt upon her lover in his every aspect, real and fictional, he began to materialise again, to gather form and shape and substance, colour and voice, to make his presence, and thus his absence, felt. Under her breath she muttered to him, soft words of abuse and blandishment, admonishing him for so impregnating her and now deserting her, his child a sprouting, curling somnolent seed so recently germinated, disturbing her digestive system and her peace of mind.

It was he who had, with his usual irresponsible optimism and childish greed, put her in this position. Even he could never argue otherwise, unless by forgetting the whole incident, refusing to acknowledge the facts.

They had been in Bruges, and again, that had been his idea. Early January in Bruges. A couple of nights in a cheap hotel by a canal. The previous night Jethro had been playing the Ravel Piano Concerto for the Left Hand in Brussels, and for once she had flown over to hear him. It had been his suggestion initially, but then he seemed to have gone cold on the idea, leaving her with the uneasy suspicion that he did not really want her there. And the work too. A work of which he was particularly fond, now, just before the concert, he seemed to turn against it, to disparage it, to make sour and rather tasteless jokes about it. If she hadn't known better, she might almost have thought he was suddenly nervous of the piece. And so she had cried off coming, made other arrangements, and listened to the Ravel in practice, standing motionless in the kitchen to hear the sudden pauses when he stopped, waited for a second and swore before taking up a passage again. This kind of behaviour made her tense and even absent-minded, lacking in attention when it came to her own job.

127

At the eleventh hour he changed. His spirits began to rise, he was all smiles, all jokes. He demanded to know why she was deserting him, why she was not coming with him. What kind of a woman was this, he asked? He had better find another, he said, putting his hand inside her jumper.

Startled and pleased, she said she would of course come. At a moment's notice she cancelled a sitting with a haughty young ballerina whose goodwill she thus lost. She bought herself a new dress for the occasion, a svelte green velvet number which set off her pale hair and milky skin, and then, in Brussels, the hall had been so over-heated she had nearly died of asphixiation and the one night's wearing had brought a bleached stain creeping under the armpits.

After the concert she had, in her ignorance, supposed there might be some kind of reception for Jethro, an affair at which she would have to shake hands and smile and speak French to the conductor, the orchestra and the promoters, and make them accept that it was her, not Kitty, whose glass they filled. But she was wrong. And if she expected, either, a select, urbane small group of musical Belgians to host the pianist and his lady in an expensive, gourmet restaurant where the patron brought the wine personally to the table and greeted Jethro (who had, after all, played in Brussels on a number of triumphant occasions before and was said by Roger to be beloved of its audiences) . . . then again, she was to be surprised, if not actively disappointed. She assured herself that she did not care for such occasions or enjoy ostentatious food, and as Jethro whirled her in a taxi driven by a wild, thin woman to a 'Tripe Bar', the wrong side of town, where he assured her 'those who knew' flocked in droves to stand in a jostling, competitive scrum on the pavement until the doors were opened, she convinced herself that this was life.

After a long and acrimonious wait, pushing half into the restaurant and being pushed out again, they finally found a table, a filthy cloth was whisked off and a clean white one whisked on with a flourish, and the menu brought by a surly Belgian brute in a striped apron. The tripe, which Jethro insisted they ordered, although the alternative dishes listed were of course legion, was in actual fact delicious, despite the nausea for which Paula, who had never eaten tripe and spent a life-time looking upon it with aversion, prepared herself.

'It's very good!' she said, feeling for his knee beneath the table to express appreciation.

'Of course,' he replied. But he showed little interest in her knee. He was entirely engaged in eating.

Seated, eating and drinking a good Alsace Riesling, Jethro fell entirely silent. Morose, he burrowed into his food, never looking up to give her even the most fleeting of smiles. Dumb, she ate, miserably, wondering whether he was now regretting having brought her. She repeated how much she liked the tripe and how clever he was to have found the place, so full of French and Belgians and so empty of tourists. She laughed gaily at her own prejudice, but he never raised his head or seemed to hear. She spilt the soft, creamy wine sauce into her green velvet lap and when she stood, in distress, to try and wipe it off, and the waiter brought water to help, thus proving that he was only in brute's clothing, he never took his eyes from his plate. Lost in thought, he ate. She sat motionless, eyes for ever returning to the mark in her dress, for something like twenty minutes with the bill lying on the plate unread. She longed to speak, but did not dare. She longed to reach across, turn up the bill and see what this odd, not very satisfactory evening had cost them; but she knew better, and so they sat, ignored by the staff, who appeared not to care whether they sat all night.

At last Jethro felt in his pockets, produced a few dog-eared notes, and rose. Hurriedly now the waiter came to the table, and picking up the plate, glancing at it, said *'Service non compris, monsieur.'*

Jethro ignored him, swept Paula out into the street ahead and, seeming now to have lost any interest in taxi-transport, marched along the pavement. In high heels she had a job to keep up. It was raining slightly and the way was slippery. Eventually they reached their hotel.

That had been their second night in Brussels, when Paula had realised, in a flash, that she had left her contraceptive pills behind in Barnes. For some reason, perhaps because her leaving had in the end been so rushed, perhaps because she had been distracted by the ballerina's shrill telephone denun-

129

ciation when she had so hastily cancelled the sitting, Paula had quite overlooked the absence of the pills the first night, not even remembering that she ought to have taken one before turning off the light. That night, the night before the concert, he had not wanted to make love to her and now tonight, she realised with relief, he seemed in no way amorous. He would have been very upset if thwarted, and while some men might have resorted grumpily to the vending machine in the hotel '*messieurs*', condoms were not Jethro's style. He had made that perfectly plain from the outset.

So – she had managed to get through two pill-less nights without disaster, but now, on holiday in Bruges, in a hotel where the drain from the wash-basin stank and the walls were spattered with what the mosquitoes had supped upon in the misty days of autumn by the canals and the hotel had failed to paint over, his libido rose to full and glorious erection. It was, he surely felt, time to make his presence felt.

She explained. He laughed. He tore her dress over her head and left it lying on the floor. She explained again, at first firmly and then more feebly, as he pressed her down upon the lumpy bolster and nibbled the softer, more yielding parts of her upper arms and bosom.

'Yum, yum,' he sang.

He ran his hand down the sides of her and made her scream when it tickled her waist and then stopped her mouth with kisses so she gurgled. It was all good clean fun, but as she said, 'No, Jethro, please, Jethro, we must be more careful, oh *don't*, Jethro, I'm sure you could buy something downstairs . . .' he entered her.

After this act of love, during which he made her the mother of his child, he reverted and became once more morose, silent, preoccupied. Exploring Bruges the next day he behaved as though she were not there at all, wandering about the narrow streets and the canals with his camera, darting away and losing her in alleys. At one point she truly lost him and was forced to return, scared and alone to the hotel. She was sure he had done it on purpose.

On the last night of their stay he made love to her in the true sense of the word, tenderly and kindly, as though he loved her. He even told her she was his 'little haddock', an odd endearment to which she had grown used and of which she had become fond in the early days of their attachment, but which now he seldom used. As he slept, she wept quietly and happily with relief. His love-making, although sweet, had failed to satisfy her, not because he could be faulted or had failed her that night, but because she was weary after the holiday and a little nervous of any repercussions there might be. Although she would love to bear Jethro's baby, his reaction was something of an unknown quantity. He had at the outset of their liaison pointed out that he already had a sufficiency of offspring and that he was terrified, if he had any more, that he might produce one with some musical gift. Thinking such thoughts, she had not been able to relax or lose herself in love.

She had indeed found herself wondering, as he bounced about the noisy springs of the bed, what she would do if she did find herself pregnant later.

On the boat he never spoke to her. He stood on deck watching the waves separate and foam and crash back against each other and the boat while she, in woolly hat and duffel coat, sat in a wet deck-chair. Most of the passengers sat below in glum ranks staring through portholes at the ginger-beer sea, or steadied themselves at the bar. It was a rough crossing and the seamen were busy with buckets of water to sloosh and swoosh away too visible distress, but Paula was not sick. She was a good sailor, a good traveller, and almost never sick at sea.

Yet now, she hurried through, once more, to the bathroom. Surely morning sickness disappeared as the day moved on. Surely. How would she cope in Slough? How would she cope anywhere, any time, without Jethro, she and her baby, his child? Nina and Tatiana's sibling. That was a thought. And Antony's. It would all seem very rum.

For a fanciful moment, as she brushed her teeth, she wondered whether he could have guessed and that could have been what had sent him running.

She passed his desk on the landing and pulled out a drawer. Old cheque books and bank statements fell out on to the carpet. She picked them up and tried to stuff them into the crammed drawer, but they spilled out again. Bundling them

131

up with an elastic band she suddenly thought . . .

'What will he do for money?'

She rang Loudoun Road. She never stopped to think or wonder why that was the number to which she automatically turned. For a long time she held on, but there was no reply and eventually, dejected, she replaced the receiver. She wanted very much to hear one of the Mannings speak. She wanted a Manning ear to listen and a Manning voice to tell her what to do.

Now she telephoned Roger's office again, and this time Tamsin answered.

'Roger's out,' she said, 'but Mr Bristol's in the office.'

'Mr Bristol? Why?'

'He's waiting for Philip. He called to see Roger.'

'And Mr Foster's out too?'

'That's right.'

'Well, I don't quite know that Mr Bristol can . . . oh well, yes, would you put me on to him?'

'What are you doing there?' she asked Theo.

'Roger's gone up to Manchester this morning to try and pacify the Hallé,' he said. 'And he's going on to Scotland after that. He seems to have some hunch Jethro could be in the very north somewhere.'

She was incredulous. 'Why Scotland?'

'I've no idea. I'm only the office boy. I know nothing. I come from Barcelona.'

His flippant tone irritated her, but she had to talk to someone.

'Who actually takes the financial loss for Jethro not turning up in Manchester?'

'The Hallé Concerts Society are the promoters in this case. They've every right to come back to Jethro, and if he doesn't pay up, they could always sue him.'

'They wouldn't!'

'They're not a charitable institution.'

'But Jethro couldn't possibly – and anyway, if he's not to be found . . .'

'It's all that Roger's gone up to try and sort out. I can't say I envy him.'

She was quiet for a moment or two. Then she said, 'Jethro

couldn't have had much money on him when he left.'

'How do you know?'

'I'd almost cleaned him out on the Saturday evening when I went to the butcher. He can't have had more than five pounds, possibly less. How's he managing, I wonder.'

'He stole from me,' said Theo. 'Actually.'

'Oh dear.'

'A mere nothing, dear girl, compared with my car. But I keep a little "cache" in the fridge and Jethro knows my habits very well. It had gone when I got home.'

'How much?'

'On this occasion, over seventy-five pounds.'

'Damn,' said Paula.

'Won't last him that long,' Theo mused. 'Has he got his cheque book?'

'That's the point. All the ones in his desk are old stubs. He must have got it. And when he cashes a cheque, then surely we can find out where he is.'

'He could always use the cash machine.'

'But he can never remember his number, and I've never let him carry it around with him because knowing Jethro he'd be bound to keep it with his cheque book.'

'It wouldn't be so easy to trace him, even then.'

'The bank would cooperate.'

'Not necessarily. What authority have you? Is it a joint account?'

'No.'

'Well then. It isn't as if you're even his wife. The bank manager's not going to reveal anything, is he?'

'Surely. With Jethro missing . . .'

'I wouldn't be so certain.'

'But if the police . . .'

'The police can ask. They can't direct. The bank is autonomous and Jethro is their client. Not you.'

'I shall go and see the manager,' she said grandly.

'You do that,' he replied, 'but you may get no change from them. After all, Jethro's meandered off of his own free will. Nobody made him.'

Paula replaced the receiver.

'I hate that man,' she said to herself as she dressed, pulling

133

on warm rust-red tights. Pulling back the bed, a piece of paper fell out of the duvet. She picked it up from the floor. It was the scrap upon which he had written details of the Cardiff engagement. She turned it over and now, on the other side, she saw a telephone number. A London number with a Bayswater exchange code.

She rang the number, sitting on the side of the bed. As she dialled, she had little idea what she would say to whoever answered, how she would cope were it a young, female voice. But she need have had no fears, for there was only a recorded message, telling her that Dr Courtney's secretary was temporarily out of the office and pressing her to leave a message and her telephone number. She put the receiver down without speaking, and sat for a while, thinking.

Picking up the directory, she pored through the Courtneys to match the name with the number, but although she ran down the list several times, most carefully, she could not find the number. It must be new, since the printing of the directory. Or else, of course, it could be ex-directory.

Kitty might know. She tried Loudoun Road again, but now the line was engaged. She continued trying for ten minutes and then gave up.

As she backed the car out of the garage, narrowly missing the cat's tail, she realised that she no longer felt sick, and that was something.

In the bank she went straight to the enquiries counter and rang the buzzer. In time a worried-looking man with hair scraped sideways across his balding scalp opened the door of the box within and came to the glass partition. He looked as though he expected her to be armed.

'Yes?' he asked.

Although she had been rehearsing her story in the car, she still found it difficult to explain clearly, and without too much hesitation, what it was she had to say. She began by explaining that her friend, the celebrated concert pianist Jethro Manning, had disappeared.

'Oh yes?' he commented.

'You've heard about it possibly.'

'I may have,' he said guardedly.

'It's been in the papers.'

He looked patiently expectant, ignoring the small queue gathering behind her.

'Would it be possible,' she asked, 'for us to talk somewhere a little quieter?'

'You may talk here if you like,' he said.

She glanced over her shoulder. 'I think I would rather not.'

He sighed. 'If you would care to wait a moment . . .' Not seeming to hear as she said, 'Perhaps I ought to speak to the manager', he disappeared.

She stood back to allow a Chinese woman to take her place at the window. Nothing happened, and in time the Chinese lady rang the bell on the counter. A young man in a pink shirt came and asked if he might help her.

Out of a mahogany-veneer panelled doorway the other man emerged after a little. He led Paula through another door into a bare room with Venetian blinds and a desk. There were artificial roses on the desk. For a moment he stood beside it, then gestured for her to sit. As he himself took a seat, he glanced at the clock on the wall.

'Perhaps I ought to be seeing the manager,' she repeated. 'This is a very difficult situation.'

He didn't respond and she continued. 'I'm in a delicate position. In a way.' She wished he could have been the young man in the pink shirt.

'I'm the manager's assistant,' he said at length. 'How can I help you?'

'Mr Manning is my . . . friend. We – er – share a house. My house actually . . .' she floundered.

Politely he attended her.

'He . . . separated from his wife just over a year ago, and came to live with me. I'm a photographer. I don't have an account with you, in fact' – she blushed – 'but he does. It's quite a healthy account – most of the time.' She tried to smile. 'He has a deposit account too. I think he has about three thousand in that at the moment. Sometimes he overdraws on his current account, but that's only carelessness . . .' she babbled.

He shifted his position in his chair and crossed his hands on the desk.

'He had this Sunday recital at the Queen Elizabeth Hall,

you see,' she explained. 'And then immediately after, he disappeared. There's been no word since. You might have thought he was just taking a break,' she said, forestalling him, 'or that he wanted to get away from it all – or even me, but you see, it isn't as simple as that. He failed to turn up for a piano recital booking at the Manchester Free Trade Hall the next night. Now that's a thing he would never do.'

He looked sympathetic.

'At first the police wouldn't do anything, but after that they've had to take it seriously and now he's listed as a missing person.'

'Ah,' he said.

'He took some cash, but not enough to last very long, so soon he should be cashing a cheque or going to a cash machine. I suddenly realised. If the Bank will authorise a search, we can presumably find out where he is – once he does that.'

He shook his head. 'I don't think we could,' he said. She stared at him. 'Surely it's not difficult. The cheques all come in.'

'Not difficult. Merely . . . improper.' The word 'improper' was, she felt, intended to be crushing. And final.

'But that's ridiculous,' she said hotly.

'Not really.'

'Supposing you were trying to trace a homicidal rapist.'

'But your friend isn't a criminal. And you are not, as I understand, his wife.'

'Would you do it for his wife?'

'That would depend,' he answered, 'upon a number of factors.'

'Then his wife will approach you,' she said with some dignity. She rose. 'And if the police tell you to trace his cheques?'

'It is not for the police to tell us what to do.' Now he seemed to be making less effort to be courteous.

'Is that really so?' She was astonished.

'They can advise us,' he said. 'We do not have to take their advice.' He paused. 'On the other hand, it could be that the bank might wish to cooperate.'

'But whatever you did, you would not act on any instructions from me.'

'I'm afraid not. 'That is correct.'

136

'I see.' She picked up the briefcase she had put on the floor. 'In that case . . .'

He rose with her. He managed a weak, small smile of conciliation.

'I do appreciate you must find all this very . . . frustrating. Distressing if I may say . . .'

Her eyes began to fill.

'May I use your Ladies, please?'

But however hard she tried, she could not be sick. And now she drove to Slough.

Eating lunch in the works canteen with the Sales Promotion Manager for Home Counties she thought of Betjeman. She felt a terrible inertia creeping up. Maybe it was Slough.

> "Those air-conditioned, bright canteens,
> Tinned fruit, tinned meat, tinned milk, tinned beans
> Tinned minds, tinned breath."

Only substitute frozen instead of tinned in today's world. The Sales Promotion Manager for Home Counties had tomato ketchup on his chin. She wiped her own.

Throughout the day, she tried to telephone Kitty's establishment, but the line was permanently engaged. For some reason she felt a reluctance to try the Bayswater number from anywhere but the security of her own bedroom. She did not know why. It was a form of personal eccentricity, and one she did not understand, a weakness, but for her a call to persons unknown represented something of a hurdle to be surmounted. A challenge from which she recoiled. Even a threat. For what might it reveal? She felt a cowardly longing to lean upon Kitty whom, she was certain, suffered from no such inhibition.

Thus it was not until she arrived home and had taken off her shoes, was lying in the safety of her room, that she tried the number once more. Again, there was no reply and this time, not even a recorded message, and she realised, guiltily, that she had very probably missed all the working hours during which, were it an office or other place of business, it might have been open. This morning she had rung too early. Now she rang too late.

However, Kitty's number now brought a voice – Nina's. Kitty, it seemed, was out and had been so since the late morning. No, Nina did not know the number or the name Courtney, but made a note of both and would ask Kitty upon her return. Yes, it was probable that their own line had been engaged for long periods. Kitty had been ringing everybody she knew this morning for news of Jethro, following every possible thread which could lead to him. She had telephoned friends in Edinburgh and friends in Bristol and people Jethro had once visited in Carlisle, but nobody knew anything. One thing – Kitty had asked whether Paula kept Jethro's passport for him?

'No,' said Paula. She made it sound as though it were an odd suggestion, but her heart sank. Of course, Kitty would have taken care of the passport.

'Where does he keep it?'

Paula began to feel flustered. 'If you'll just hold on,' she said, and went to rummage through the drawer of his desk where he kept a box-file marked 'J.M. Attention'. In Kitty's writing.

She came back to the telephone. She didn't tell Nina that the box-file was stuffed with old photographs of Jethro, including those she herself had taken. And nothing else at all.

'I'm afraid I can't find it,' she said. 'But that doesn't necessarily mean it isn't here. It could be anywhere. He's not terribly tidy.'

'I see,' said Nina. The words sounded like a condemnation. 'Oh, well . . .'

'I'll ring you if I find it,' said Paula.

'Do that.'

Nina was not unkind, but Paula, lying on her bed with an Irish whiskey in her hand, felt bleak with self-contempt. She was so useless. She couldn't even help to establish whether Jethro had the capability of leaving the country. She felt she was contributing very little to the search and no doubt, in the condition in which she was sure she was, *enceinte*, she ought not to be drowning her sorrows in the bottle. Pregnancy, if confirmed, would have to be taken seriously.

She lay back and closed her eyes and tried to visualise life without Jethro and with a baby. She found she could not concentrate. Both Jethro and his offspring retreated into unreality. All that was real was a growing hunger pain. The canteen lunch in Slough had been curiously unsatisfying although it seemed to have swollen her at the time. Now she rose to cook herself a toasted cheese dream for which, quite suddenly, she felt an uncontrollable yearning. She ate four, quickly. And suffered all night.

Chapter Ten

Wednesday. Tatiana on her way to work walked briskly, just before ten o'clock, through Maiden Lane, past Rules and the little Roman Catholic Church, and on round the Covent Garden Piazza, just awakening, to Floral Street. A chill day, the kind where, unless you wear a scarf, the dirty damp of London gets down your neck. Tatiana wore one of Kitty's cast-off furs, the raised collar stuffed well with one of Antony's Charterhouse scarves. A woolly hat came right down almost over her eyes.

She was one of the thousand-odd staff employed by the Opera House, one of those citizens belonging to the whole world so busily and fruitfully engaged somewhere in the labyrinth behind the noble cream neo-Palladian porticos in Bow Street.

The Garden's thoroughfares were grubby. There were signs of last night's revelry, refuse left from take-aways and an offering left on the pavement by a visitor who had been unable to hold his English beer.

She pushed open the heavy glass panels of the stage door. Already the warm, well-lit lobby was crowded, full of chatter, alive with greeting. A long-legged ballerina with a cloud of dark hair and skintight jeans was leaning against the desk, talking earnestly to a bearded man in a long dark coat, a cashmere scarf and high boots. A policeman on the beat had come in from the cold and seemed reluctant to leave. He had no business. The door-keeper appeared to know him. Three women, one black and young, beautiful and sulky, sat on the bench seat staring at nothing, waiting.

Tatiana took the bundle of mail the stage door keeper handed to her and went out into the damp street again, the door held for her by the young copper, who still did not follow. His walkie-talkie whispered messages at him. She crossed the road to 45, Floral Street, where the administrative staff are housed, flashed her identity card at the door keeper there and ran up the stairs, running her hand up the red plastic rail, across the wide landing where stood the copying machine and its attendant paper stores, past production wardrobe where all the costumes were either waiting to go out on tour, or just returned, shrouded in covers, and along a couple of narrow passages until she reached her own office. It was a building in which the uninitiated could easily lose themselves, but to Tatiana it was now home. Here, it seemed to her sometimes, her world had more substance than in Loudoun Road, since Jethro had left and the music room had fallen silent.

Sally MacKinley shared an office with Tatiana and another girl who was today away ill, the winter flu epidemic having decimated the staff. She was toasting her feet at an electric blow heater.

'My feet are blocks of ice,' she said. 'Dear brother brought me on the back of his motorbike. He sends his love. You better?'

'Send it back,' said Tattie. She hung up her coat and kept the scarf on. 'I mean – send him mine. Yes, I'm fine, thanks.' She began to open the mail. 'This shouldn't be here,' she said. 'It's from one of the Friends.'

'I'm going along there in a moment. I'll take it for you.' Sally held out her hand for the letter and then hesitated. 'Any news of your father?' she asked.

Tatiana shook her head. 'You saw the piece in the paper?'

'Yah.' She sighed and shook her head. 'What a thing! I really don't know what to say. How's Kitty? I hardly liked to ask.'

'OK on the surface,' answered Tattie, a little carefully.

'Irene rang. She wanted to speak to you because she's not been able to get through to Kitty.'

'Why does she want Mother again? She spoke to her late last night.'

'She didn't say. But she may pop up later, or see you in the canteen, she said.'

'I wanted a quick, quiet lunch to myself. Irene's a drag.'

'Only passing on the message. The orchestra are rehearsing in the Crush Bar this morning. Ballet's on stage. By the way, Alerick had a brush with the fair Paula last night.'

'Oh?'

'He was scheduled to have a lesson. He duly trekked over to Barnes and of course there was no Jethro. So he took it out on her.'

'It wasn't Paula's fault. Not that I hold any brief for the woman, but . . .'

'I suppose she could have rung him.'

'She had more to worry about yesterday than Father's pupils.'

'Well – Alerick can be quite petulant at times. As you know, he idolises Jethro, but he does get a bit fed up the way he's always forgetting lessons. It's a habit of your Pa's. Incidentally – do you think he could have forgotten about Manchester?'

'I suppose he's capable of anything, but I'd hardly have thought so. Roger'd not let him forget, anyway. And presumably Paula . . .'

'How competent is she?'

'Not very, I suspect. Incidentally, Theo says Roger's gone rushing off to Scotland, after he's been to see the Hallé Concerts people.'

'Why Scotland?'

'Seems to have some hunch. It's all rather mysterious.'

'Who's Theo?'

'Don't you know Theo? He's a sort of family friend right back. Much older than my parents. I think he had something to do with concert management a hundred years ago and he seems to know everybody. He's kind of retired, but he hangs round Roger. Ma calls him an elder statesman and Pa calls him an old woman! He knows Arthur and Irene, too. I believe Kitty's having supper with him tonight. He goes to the best places and she finds that comforting.'

'Is he your mother's lover?'

Tatiana smiled. 'He's not that way. Anyway, Kitty doesn't

142

have lovers. She's worn her chastity belt since Father walkd out.' She paused. 'Or even before, possibly,' she muttered.

Sally shot her a look. 'Oh dear!' she said.

'You know my father.'

'Not as well as some!'

'That makes you quite a celebrity!' said Tatiana. 'Anyway, thanks for the delicacy. One never can be quite sure with Jethro.'

'You ought to be sure of me.'

Tattie smiled. 'Perhaps,' she said.

'I suppose we ought to get down to something useful.' Sally shuffled papers on her desk. ' "His Nibs" has been here for hours.'

'Weren't you going along to Friends?'

'Yah.' Sally stood up with the letter in her hand as the door opened and someone from Publications breezed in waving a proof of a Deutsche Grammophon 'ad' and put it down on Tattie's desk. 'Did you know about this?' he asked.

She picked it up, and shook her head. 'News to me,' she said.

He hovered by her chair. 'What's all this about your papa?' he asked.

'Presumably you know as much as I do.' She was short. 'From what you say you've read the newspaper reports.'

'Well, yes but . . .'

'I know no more.'

'Oh dear. Oh God. Sorry.'

He looked apologetically at the top of her head, which she refused to raise. Sally indicated the door and he left with her.

'Cretin!' she said in the passage, leaving him standing.

On her way back from Friends she bumped into a girl from Postal Bookings. 'That violin was looking for Tatiana earlier,' she said. 'Irene someone.'

'She knows.'

The girl paused for a moment. 'Isn't it awful about her father!'

'Awful,' agreed Sally. 'But I shouldn't mention it to her. She's a little upset about the way people keep on about it.'

'I wouldn't! Do you think . . . do you think he could have killed himself?'

'Now why on earth,' snapped Sally, 'would he do a thing like that?'

Indeed why – she asked herself on her way back to the office, where she found the telephone ringing and Tatiana disappeared. She picked it up. A newspaper reporter asked to speak to Miss Manning. 'Out!' she told him.

'Do you know when she'll be back?'

'Haven't any idea.' She rang off. Then came back to the switchboard to ask them to keep any Press off the line today. 'Ask who's calling,' she directed. 'If it's a journalist say we're out.'

Tattie came back with a long face. 'I had to run over to give an urgent message to Sir John,' she said. 'He's watching the ballet rehearsal this morning. Everywhere I go, people ask me about Jethro.'

'I suppose it is to be expected,' said Sally quietly.

'Why can't people mind their own business?'

'Jethro, my sweet, is everyone's business! That's what it is to be a household name. By the way, a reporter rang. I said you were out and I'd no idea when you'd be back. Was that right?'

'Of course it was right, but how've they got on to me here for heaven's sake?'

'Not difficult. Journalists are like ferrets.'

Tatiana scowled and settled down to her typewriter and the sheaf of papers before her.

At one o'clock the door of the office opened and Bridget put her head round. She was wearing a fur bonnet tied with fur bobbles.

Sally glanced at Tatiana who was studiedly not noticing the arrival. 'You're early,' she said to Bridget.

Tattie looked up, veiled warning for Sally and a civil enough acknowledgement for Bridget. 'Hello Bridget,' she said.

Bridget took off the bonnet. Her hair was flattened and had not, apparently, been washed very recently. She swung the bonnet in her hand. Tattie looked at it with distaste.

Bridget held it up. 'It was my Great-Auntie's' she explained. 'Most of her things went to Help the Aged when she died, but I kept this because it's so cosy.' Now she took

144

off her grey simulated tweed coat and hung it behind the door.

'Are you two not going out?' asked Tatiana.

'No,' said Bridget eagerly. 'Sally's taking me to the canteen.'

'Oh dear, what a pity.' Tatiana rose and smiled pleasantly. 'I'm running out today. So I shan't be able to come with you.'

Bridget's face fell.

The door opened again, and Kitty put her head round. 'Tattie,' she said. 'I want to talk to you.'

'Darling! What are you doing here?'

'We'll have a quick bite in the canteen. I've left Nina doing some telephoning and I've popped up to see Masius.'

'Masius?'

'Daddy's solicitor.'

'He won't see you, will he?'

'He will!'

Tattie couldn't help smiling. 'Them's fighting words, pet. But I was going out, actually.'

'I'd rather not. No time.'

'How are you, Mrs Manning?' asked Bridget.

Kitty stared at her and took a moment before she replied. 'I'm not entirely sure. Have we met?'

'I'm Bridget. Is there any news of Mr Manning?'

Kitty raised an eyebrow and glanced at Sally. 'Not yet,' she said crisply, not inviting any further enquiry.

Bridget clicked her teeth. Tatiana held her breath. Kitty's control could be a fragile thing and she was never fond of such mannerisms. Tattie remembered when she had been driven to screaming point by a habit of blinking that Nina had acquired when she was thirteen. Kitty had taken the girl, protesting, by the hand and dragged her into her bedroom, where she was made to lie in darkness, curtains drawn, because Kitty insisted, with some ferocity, that it must be due to eye-strain. Long after Kitty had forgotten her, Theo, a dinner guest, had crept upstairs and released her. By then it had indeed been dark, and the fretting Nina had been alone, meditating upon nervous blinking, for something like three hours.

'Alerick must be ever so upset,' blundered Bridget.

Kitty whisked round to stare at her. 'Must he?' she demanded. 'Why especially Alerick?'

'He thinks a lot of Mr Manning,' said Bridget stupidly.

'So do we all,' Kitty replied with dignity. 'And so do most of the musical world.'

Sally stood to receive Kitty's fur should she decide to take it off. She drew close and waited for anything. She was fascinated now, as indeed she always was, to see how Kitty would react. Fascinated but not embarrassed. It took a great deal to embarrass Sally, who viewed life with all its humours as a spectacle to be enjoyed; and the Manning family, providing entertainment and excitement and a *soupçon* of mystery at every level, were often a bonus.

'Do you think it's amnesia?' asked Bridget.

Kitty ignored the remark.

'My Great-Aunt Edith – the one I got the hat from – she had a breakdown once and lost her memory for two months. She forgot who she was and where she lived and everything about herself – in Tottenham Court Road. Just outside the Dominion.'

'No, I think I'll keep my coat,' Kitty said to Sally. 'I'm feeling the cold especially today.'

'It's wicked,' agreed Bridget and clicked her teeth at the weather.

Kitty gave her a long, hard look. 'Are you having trouble with your teeth?' she asked.

Tattie took her elbow and gently propelled her out into the corridor. 'Couldn't we nip up the road, Mother love?' she asked. 'That ghastly girl's going to eat in the canteen.'

'It makes no difference to me where she eats, darling. I can see no reason why we should have to speak to her again.' And knowing the way very well, she marched across the road and into the Royal Opera House with Tattie after her, down the passage which led to the canteen, now filling up with dancers post- and pre-rehearsal. On the way she kissed one or two people and was embraced by others who promised they were thinking of her and Jethro every minute of every day. An emaciated choreographer wearing an outside crucifix stopped to clasp and press her hand for some minutes in silence.

'Darling!' said Kitty. 'I remain convinced he's all right and simply run away from that dreadful woman.'

'Hell-cat,' he agreed. 'Hag! It's just too frightful. You're so brave, darling. I say to everyone how brave you are. I suppose you never think the worst.'

'Never,' said Kitty.

They embraced and he went his way, his crucifix bumping on his bony chest. A springing young man in an emerald tracksuit ran after him, put a hand on his shoulder and together they disappeared.

'People are so bloody stupid,' grumbled Tatiana. 'You can hardly believe the things they'll say.'

'Don't worry, treasure. I don't mind a bit. He was quite right to suppose I never would think the worst. He knows me. He knows I would never give in to morbid fancies.'

Tattie gave her a sharp look. She seemed to be serious. And thus they came into the canteen. Eyes turned as Kitty, her fur now loosely over her shoulders, made her entrance. She passed a pile of trays and made for a table. 'Get me something you know I'd like,' she told Tattie.

And when Tattie came back, first with one loaded tray and then with another, full of sensible and slim-worthy goodies, she found Kitty in conversation with a young male dancer who was devouring an odd luncheon of suet pudding and yoghurt, washed down with Perrier. When he had finished he went back for a second helping, saying he never bothered with a first course and loathed salads and all that beastly health stuff. When he had finished that he pulled a Mars Bar out of the child's school shoe bag in which he seemed to carry his wordly goods.

'I came to your father's Q.E. Hall on Sunday,' he told Tattie. 'I'm a fan. I thought it was rivet-inducing.'

'Oh. Great,' said Tatiana, putting her knife into her beef casserole. 'Old boot leather!' she said.

'I've never thought of dancers as being all that musical,' said Kitty, rather aggressively, Tattie thought, considering where she was.

'If I hadn't been such a good dancer I might have been a pianist,' said the youth modestly.

'What a choice! Who thought you could make it as a pianist?'

'Mummy. She was despairing when I got into the Royal Ballet School. It wasn't what she wanted.'

'Why did she let you audition for it, then, if she didn't want you to go?' Kitty seemed fascinated, surprisingly, by this little story.

'I was too good to overlook,' said the dancer.

'Well,' Kitty acknowledged, perfectly seriously. 'A real gift will out. Are you going to be a big name before long, do you suppose?'

'Oh I'm sure I will.' But a cloud passed, momentarily, over the young eyes. 'Mind you, there's always so much luck.'

'True,' said Kitty.

God! thought Tattie. What a drag he is!

'And ballet,' he went on, 'is, after all, such a bastard art.' He said it as though ballet made him want to throw up his suet pudding and yoghurt and Mars Bar.

'I don't agree at all,' said Tatiana. 'What nonsense. What a silly thing to say.'

The canteen suddenly filled up with orchestra, hungry from rehearsal. The queue was instantly swollen and the decibel level raised.

He shrugged and looked offended. 'It is,' he said. 'Of course, you're not a dancer, so you probably don't understand how one feels.'

'I know a lot of you,' she persisted. 'I know a lot of dancers who believe totally in what they're doing.'

Kitty was beginning to look around the room. Boredom was plainly starting to creep in round the corners of her consciousness. She waved at somebody in the queue, and shook her head as though in despair.

'It's nothing in its own right,' said the dancer, haughtily. 'Music is pure sound. Painting, sculpture, they're pure visual art forms. But what do we do? We prance around to somebody else's music on somebody else's set doing somebody else's choreography.'

'You're exponents. Like my father's an exponent of somebody else's music.'

But like Kitty, his attention had wandered while she was lecturing him and now he rose to greet a girl with a blonde crewcut and a vast amount of Kohl on her eyes. 'Darling!' he

148

said as they embraced. 'You look dreadful! Who told you to make up your eyes like that. Why do you never listen to me. I told you before eye-liner makes you look like a lemur!'

She put her tongue out at him. A friend joined them. Plainly he had forgotten Tatiana and the argument. He stood up and with his peers he left the table without saying goodbye.

'What a stupid, pretentious boy,' said Tattie crossly.

'Yes,' agreed Kitty, absently. 'That bassoon player over there is someone your father could never stand. He's been making sympathetic gestures over the tables. I find all this very unnerving. The way everyone knows.'

'Well, sweetheart. It was in the papers. People were bound to start talking.'

'I hate people,' said Kitty with sudden passion. 'I hate them all. None of them really care a fig for Jethro. They just want to get in on the act. I believe half of them are secretly longing for the river police to find him lying in a bed of Thames mud with an anchor round his neck.'

Tattie winced. 'You mustn't say such things, love. Really you mustn't. It doesn't do to start even talking like that.'

'Maybe,' said Kitty, 'we keep too tight a hold on ourselves.'

Tatiana looked at her quickly. Could she detect a wild glint to the eye, the wild glint she had been dreading? Possibly not. Kitty seemed in command.

'One must always,' suggested Tatiana gently, 'be in control. 'Especially when things are bad. It's the only way to get things done.'

'I am not,' said Kitty, 'entirely clear what there is to be done. If I *did* know – life would be easier. It is feeling so very helpless . . .' She looked away. Tatiana put a hand on her arm. 'No, darling. Don't touch me. If you do I could cry or something quite absolutely frightful and at this moment in time it is imperative I do nothing so totally blush-making. For God's sake don't let us be physically sympathetic. Not for a moment.'

Tattie withdrew her hand.

'Apart from feeling impotent,' Kitty continued, 'I feel so guilty.'

'You? Guilty?' Tattie looked incredulous, but somewhere in the deeper regions her heart sank. She had been wondering

149

when her mother might begin to say this. For how long had she been feeling it? In Kitty's case one never knew.

'Yes, guilty. Guilty. Guilty!' Her voice raised and one or two people turned interestedly. Tentatively Tatiana barely touched her arm again and this time it did the trick. The voice was lowered and Kitty thought a while before going on. 'For being such a useless, futile wife.'

'No, darling,' Tattie cooed. 'You!'

But Kitty shook her head. 'If I had given Jethro what he needed he would never have left us for that Paula. And he wouldn't have run away like this from his home.'

Tattie didn't quite know what to say. There was little logic in this. Jethro, after all, *had* run away from his home. For another.

At ten to two Irene Heygate hurried into the canteen and came over to where Kitty and Tatiana were sitting. She kissed Kitty.

'How fortuitous!' she cried. 'I've been trying to get you on the telephone since early this morning!'

'I've probably been engaged.'

'I'll find something to eat,' she said.

'Why did you have to see her, Ma?' complained Tattie as she went off to join the queue of musicians newly in from the rehearsal. 'Don't we want to be alone? You were positively welcoming.'

'One is never alone,' said Kitty, histrionically. 'One leads such a public life.'

'It's a matter of how much you choose to,' muttered Tattie.

'I feel better with my friends around me,' said Kitty.

Tatiana made no comment and Irene returned with limp salad.

'This is all that's left by the time we come in,' she grumbled.

'What've you been doing?' asked Kitty.

'*Don Pasquale* in the Crush Bar.'

'Why there?'

'We rehearse in there the days we don't have the orchestra pit.' She dropped her head and ate with remarkable enthusiasm.

'How bizarre!' said Kitty, her eyes wandering again. 'The things you get up to.'

'Not for Wagner, of course.'

'I suppose not.'

'It's about Paula . . .' began Irene.

'I always feel,' said Kitty, 'that Paula's a kind of a dusk person. The edges are blurred. It's difficult to make out anything definite. It makes communication difficult. I really don't know how much she feels.'

'I told you she came to see us.'

'Yes.'

'I lay awake all night worrying, wondering whether I ought to tell you.'

'Tell me what?'

'I have a hunch she could be pregnant.'

Kitty stared at her. 'You're always having hunches and they're almost invariably wrong. On what do you base this one?'

'She wouldn't drink any coffee. She said she had mysteriously "gone off" coffee.'

'One can go off things.'

'I went right off coffee when I was pregnant. Both times.'

'It doesn't mean a thing.' Kitty laughed coldly.

'She left us in such a state. She seemed quite hysterical. I had to come in for rehearsal, but Arthur was working at home and he watched from our window and saw the warden give her a parking ticket. She was parked on a yellow line.'

'So?'

'She had a screaming match with the warden and tore up the ticket.'

'Good gracious.'

'Arthur saw her go into the police station with a constable. He left it for a bit and then went over to see if there was anything he could do – very decent of him, considering how rude she'd just been to him – but you know Arthur, heart of gold beats there under a crusty exterior.'

Tattie wanted to add something about a beady eye and a curious nose but she kept quiet.

'Anyway, she'd gone. But they said she'd been sick. I'm sure she's expecting a baby, Kitty.'

'Pouf!' said Kitty. 'Upon what evidence? I don't believe it for a moment.'

'If by any chance Irene's right,' murmured Tatiana, 'it could be enough to throw Father into a tizz.'

Kitty's startlingly blue eyes widened. 'He wouldn't care for it,' she agreed. 'He certainly wouldn't be pleased.'

'He'd go bananas,' said Tattie. 'You've always said he loathed us when we were little.'

'He certainly did.'

'And now he's that much older. Honestly, I think he'd take news of that sort very ill.'

'That's what I thought,' said Irene. 'That's why I felt I simply had to tell you.'

'It still doesn't explain Manchester.' Kitty shook her head. 'He might walk out on a pregnant mistress. He might have gone off to stay with Theo, or come home, or even gone to some other girlfriend for a few days while he worked out what to do, but he'd never let down a professional engagement because he'd been told he was going to be a father again. It's not Jethro.'

'Do you think he'd try to persuade her to abort it?' asked Irene.

'Frankly, yes.' Kitty turned the gaze on her. 'I don't think he'd have any hesitation. But I'm not sure she'd . . . I think she'd stick out if she wanted it. When she wants something . . .' She looked away. For a moment, Tattie was apprehensive.

'What makes you sure she would want a baby, Mother darling?' she asked.

'I'm just sure she would,' said Kitty simply. 'Once she found she was pregnant. I think she'd get broody. That kind of a woman stops being the mistress once she becomes the mother.'

She suddenly stood, angrily reaching for her fur. The conversation appeared to be terminated. Tattie helped her into the coat.

'If he had another child,' said Kitty, quite savagely, 'I'd fight her every inch of the way.'

'What d'you mean, darling?' Tattie looked puzzled.

'For you girls and Antony.'

'Why would it worry us?'

'You're very naïve, sweetheart. It does you credit, but if

152

Jethro thought he was going to start changing his will in favour of her brat . . .'

'It never occurred to me,' said Tatiana coolly, 'that Father had anything to leave but debts.'

'Well he has. And I'm having no nonsense from him. That's one reason why I want to see Masius. Even without her child, he's not getting away with neglecting you girls.'

'But darling – we're grown up. Nina and I are both independent and he still pays Antony's school fees, doesn't he?'

'You've forgotten, or perhaps you never knew, that Nikolai and Natalia paid the Charterhouse fees in a lump sum when he went there. All Jethro pays is the rise in fees since then, which isn't inconsiderable but the main burden fell on my parents. And as for you girls, if you think the pittance I ask you to contribute to the housekeeping really covers the costs . . .'

'We'd better give you more,' put in Tatiana, stiffly. 'I had no idea you felt we weren't paying our way.'

'I never said anything of the sort,' snapped Kitty. 'You're twisting my words. I simply said he does nothing to help you girls. I wouldn't accept another penny from either of you.'

'You put me in an impossible situation, Mother.'

'I don't see that at all.'

'Then you're not being very sensitive.'

Kitty raised her chin. 'This is a ridiculous conversation,' she said. 'Let this be an end of it.'

Tatiana bit her lip. Irene caught her eye, but the girl looked away. 'I suppose he's free, ultimately, to leave his money where he wishes. You really have no control over that. And I don't like talk of wills and money – it always seems to bring out the worst in people.'

Kitty marched out and up the stone stairs, past the Green Room.

'That woman Paula is a parasite,' she was muttering as they came up into the stage-door lobby.

'Oh,' sighed Tatiana to Irene. 'I wish you could have kept your mouth shut. Now we'll never hear the end of this and the chances are there isn't a baby on the way anyway.'

'Alley-cat!' hissed Kitty. People in the lobby turned and

stared. 'They're the ones who breed, too,' she added. 'Breed like fleas.'

Tatiana put a hand on her mother's shoulder. 'Honestly, love,' she said, 'let's not assume anything yet.'

'She's after a meal ticket right through life for herself and her nasty little brat.'

Tatiana froze. 'I do find this a little distasteful,' she said quietly, conscious of eyes.

'Prig!' cried Kitty. 'My daughter's a prig,' she told a laconic man standing by the desk.

And with that she swept out through the weighty glass doors only to back in again.

'Who are those men out there?' she demanded of the stage-door keeper. 'There are six of them.'

'They're the Press, madam. They're waiting for you.'

The clutch of reporters pressed forward to the door, aware now that something was up. Kitty turned and fled up the stairs, with Tattie after her.

'You can't go up there,' she urged. 'Come down, Mother. I'll take you round to Bow Street.'

'They'll be there too.' Kitty had lost all command of herself. She ran her hands through her hair.

'Not if you wait for a bit. They'll go away.'

'They won't.'

Tattie looked at her watch. 'Can I leave her with you, Irene?' she begged.

'Not really. We've got to have another rehearsal, I'm afraid.'

'When?'

'Now.'

Kitty seemed to be walking purposefully. She pushed her way through a pair of glass doors.

'You mustn't go in there, darling, you really mustn't.'

'There's someone singing,' said Kitty. 'It sounds like Joan.'

The golden voice spilled out from the rehearsal room. Tattie tugged on Kitty's fur, as Kitty peered through the glass panel into the huge studio.

'Kitty,' whispered Irene. 'Come away. Please. It's Joan Sutherland. Do be careful she doesn't see you.'

'She gave me a most beautiful camellia for my birthday,'

154

said Kitty with hauteur. 'And she's a great admirer of Jethro's. She wouldn't mind.'

'That's the trouble,' hissed Tattie. 'She's too nice. If she knows about father, she might even break right off and come and speak to you and that'll interrupt the whole rehearsal. You can't abuse her warmth just because she's a good friend.'

'But this . . .' began Kitty.

'Nonsense,' said Tattie sharply. 'You'd half kill anybody who interrupted Father.' And Kitty allowed herself to be led away and down into the stalls circle foyer, where Tattie left her sitting on a sofa.

They kissed goodbye. Irene fled to her rehearsal and the front desk of the violins.

'Will you be all right?' asked Tatiana. 'I'll pop down to the street later and see if they've gone and come and tell you. I don't see you're going to get to Masius this afternoon. Did you have an appointment?

Kitty shook her head.

'I don't suppose he'd have seen you then, anyway.'

She hurried back, through corridors and passages, to the stage door. Through the doors she saw the reporters standing and chatting. They looked cold and bored. She drew herself up and pushed open the doors. At any rate, she thought, they won't know my face.

'That's one of the daughters,' called out a female reporter newly on the scene, and the whole clutch bore down upon her.

She ran fast, pushing her way through them, as a taxi sped down Floral Street, hand hard on horn. The driver lent out and shouted something like ' 'ave an 'elicopter next time, darlin' ', but he had divided them. Tatiana was home and dry inside number 45.

At five o'clock she rang through to the house manager and asked him to send someone to see if Kitty was still in the stalls circle bar.

'No,' he said. 'She's sitting in my office. I'm telling her, I don't think she's going to be able to go out for a bit.'

Eventually, just after six-thirty, three people from front of house helped Kitty and Tatiana out, through what was now a small mob of journalists, and into a waiting taxi. Sally slammed the door on them.

'She'll give you the address in a minute,' she said to him, 'if you start up northwards. St John's Wood,' she added, leaning right into the cab.

When Kitty gave him the address through the sliding window he began to say he couldn't go that far out, he'd been on his way home to Penge anyway, but she threatened to take him through every court he cared to name if he refused. He drove on, up Tottenham Court Road and across the park behind Mornington Crescent.

Kitty sat back, pale, spent.

'So much for today,' she said. 'So much for Masius.'

'I can see this is going to be a hazard from now on,' sighed Tattie. 'God I'm exhausted. I don't think I've shaken off my bug.' But if she was wanting sympathy from Kitty she didn't get it, for Kitty seemed not to have heard. 'You'll just have to stay at home for a while,' she added.

Their taxi driver turned into Loudoun Road and drove slowly up towards a small crowd of newspaper men collected on the pavement.

'That where you live, lady?' he asked.

As they alighted and hurried up the steps, Nina came to meet them. The two girls brushed the reporters off like flies. Nina slammed the door and bolted it. Tatiana put on the chain.

Kitty sat on the stairs while Nina placed a whisky in her hand.

'It's been like this all day,' she said. 'What price fame?'

Chapter Eleven

Roger Dilke had caught the nine-fifty a.m. from Euston that day. Unlike Philip, he always travelled second class on an Inter-City Saver; Philip's grandiose ideas about the comforts becoming to an agent were a bone of contention between them. Philip always took the line that his life-style was an 'in-joke' everyone enjoyed, ignoring the fact that Roger was actually irritated by his extravagances.

Settling himself into the seat Tamsin had reserved for him, he looked around with distaste at his companions. Regretting his stance for economy? Opposite him sat two youths, one stolidly ear-plugged; but the trouble was that Roger could hear, nevertheless, a dim murmur of Radio One which was, in a way, more maddening than the unleashed frenzy of pop. The other boy, wearing a check shirt over a black vest, smelled of armpits and picked at a mole on his neck. Across the way sat a girl with a curly perm and a child. The child had a cold and sneezed on to the table before it. Roger looked away and then, compulsively, looked back.

Briefly, an image crossed his mind – of Philip and Theo off to Paris together on The Golden Arrow just after the war, while he was still at school. When those two got together they fed each other's nostalgia and he would listen with one ear, telling himself he was amused. On the wall of Philip's office there was a photograph of the interior of the train, all inlaid wood and luxury, with Theo and him sitting smug as tomcats. But there were advantages to today's world. Caroline was one of them. In Theo and Philip's peak years, a Caroline would have had to have been fed in expensive restaurants and visited discreetly, whereas now she was served up with coffee and bran flakes at breakfast. She would have kept him a wicked secret from Mummy and Daddy. Now she threw their coats on the double bed with no apologies when they came to call, bearing wine. Was all that an advantage? And was Philip, for all his air of amiable disintegration, past his peak? Roger happened to know that, in addition to having a charming French wife, a sculptor pleasing to the art critics if quite unknown to the public, he also visited a rich widow in Wilton Crescent. Neither woman washed his socks. Some people asserted, too, that he had once been one of Diana Casimir's lovers, although Roger, for one, disbelieved the rumour.

He sighed and looked out of the window. The prospect of the meeting ahead of him was not pleasurable. He had rung the deputy general manager of the Hallé Concerts Society and asked if he would eat a bite of lunch with him at the Midland, but the other man had politely declined, suggesting that time was precious and that maybe a short chat in the office in Cross Street would be helpful. Roger, staring glumly at the landscape as it spun past the grubby window, stained with dirty rain-streaks, doubted whether anything could be helpful. Other than a veil drawn over Jethro Manning and a swift booking for another prestigious client.

Feeling so jaundiced, by rights the passing countryside ought to have looked ugly, a wasteland with the breath of chimneys hanging over it. But the day, dancing with winter sunshine, betrayed him. The Trent and Mersey Canal ran like a blue ribbon alongside the railway, threaded with pleasure launches and long boats smart and jolly as a primitive painting. Horses grazed serenely in hazy fields, while the wooded hills framed the view. It all looked innocent, domestic and very English.

Manchester was only a stop-over en route for Scotland, and Scotland would probably prove to be a wild goose chase, but one had to pursue every possibility. It was quite on the cards that Jethro had never seen the damn girl since he had shacked up with Paula, but at the time he had seemed obsessed with her, a slight blonde with green eyes and an unnerving stammer, from the front desk of the violins. What the devil was the girl's name? Oh well, he would have to be open about

158

the reason for his visit when he called on the conductor of the orchestra. The whole operation was extremely distasteful.

He shifted in his seat, rested his hand on the arm by the window, and felt something sticky. He took his hand away and found a lump of chewing gum sticking to it. Removing it, he put it in an empty coffee carton on the table and looked back out of the window as the train pulled into Stoke-on-Trent, past the Stoke City FC, and into the nineteenth-century station, laced with black diamond decoration over the red brick, under the fairy glass roof thrown over the lines by Victorian dreamers. Cold passengers with cheerful faces crowded on the platforms. A stone pillared arch over the entrance bore a reminder – '1914 – In Memory of the Men of the North Staffordshire Railway who Fell in the Great War – 1918'. The train filled up with travellers with loud voices. A stout lady in a mauve coat with a fur collar squeezed in beside Roger and smiled at him with gold teeth. He shifted his glance out of the window once more as the train pulled out, past dereliction of immediate railway land, out to pasture again, until it whizzed past a municipal sports field where an unimpressive pavilion bore the legend "Stoke Kill".

Past birch woods with a view of greater, grander hills building up towards the backbone of England. Roger was often struck, travelling into the provinces, with a sense of sharp surprise at the reality of the world outside London: that people lived and drove to work and walked on hills and listened to local radio and felt themselves more real than him. Today their substance invaded his own presence more forcibly than usual. He looked down upon his own Liberty's tie and Jermyn Street shirt and Gieves coat and wondered whether, if he lived in Stoke, he would buy his clothes from Marks & Spencer, that universal leveller.

Caroline had given him the shirt for his birthday. He had twitted her that the firm must pay her too much if she could afford such presents.

Macclesfield looked a charming town, viewed from the train, its streets clambering up its hill. For a moment he wondered what it would be like to be one of them, a friendly man with generous vowels and a tough core under geniality, with a plump little wife like a suburban pigeon and a high tea

159

to return to, a substantial car and not too much traffic on the roads; and for that moment he ached with a most improbable envy, a kind of yearning for roots buried so deep he hardly knew they were there. His great-grandfather had come from Clitheroe. Could that be it? The old man had been an amateur bassoonist and had sung with an excellent bass, so he had been told. A sepia photograph of him had been among the cases and trunks of clutter found in his mother's loft after she died. He wondered what he had done with it and suddenly wished it were framed upon the wall of his office, in dignified competition with Theo and Philip lounging in the Golden Arrow.

In an unwary moment he smiled and the lady in the mauve coat, taking it for herself, smiled back.

In Manchester he walked, fast, to Cross Street. In the pedestrian precinct he passed street musicians, old men and students, groups and a little fiddler who looked no more than thirteen. Past the Woolworths and the British Home Stores and the Littlewoods and all the cheap chains and eventually out into Cross Street, where he crossed the road and entered the Alliance Building, taking the lift up to the Hallé offices.

The deputy general manager greeted him with a rueful but not belligerent handshake.

'Well, well . . .' he said.

'Well indeed,' replied Roger.

The telephone rang almost immediately and the other man, waving a hand at the chair the other side of the desk, answered it.

'Ten wheelchairs!' he was saying. 'Plus attendants?' He made a note upon a pad. 'Right. I don't think we ought to have any problems there, except that we'll have to bring them in by the side entrance and there's the danger they'll end up at the back of the hall. Still – we'll have to see about that.'

Roger sat, looking out of the window at St Anne's Church, mellow red sandstone, with the bare branches of the tree before it spreading. On the wall of the office, before him, Hans Richter looked sternly from his portrait. Roger felt the accusation and moved uneasily, wishing the telephone call would finish.

'Right,' said the man standing at his desk. 'No problem.

160

We'll see to these folk. Leave it to me.' And he replaced the receiver, smiled a half-smile, and sat down.

'What a pickle!' said Roger. As he said it, he thought how stupid it sounded.

The other man nodded, but gravely now. 'Yes,' he said. 'Your Jethro gave us a nasty evening.'

'*My* Jethro!' Roger tried to laugh. 'I'm not his keeper.'

'Only his agent!'

There was a short silence, which Roger broke. 'Presumably the insurers will look after the loss,' he said.

'That's true, but it doesn't detract from the hassle of cancelling and now the whole business of making the claim. Very time-consuming. By the way, we'll need a doctor's certificate.'

'How the hell can I get you that? We've no reason to suppose he's ill.'

'I assume you've talked to his doctor?'

'He says he hasn't seen Jethro for eight months,' Roger said.

'Hm. Isn't that surprising, knowing Manning?'

'It is. Yes. I'm puzzled.'

'Does it suggest he's gone to a new doctor?'

'It could.'

'Would Mrs Manning know who that could be?'

'Surely you know they're not living together.'

'Are they divorced, actually?'

'That's the kind of tidy detail the Mannings don't get around to. I don't think Kitty intends to give in easily. That's what it amounts to.'

'What about the . . . er . . . other woman? Would she know?'

'I asked her. She seemed surprised, and knew nothing about Jethro leaving his old doctor. She said they "didn't talk much about things like that".'

'What is she like?'

'Fey.'

The other man reflected. 'Jethro does pick them,' he said, and Roger nodded, glad of any area of agreement.

'So. Did the doctor have any light to throw upon Jethro's health when he did last see him – eight months ago or whatever?'

'He said his blood pressure was higher than it ought to be.'

'I don't think that surprises me. Does it you?'

Roger shook his head.

The door opened and the general manager of the Hallé Concerts Society put his head round it. 'Ah,' he said. 'Come to try and pour oil on troubled waters?'

Roger rose and held out a hand. He had been rather dreading this.

'I felt I'd like to come up and say how upset we are our end,' he said. 'And mystified.'

'You've come all this way just to say "sorry"?' asked the general manager, with the ghost of a smile.

Suddenly Roger grinned. 'I can't afford to lose your good-will,' he admitted.

They all laughed.

'Who are you trying to sell us now, then?' he enquired.

Roger coughed. 'I thought I might have a word about Emily Hardcastle while I'm here.'

'Ah. A concerto.' The other two glanced at each other. 'Well,' said the man at the door, 'she's a fine artist. I don't know what you have in mind, but I'm pressed for time so I think I'll leave you two together to chat about it.'

'I didn't know she was with you,' said the deputy general manager.

'She joined us recently,' said Roger, relieved at the way the conversation had turned. 'Considerable acquisition. And – er – a somewhat different kettle of fish.'

'From our friend?' The other man sat back. 'Yes. I'll allow you that. Why did she leave Traversi and Elliot?'

'Clash of personalities with Bruce Elliot. Not her fault. His. She's straight, reliable, punctual, a decent sort. Her word's her bond.'

'Doesn't sound much like a soloist!'

Roger giggled. Things were definitely easing. 'Truly. Emily never let anyone down yet. Lovely lady. Lot of people thought she ought to have won at Leeds, but you know that as well as I.' Relief surged over him in waves. 'Very intelligent artist,' he added, for good measure.

'Still, we can't ever expect performers to behave like bank managers,' said the Hallé chap.

'No, but it helps if they're moderately sane.'

'Do you think Jethro's mentally ill?'

Roger was alarmed. 'I never said that – did I?'

The other man laughed, but soberly. He shook his head. 'I just wondered whether he'd been having any psychiatric help or anything.'

'Not so far as I know. Jethro's eccentric, but I've no reason to suppose he's round the twist. Any more than any of them.'

'But I wouldn't swap the job one does. Would you?'

'I have my moments.' Roger hesitated. 'Perhaps not.'

'The strain of their lives. The pressures. The packing and the travelling and the projecting and the notices. And the fears. It's surprising any of them remain sane at all.'

'All those things get the adrenalin going. Stuff of life. Performers are a special breed. They have to be.'

'They're still human beings. And they vary.'

'If Jethro weren't a born performer he wouldn't have chosen the life.'

'But did he? Choose it? I remember a chat we once had, one of the few occasions he and I ever really got talking. We were sitting in the back of the hall while the tuner was voicing the piano and Jethro suddenly became rather intense and articulate. He told me a bit about his father. I gathered the old man was the motivating force. He said it all went back to him.'

'That's true. His father picked up the child's talent very early. To begin with he taught him himself . . .'

'I hadn't realised he was a pianist.'

'Small-time teacher in Sussex. He didn't go far with Jethro himself because he realised he wasn't up to it, so then he had him taught by Mike Fardel for quite a time until he thought he ought to go on from there and began to trot him backwards and forwards to Paris for lessons with Alain Dartoy.'

'Oh yes – of course. I remember now reading about where he studied.'

Roger continued. 'Eventually he ended up in Budapest, after he left the Royal College. But the years with Dartoy every fortnight must have set the parents back a lot, and they weren't made of money. I believe the wife resented the inroads it made into their life-style and there was some conflict. I've always understood Jethro's childhood wasn't too happy – on the parental front, that is. Then there was a little sister who was a mongol and the mother insisted on keeping her at home and looking after her herself, which made life very arduous.'

'Good heavens! What a background for an artist of his calibre!'

'Mm. It can't have been easy. The sister died before Jethro went to the College. But while he was a child himself the father stood over him, literally, watching him practise – very strong character, forceful. I suspect he began by driving Jethro until he learned to drive himself.'

'He loved his father, I felt.'

'He adored him. Almost slavishly. And then of course the old boy had his stroke the very morning of the Wigmore Hall debut.'

'It must have knocked Jethro sideways. Couldn't they have kept the news from him? It was a pretty bad stroke, wasn't it?'

'Complete paralysis down one side. No, they couldn't really. After all, he would have been there, wouldn't he? Knowing him, he'd have been with Jethro right up to the last minute, almost hovering over the piano in the Green Room. The mother could hardly hide it.'

'Did she turn up?'

'No. The person who carried him through it was Kitty. That's really when she came into her own. *And* she's never forgotten her moment of glory. But you see – the mother was always hostile to his career.'

'That was the impression I got, listening to Jethro. Why?'

Roger shrugged. 'I suppose she had her own problems. Jethro cost so much, and there was the other child. Anyway, there was constant warfare between husband and wife.'

'Now history repeats itself! As between Jethro and *his* wife.'

'Oh no. Not the same thing at all. Kitty and Jethro fight on the surface, but there's a strong bond beneath. I don't think it's broken even now, not despite the Paula creature.'

'Mm.' The man at his desk was ruminative. 'Some people thrive on battle.'

'Too right. Kill most of us the way they go on. But I've always thought there's an integral toughness about Jethro – a capacity for self-preservation that all artists must have or they would indeed go bonkers.'

'Learned at the father's knee, eh? Well, well. . . . All very interesting. I'm not sure it helps us now. I wonder where he'll turn up – and when. Or if . . .' he added.

'He'll turn up,' said Roger. He sighed. 'Sometimes I feel like a nanny,' he said. 'A nanny and a daddy and a shrink all rolled into one.'

'I'd be surprised, you know,' said the other man suddenly, 'if Jethro'd done himself an injury.'

'He would never kill himself.' Roger stared out of the window. In Half Moon Street below, a delivery van reversed. Manchester was humming at mid-day. Despite his words, he had a sudden vision of Jethro lying huddled somewhere, in a quarry, by a road, in the back of a car, in some bleak hotel room, in a winter wood on dead leaves. He struggled away from the image and back to the room, under the eyes of Hans Richter. 'Yet he lives with fear. Fear that one day this thing, this fragile little thing called genius, could just dissolve.'

'He's so frightened?'

'Any real artist must be. I do believe it's built into the creative instrument, the heart and mind. That's why I think Kitty was necessary for him. I honestly do think her belief in his reality and worth sustained him more than he knew. Even the fighting nourished him.'

'And this other woman?'

Roger shrugged. 'One feels that a puff and she'd dissolve.'

'Into mist?' The deputy general manager smiled.

'Into old-fashioned London smog.'

'You don't like her!'

'Not much.'

'And do you like Kitty?'

'Like?' Roger laughed. 'What a word to use about Kitty! Kitty lives. Kitty rules OK. I suppose that while at times I detest Kitty, I love her after all these years – in my fashion.'

'There's nowt so strange as folk.'

'True.'

'Of course I haven't seen Jethro for over a couple of years but I had heard he was drinking more than was good for him.'

'Reports get exaggerated. If it had been serious it would have shown. No, I think it's simply been that the bogeys have come out from behind the corners more since he left Kitty and just occasionally, spasmodically, he has drowned his terrors.

165

Perhaps too much and too often, but he's no drunk.'

'What are his bogeys?'

'Fears about his hands, all that kind of thing. The usual, really. Jethro's always been prone to panics about hands but I've noticed recently . . . I'll tell you something – a while ago, he was sitting in my office and Tamsin brought him a cup of coffee. He took it from her and – just dropped it. Opened his hands and let it fall through. She was completely thrown. He sat there with the cup and saucer on the floor at his feet and coffee swimming all over my green carpet and stared at it. She cleared it up and nobody said anything at all, but afterwards he kept muttering to himself – I could hardly hear – something to the effect that his hands were asleep.'

'Asleep!'

Both men were silent for a while.

'He got up and left after that,' said Roger. 'We were in the middle of discussing a recording session and he just upped and went.' He paused. 'And that reminds me that he was due to record at EMI tomorrow, but I've had to cancel that – along with everything else.'

'Is there any chance he could simply turn up at Abbey Road?'

'There's always a *chance* of anything.'

The deputy general manager rose. 'So. Are you off back to London now?'

'No. I thought I'd said. I'm on my way to Glasgow.'

'I don't think you mentioned it.' The man was always courteous.

'There's just a slim possibility of a lead there, and I have to follow everything, however slight. A girl. A young fiddler.'

'Ah.'

'BBC Scottish. At one time Jethro was very taken with her. I can't remember her name, but she's a sensitive lass and I didn't feel it would be appropriate in her case to start asking questions from London which would cause her distress. She's a parson's daughter and shy and it seemed important to protect her privacy.'

'Fiddler, you say?'

'Uh-huh.'

'Fair lass? Does she stammer?'

'That's the one.' Roger was surprised. 'You know her?'

'She's with us now.'

Roger's mouth fell open.

'I don't think you need go to Glasgow,' said the other man. 'Cynthia's on our front desk and she married a viola last week. Splendid occasion. You won't find Jethro through her.'

Roger picked up his coat.

The two men shook hands.

'Remember me to Philip,' said the Hallé man.

But at the door Roger paused. 'About Emily Hardcastle . . .' he began.

In the evening Antony, who was finding it progressively difficult to divorce himself from his anxiety, rang his grandmother.

'Hello, my pet!' She sounded delighted. 'How are you?'

'What's happening at home?' he demanded. 'They've been engaged all day. Is there any news?'

'None as yet, my sweet,' Natalia replied calmly.

'So what's being done?'

'Well, it was a job to get the police to do anything at all to start with, but now the newspapers have taken it up they've begun to make enquiries – whatever that means. Kitty and the girls have been contacting everyone they know who could have any idea where he might be, and of course Mr Dilke's running round in little circles. Your mummy's very exhausted, of course.'

Calling Kitty 'your mummy' was one of the few things capable of irritating Antony about Natalia, but today there was something soothing about the familiarity.

'It suppose I had better try again. I've got a mountain of work here with mock A's coming up, and it's awfully time-consuming keeping on coming down to the phone, but I can't settle to anything. Do you know if they're in?'

'I have a feeling Kitty was dining with Theo tonight. He's being very kind. But no doubt one of the girls will be there. I wouldn't have thought they would leave the telephone unattended at a time like this.'

'Mother can't be all that tired if she's going out on the

167

town.' He sounded fretful.

Natalia laughed lightly. 'I don't suppose dinner with dear old Theo constitutes a rave-up, my sweet, but you know with Kitty, she's full of nervous energy and even if she's dead on her feet she's still rushing about.'

'I'm surprised Dr Penfold doesn't give her something to calm her down a bit.'

'I don't suppose for a minute she's been to Dr Penfold.'

'Shouldn't someone suggest she ought to?'

'Darling – I really don't think things have got to that state. Kitty wouldn't like to hear you talk like that.'

'For heaven's sake,' he cried. 'In this family we all always have to consider what *Kitty* would like! It's an obsession!'

'It is her body,' said Natalia mildly.

'She's never been much good at looking after it. You know what she's like and how she punishes it. What she needs now is a bit of a rest and what does she do – goes out wining and dining with that stupid old man. I can't stick him anyway.'

'What a pity. He's always so nice about you.'

'Oh is he? Well, that's enough to get me worried! Knowing him!'

'You've got to let people manage their own lives, darling.'

'My parents have made a pretty good cock-up of managing theirs, haven't they?'

'This doesn't sound like our Antony.'

There was a pause, then . . . 'Sorry, Granny. I didn't mean to bark at you. I'm just . . . a bit worried.'

'I know, darling. We all are. I wish I could say something more comforting.'

'Just hearing your voice is comforting. It always is.' He surprised himself by the admission, and her too. When he rang off she went and told the dogs about it. In every way, Antony was not running true to form, worrying like this. Recently he had seemed so remote, separate, almost as though he had cut himself off from his family. And there'd never been much evidence over the past year that he cared for Jethro or wanted him back. It just showed that blood, in times of stress, was thicker than one thought.

She stood by the piano for some time with the photograph of Uncle Evgeny in her hand. Unused to weeping, she had no hanky to hand and had to wipe her tears away with the corner of the pink curtains.

'Well, Evgeny?' she whispered. 'What about that?'

Antony, feeling for some irrational reason slightly consoled, tried his home number once more and did a double-take when a strange voice answered 'This is the exchange. What number are you calling?'

He floundered. 'What number are you calling?' the anti-septic voice insisted.

He told her, stuttering. Panic had hit his chest. What could this mean?

'Who are you calling?'

'What is this?' he demanded. 'I want to speak to Mrs Manning.'

'May I have your name, please, and the exchange you are calling from?'

'For heaven's sake,' he shouted. 'I'm Antony Manning, her son. I'm calling from my school in Godalming. What's all this about?'

'If you would hold the line, please . . .'

Fuming, he waited. The voice seemed to have vanished. When it came back it said, 'I'll put you through now', and soon Nina was on the line.

'What's happening?' he demanded of Nina. 'I got this mad woman on the line asking who I was calling.'

'I've arranged for our incoming calls to be intercepted by the exchange,' she told him. 'We've been being persecuted all day. People we've never heard of keep ringing to ask about Father, and some of the calls are really beastly. I knew it would upset Ma terribly, so I got this arrangement lined up with British Telecom today.'

'How do you mean, beastly? Threatening?'

'A bit. Suggestive, anyway. Alarmist. Everything. People seem to think they have some kind of a right to interfere with our lives and tell us what to do or – worse – what Mother did wrong in the past. And oh yes . . . several have said they're sure they've seen him. In the oddest places!'

'I didn't know so many people cared!'

'Jethro's a public figure, you know.'

'Wouldn't you think strangers'd have more to do, though,

169

than bother about what's happened to him, or us?'

'No,' said Nina. 'Nothing surprises me. A lot of people haven't enough to do. They live vicariously.'

'It's sick.'

'Yup.'

'Have you followed up any of the places people have said they've seen him?'

'You're joking.' Her voice was very flat. 'Would you believe it, one very nasty character asked if there was a reward for any information.'

'What did you do?'

'Well, I had to let the police know, didn't I? But I never took it seriously. One learns not to.'

'Oh dear.'

'Mm. Oh dear.'

'So have I got to go through this rigmarole every time I ring home?'

' 'Fraid so. When you say who you are they check you off on the list we've given them of people we'll take calls from.'

'List! I'm on a list! Oh great. Ta. That's fantastic. Big deal. I'm on a list.'

'Don't be an idiot,' said Nina.

'It's all right for you to talk. You're at home. I happen to feel a bit cut off down here.'

'You're always telling us you like being away. You say you find home a drag these days. Well, I can tell you, you'd find us all a lot more of a drag than usual now!'

Antony sighed. 'I don't think I'd feel it now. I want to be with you.'

'Poor old Antony. Actually, you're probably in the best place. It's pretty good hell. But don't you think it was clever of me getting this interception business? I was jolly pleased.'

'I suppose so.'

'It'll make life far easier for Mother. You should see the Press outside.'

'Press?'

'Clamouring at the gates.'

'You serious?'

'Of course. Hang on – I'll look through the window. Yes. There are still half a dozen of them there, even now. There

170

were far more earlier. When Tattie brought Mother home . . .'

'Brought her home?'

'From Covent Garden. They'd been together. Kitty went up. Look – this is costing you money.'

'Does this interception business cost a lot?'

'No. They don't charge.'

'Free service? Well!'

'They don't give it easily, though. I had to tell them just how awful things were here. Apparently whatever instrument they use their end to do this is in short supply and the public queue up to ask for them.'

'Why?'

'Don't ask me. I suppose they get obscene calls.'

'Have ours been obscene?'

'Not so much obscene as unfriendly. Or interfering. Anyway, I was able to say we were "helping the police with their enquiries" . . .'

'That sounds as if we're criminals!'

'Do you want to speak to Ma?'

'Granny said she thought she was out with Theo.'

'She couldn't face it. She was finished when she got home and those reporters were the final straw. I don't think she'd have wanted to battle through them again. We rang Theo and put him off.'

'Is she talkable to?'

'I'll go and look. She's in bed but I shouldn't think she slept through the phone ringing. Hang on . . .'

Nina came back quickly to say that Kitty was fast asleep and she thought it better not to wake her. Tattie had braved the gauntlet outside and gone out with John, so perhaps Antony had better ring again tomorrow.

'And go through all that do-dah with the exchange?'

' 'Fraid so,' said Nina. 'Be good.'

With his evening plans cancelled at such short notice, Theo felt at a loss. Normally speaking he was increasingly happy to spend the dark hours at home. The warm flat and the television or a good book, with a bottle of decent port beside him,

171

seemed a deliciously indulgent way to pass the time. But it was different once one had made the effort to prize oneself from the shell, had a bath, laid out a clean shirt and a fresh pair of socks and booked a table at a quiet, expensive restaurant in Hampstead. Admittedly, Kitty had been an exhausting prospect, but vaguely he felt let down. He must have shown it on the telephone when he spoke to the girl Nina, who had been delegated, it seemed, to ditch him.

'Why don't you take Granny instead?' she suggested.

It was an excellent idea, but he was not absolutely sure how much he liked her suggesting it. Did she see him as Natalia's contemporary? Well – wasn't he? He looked in the gilt-framed mirror above his fireplace and came to the conclusion he might as well accept that he and Natalia would make a pair of a piece in any restaurant, a handsome period couple.

She received the invitation warmly, in no way dismayed that she was to play second fiddle, and so, just after eight-thirty, Theo picked her up in a taxi to take her up the hill to Hampstead. At the door, he handed her a bunch of pale pink carnations which she clasped prettily and plopped into a jug before leaving. She wore a dress in petunia fine wool with a matching jacket, pink stockings and petunia shoes. Around her neck hung her favourite string of rose quartz. Her gloves were of rose suede.

Theo thought what a pleasure it was to take out a woman who looked as though she was being taken out. It was a charming compliment to dress up with rings and things. Kitty, if tired, would have been capable of slinging that fabulous fur over a black tracksuit and sitting down to a gourmet dinner with smudged mascara and gym shoes. You could never tell. Whereas, you could depend upon Natalia.

He patted her hand in the taxi. 'Bad, all this,' he muttered. 'All very, very bad. What d'you make of it?'

Over the avocados he told her that he had never seen the Paula woman as a permanency. Too stupid for Jethro, by far. But surely, Natalia put forward, Jethro preferred a stupid woman. Had that not been half the trouble with Kitty? No, Theo considered, that had not been the trouble. He didn't want to cause any offence to her mother, but he himself had never thought Kitty over-intelligent, either. Not stupid, mind

172

you. That would be going too far. Jethro, in his opinion, was of a very superior order of intelligence – a clever man of the kind who so often sought out a woman of inferior intellect.

'You're not telling me that Jethro dominated my Kitty, are you?' smiled Natalia.

'I think that might be going too far,' he agreed. 'But I think, in a sense, her quality of – how shall we say – fecklessness, irrationality, her histrionic side – all that – governed always by the emotions rather than the head . . . I think all that amused him. I think he found it agreeable. Do not you?'

'I think,' said Natalia quietly, 'that possibly he found it a relief to get away from his mother, and Kitty was very different.'

'You knew the parents, did you not?' Theo poured his guest some wine.

'A little. We moved in rather different circles.' She said this simply. 'At that time, when Kitty first met Jethro, Nikolai and I were living near Lewes, with a flat in London, and the Mannings had just moved to Brighton from Haywards Heath. Had it not been for our children, there is little likelihood we would ever have met.'

'Did you not care for them?'

She shrugged. 'It was a depressing household. Nikolai and I – perhaps we had already seen too much – we never saw any reason to seek unhappiness. It was not that I felt nothing for the poor woman's plight, but I think – I think she was the sort who would have been unhappy wherever she had been, whatever her lot. She certainly had a strong feeling for the girl, the daughter, the one who was born with the big head and the vacant eyes and was helpless like a little child. She loved her – would do anything for her. But perhaps there is a limit to the energy a woman like her can give out in loving, and she had none left for the boy, for Jethro. Or for the husband. There was a kind of hatred there, destruction. The father wanted Jethro to be a pianist, so the mother, Wynn, fought him all the way. She thought all musicians were mad and all art was pretension. She thought it was an expensive indulgence, and every penny spent on Jethro was less to spend on the little girl. Jethro was good at science, too . . . his school always thought he ought to study physics . . .'

173

'Bright lad!'

'People who are clever in one way are often clever in others, don't you think?'

'Possibly. So Wynn was opposed from the start?'

'She came from a medical family. She'd been a nurse herself and nobody would let her study to be a doctor, which is what she really wanted. Her own father had been a heart surgeon, but he thought it was a waste of money to train a woman. She was very bitter. All through Jethro's childhood, when her husband was spending their savings taking him backwards and forwards from Paris for piano lessons, she poured scorn and contempt on the little boy. He played a concerto in Brighton when he was ten, and she never even went to hear him. I didn't know them then, but I heard about it. And all that night – Jethro has told me – he lay awake listening to them quarrelling. In the morning his father was ill, which was very unusual. He went to his bed and stayed there for one week while Wynn more or less ignored him. Little Jethro's triumphal day fell flat, you might say. While his father lay in bed, all he did was trot up and down the stairs with trays of food he had himself got together in the kitchen.'

'She sounds a monster!'

'Perhaps life had turned her into one. But the funny thing was that Jethro seemed under her spell. I don't know whether you would call it love, but he cared for her, right up to the day she died. She finished in an old people's home in Brighton. I used to go and see her.'

'You!' Theo made no attempt to hide his surprise.

'Yes, me!' Natalia smiled. 'I *can* do things I do not like! She was not a woman I would choose for a friend, but when somebody is very lonely – and unhappy. . . . And in a way, you might say we were sisters – in marriage.'

'Hardly.'

'Her son was now mine, too.'

'You're a good sort, Natalia.'

She waved a dismissive arm at him and he caught her hand, kissed the finger tips.

'I can never see you in an old people's home – not ever,' said Theo.

She pulled a face. 'Who can tell, Theo, where we all shall

end. You and I. Perhaps we should book our places now, before we become too difficult and dirty. But no, I did not like going there. There was one old man who used to shout, all the time. He sat in a chair by the television and shouted angry words, but to nobody in particular. He had some energy left. So many of the ones with energy were angry. The calm ones were too tired, too tired to shout. Wynn was angry, right to the end. She told Jethro, shortly before she died, that she especially disliked his kind of piano playing, that it was all hollow, sounding brass and tinkling cymbals . . .'

'Where was her charity?'

'She said it was only the people who could produce tangible evidence of making the world a better place who counted for anything at all. She said people who played other people's music were simply a passing shadow.'

Theo sighed. 'What a very sad story,' he said.

Natalia smiled and twirled her glass. 'It is very naughty of you to give me this,' she said, sniffing the glass. 'I'm not at all sure what we are celebrating.' She sipped the pink champagne.

'We are celebrating,' he said gallantly, 'that we two, in every way brighter than the next generation, are still in good health and able to be here to support them when they need us.'

'Ah,' she said.

They drank to it.

'I'm feeling utterly lousy,' sniffed Tatiana, over her pilaf. 'I think I want to go home.'

John signalled to the Cypriot waiter for the bill.

'I'm a rotten companion tonight,' she said, yawning. 'It all seems to be catching up on me.'

'Not surprised,' he conceded. 'Even I feel a bit battered. This Scotland business confuses me. What does Roger know that we don't?'

She shook her head and rubbed her eyes. 'Honestly, I'm past making a useful contribution. Put me in a cab and send me home.' She felt in her bag and brought forth her wallet.

When one went out with John one paid one's way. It was a tradition, somehow. She always wondered whether it was the same with all his friends.

'Do you want me to see you to your door?' he asked.

'Waste of energy. You need your beauty sleep too.'

'What if all those newspaper people are still there?'

'I can fight my way through.' She raised a weak fist and grinned.

'In your state?'

She closed her eyes and shook her head, wearily. 'Stop fussing,' she said. 'I just want to be in my beddy-byes.'

'Not mine?' he queried.

But again she shook her head, more vehemently.

'You wouldn't like me to take you home to my place and make you feel better?'

'It wouldn't. It would make me feel a lot worse.'

'I see.'

'Stop being so hang-dog,' she said suddenly and crossly. 'I'm not in the mood for it.'

He rose. Pulled a rueful face. 'Sorry, miss.'

She flung a handful of notes down on the table. 'There,' she said.

'No thanks.'

'What d'you mean, no thanks?'

'Not tonight.'

'Why?'

'Because I say so.'

She mustered a kind of smile. 'Very masterful all of a sudden', she said.

'That's it.'

She kissed him goodbye briefly as he put her into the taxi.

'Take care of yourself,' he said. 'I'll give you a ring tomorrow.'

'No, don't ring me. I'll ring you.'

'Oh. I see. Like that, is it?'

'Don't be daft. It's just all this carry-on with the exchange. You'll find it so frustrating.'

'Will I? OK.'

He watched her as the cab drove away, sighed, and turned on his heel. He felt no desire at all to go home alone now. He was restless. He found it difficult to get Jethro from his mind. What the hell was the man up to? What had happened? Jethro, for all his eccentricities, had always seemed to him to be a survivor, one of those people who could lay waste the population around him but never come to any irreparable harm himself. Yet there was now the possibility – it had to be taken seriously – that he could be sick, mentally ill, suffering from amnesia, in some kind of dire trouble. Even defunct. Walking slowly along the pavement, along Old Compton Street and down Charing Cross Road towards Leicester Square tube station, he thought of the good times he and Jethro had had together, he thought of the laughs, and the arguments long into the nights. Thinking soberly, it disturbed him somewhat that when he compared his feelings for father and daughter, it was the man to whom he felt more closely bound. If he had to choose, it would be Tatiana he would discard. He winced from the thought. Indeed, comparisons *were* odious. The combination of lust and liking he felt for Tatiana was a good one, and better, possibly, than anything he had encountered before with a woman. They understood each other and gratified each other most agreeably, with little or no blood spilt. He never fought with her, although they enjoyed a friendly bicker occasionally. But with Jethro gone he was bereft.

It all seemed to say something about his attitudes to men and women. Maybe it was true that men found in men their truest friends. He didn't entirely like the thought, not seeing himself as a 'man's man', indeed, shying away rather from the type in general.

It was difficult to tell how Tatiana herself felt about Jethro's disappearance. She never wore her heart on her sleeve and wringing of hands was not her style. There was, in fact, a curiously resigned quality about both of Jethro's girls. Maybe it was something to do with living with their particular parents. And yet – the very fact she felt so played out tonight must reflect something of the strain upon her at the moment. For himself, he didn't believe in the bug. Those things only hit you if you were already in a vulnerable state, and perhaps Tattie cared more than she showed.

Finding himself outside the Lamb and Flag just off Garrick

Street, he went in and bought himself a beer. The pub was packed and steaming with body-heat. Wedged up against the wall he drank reflectively, still thinking of Jethro, which it was easy to do here because he was on the man's stamping ground, Jethro being a member of the Garrick, and this being a pub they frequented together. Not quite so much of late, come to think of it.

Kitty, he remembered, didn't like Jethro's membership of the Garrick. She had shown a quite unbridled jealousy and on one occasion, when he had invited her to dinner there, and she had arrived before him and been shown upstairs into the morning room to await him, she had created a quite unpardonable scene because he was late. She said, audibly, that she thought the Club servants were a lot of frog-faced fools. Jethro had taken her by the arm and escorted her out, dragged her to his parked car, flung the keys on her lap and walked back to the Club fast. He felt that if he was going to show his face there again, he had better do it quickly, but it had pained him, hit him where it hurt, for he had an affection and a respect for the servants she was abusing. He had dined alone and not come home that night.

John had a feeling Jethro had already been sleeping with Paula by then, but could not be sure. He chuckled when he thought of Kitty creating havoc in the Garrick, and wished he had been there. There was no doubt that Jethro had a style all his own. John wondered whether he was still a member. And if so, whether Paula had ever been inside its portals.

Paula, the pale mystery woman. He wished now that he knew her better, understood more about the relationship she shared with his friend. It could throw light, perhaps. He took his tankard to the bar and had it filled. Gently, he loosened his belt, and very quietly he burped. He glanced over his shoulder to see whether anybody had noticed. If Jethro had found this female to his taste there must be something to her. He had some glimmer of what that could be – a softness, a yielding acceptance, an acquiescence. Jethro might find this beguiling after Kitty. Certainly he didn't see her as the kind who would bawl like a fishwife in a man's club.

After his second pint he went to the telephone and rang Paula in Barnes.

178

'I was wondering,' he began, 'whether you had by any chance heard anything of Jethro?'

He thought she sighed. 'No,' she said. 'Nothing.'

'How are you bearing up?'

'I can't sleep. But I suppose that's to be expected. Have you seen Kitty today?' she asked suddenly and unexpectedly.

'Actually I haven't. But I think she's beginning to feel the strain pretty badly, according to Tattie. I suppose everyone is. And they're being besieged by reporters. which makes it worse.'

'I thought it was only me!'

'What? Are they hanging round your house too?'

'I can't get in our out. It's a nightmare. The telephone never stops going and these awful Press people pounce out from behind the rhododendrons if I set foot outside the door. It's a complete persecution.'

'What have you said to them?'

'Nothing. I told them – I've no statement to make.' She giggled weakly and then was silent.

'Good. That's best.' He wondered, uncomfortably, whether his voice sounded at all slurred.

'I tried to ring Kitty but there was something funny about the number.'

'You tried to ring Kitty!'

'I went there, you know. We have spoken.' She giggled again. He wondered whether she might be losing her grip.

'I hadn't realised.'

'We felt we needed to talk,' she said, which was not exactly truthful. *She* had felt she needed to talk. 'But I never got through because of this funny thing.'

'Did they ask you who you were calling?'

'That's right. I rang off.'

'You shouldn't have done that. It's simply that she's getting so many troublesome calls that Nina arranged this intercepting lark.' He had a little difficulty with 'intercepting' but came to the conclusion it was only nerves.

'I felt scared.'

'There was no need to feel scared.'

'Well, shy perhaps.'

It was then he decided to go and see her. Something about

179

that word drew him. He felt she needed help.

'Shall I pop over?' he asked.

'What – now?'

'Why not?'

'I suppose it would be – nice.'

'Right. Bye,' he said. He was amazed at his own decisiveness. He felt marvellous as he marched off towards the tube. He felt he was going to the rescue. And, in all the flurry of decision, he had quite forgotten about the Press at the door.

Chapter Twelve

It was a starlit evening as John, with a sense of self-importance not unpleasing to him, walked up Paula's avenue past the street lamps and the parked cars and the February front gardens. Already a frost was forming over the pruned roses and the winter-shaggy front lawns, and the bird baths were frozen. Curtains were drawn. Husbands home and children upstairs pretending to do their homework. The road, which was a long one and undistinguished, a staggered procession of houses built some time between the wars, with glazed front porches and wrought iron gates, was at first deserted, until he saw, coming towards him, four large youths with little hair and big boots. John was not a foolhardy man and, being short and by no means nimble on his feet, he crossed over the road, pulse rate quickening slightly. However, they never even looked his way and when they had passed, one of them flinging an empty polystyrene fast-food container into a front garden, he crossed back and continued.

There was a bend in the road and it was not until he came almost to Paula's house that he saw the group of people sitting on her steps and leaning against the garage doors. They looked cold and dispirited, wearing woolly hats and scarfs, parkas, hoods and ear-muffs. There were two young women among them. As John padded in through the gate, catching hold of an upright to support himself when he slithered on an icy patch, they all began to move, like animated puppets who had been activated. He felt they were pleased to see him. He almost warmed to them.

'Are you a friend of Miss Kingston's?' asked a man.

'Are you Mr Manning's agent?' asked another.

'Who are you?' demanded a girl. 'And can you ask Miss Kingston if she'll have a few words with us?'

'Is there any news about Jethro?' called a man from the drive.

'If she'd any heart she'd have us in and give us a cup of tea,' said an older man.

'A Scotch'd be more to the point!' shouted a man sitting, improbably, on a shooting stick prodded into the small patch of lawn round by the side door. And they all laughed, bleakly.

'Sorry, you guys,' said John, pushing his way through. He tried to sound the kind of person who spoke their language and knew how to be hard.

'Come on . . .' pleaded a middle-aged man with a blue, bulbous nose. 'What's the point. If she'd only answer half a dozen bijou little questions very delicately posed we could all go home.'

John saw Paula pulling away the curtain slightly from the front room. She looked pale with a streak of lighting behind her and the street lamps in front.

'There she is!' called the man from the garage walking forward and stepping on to the flower bed beneath the bay window, where Paula's wallflowers were sullenly holding together, yellowing, through the winter. 'Come on, dear. Have a bit of pity for the poor old Press.' He threw his cigarette end into the speckled laurel.

Hurriedly she drew back, closing the curtain. John could imagine her inside, cowering into her sofa, wondering whether, if she opened the door, they would all push into the hall.

'Aren't you a musician?' asked the other girl. She looked brighter, tougher than the others. Younger.

John was not sure whether to be gratified or worried.

'I know,' she cried. 'John Sorensen.'

'Who's he?' one of the men muttered to another.

'The cellist,' she said with awful clarity. 'Friend of Jethro Manning's. Very celebrated musician. I went to his Smith Square recital just before Christmas. Do *you* know where he is?'

John began to relax. She seemed civilised.

'I've no idea. None at all.' John tried to sound jovial and dismissive. 'Why d'you suppose I've come round here?'

'Ah-hah!' said a man, suggestively, and the others looked interested or tittered.

'Don't be absurd,' said John. 'I don't know his whereabouts and neither does the lady inside. If I did, I expect you would already too.'

'Then why are you coming to see her?'

'To protect her against you lot,' he joked.

'She's paranoid,' said one, sourly. 'They all are. Jethro's common property and they can't expect the public not to want to know.'

'Know what?' Suddenly John found he was beginning to get angry. 'What is there to know?'

'That's what we're asking you.'

'And I'm telling you I don't know. I'm in the dark, like everybody else. Look, you lot – for God's sake go away and give this poor soul in here some peace. How would you like it if you were her?'

'Why are you coming to see her?' repeated the same questioner.

'Aren't you a friend of the wife's?' said the one from round the side, folding up his shooting stick and carrying it under his arm. 'Does she know you're here?'

'Is he a friend of the wife's?' asked another. 'Is that so?'

'And the daughter's. He's the daughter's fella.'

Suddenly John saw red. He took his umbrella and knocked lightly on the window with it. He shouted through the letterbox. 'Paula,' he shouted. 'Obviously these bastards aren't going to let you answer the door without pushing in, so I'll have to go away.'

'We shan't push in,' said one of the women. 'We only wish she'd tell us what we need to know so we can go home and get a hot meal. She can open the door to you.'

John look round, a little unbelieving. 'Go on,' said the girl. 'We're not hooligans.'

He called through again. 'Paula. Paula. They say they won't try to get in.'

There were footsteps in the hall. Through the letterbox he could see her feet. 'They only want you to answer a few questions,' he said, 'and then they'll go away.'

'And you believe that?' she said. She sounded fearful, though he wasn't entirely sure whether she was being sarcastic at his expense.

'We're not coming bursting into your house,' called the girl.

'Not unless you invited us,' shouted one of the men.

She moved closer and John heard her put the chain on the door. She opened it just a little, and the reporters all crowded near, closing in. John, panicking, hit one of them on the legs with his umbrella and the man shouted, 'Ouch – stop that, you nasty vindictive little man, or I'll have you up for assault!'

'Then stand back so she can let me in,' John shouted back. 'Or I'll have the lot of you!' he added, with sudden bravado.

Somebody laughed and it seemed they slipped back a foot or two, while Paula unchained the door and rapidly allowed him to squeeze through into the bright, safe warmth of the house. Quickly she put the chain on again and he lifted the letterbox from within. 'Go away,' he shouted, 'or I'll call the police. You're trespassing. Don't you know that?' But to her he turned and said, 'Are we being a bit horrid? It's awfully cold out there.'

'That's their funeral,' she said, thinly. 'I never invited them.'

'But I suppose they've no option,' he persisted. 'They're not really behaving all that badly, though I suppose we could insist on them standing in the street.'

'What are you suggesting?'

'Well, couldn't you tell them whatever they want to know?'

'I *have* nothing to tell them.'

'But is there any harm in just answering any questions truthfully?'

'I'm scared of reporters. You never know how they'll twist things.'

'Look,' he said. 'I'm quite wily. I'll not tell them anything stupid about Jethro or you or Kitty. I'll just answer any factual questions about Sunday and what happened. Wouldn't that be best?'

'It won't be Sunday they want to know about. They've got all that already. There's nothing new.'

'Well then, there can't be any harm in co-operating, can there? You know, I think we've been a bit prickly.'

'You'd be prickly if you were a prisoner in your own house,' she complained. 'Excuse me. I think I'm going to be sick.' And she turned and hurried away down the hall.

John made up his own mind. He opened the door on the chain again and said, 'Right, chaps. You fire the questions. I'll do my best, but don't expect a scoop because there isn't a story here at all . . .'

They crowded forward. 'How long have you known Miss Kingston?' a man began. 'Does Tatiana Manning know you've come?'

'Is it true Jethro's under psychiatric care?' shouted someone.

'Do you know if he's planning to go back to his wife?'

'Is it true the Russians won't give him a visa for Moscow?'

'Has he gone to that Polish girl he was having if off with when he was one of the judges for the Rubinstein competition?'

'Is there any truth in the rumour he planned not to give any more performances after the Queen Elizabeth Hall last Sunday?'

'What!' cried John, incredulously. 'What nonsense *are* you talking? This is mad!'

'There's a story going around that he was going to refuse to do anything except make recordings in future. Like Glenn Gould.'

'How ridiculous! Nothing of the sort,' he snapped. 'Jethro hadn't made any plans about anything to change his career. Everything was going quite normally.'

'Do you think he's been kidnapped?'

'No. Who'd want to kidnap him?' John's back was hurting, crouching at the letterbox.

'Was he being blackmailed?'

'Of course not.'

'Had he any secrets from Miss Kingston?'

'Are you Miss Kingston's lover?'

Hotly, John pushed the door close and bolted it. He was shaking, quivering. Paula stood behind him.

'I've heated up some soup,' she murmured. 'It's in the

185

kitchen. You see what I mean?'

They walked together into the back of the house and closed the kitchen door.

'My God!' said John. And began his soup, tucking one of Aunt Virginia's big white table napkins absent-mindedly into his collar. 'My God!'

He burned his tongue on the Crosse and Blackwells.

Kitty had been crying for well over an hour.

Tatiana sat on the bed, holding her hand. She found it deeply disorientating to see her mother, whose hauteur forbade any show of emotional frailty under normal circumstances, and who could reduce lesser mortals to tears with a shaft of sarcasm or a flash of the glacier-blue eyes when she wished, in this weak state, tucked up, watery, with the duvet close under her chin and her hair limp on the pillow.

'Don't, sweetheart,' she said.

But Kitty only turned her head and allowed the tears to roll down, until the pillow was so hot-wet that Tattie turned it for her.

'You've had nothing to eat,' said Tattie helplessly.

'I don't want . . . anything.'

'It might make you feel better. What about a little omelette?'

Kitty simply shook her head.

'Would you like me to call Dr Penfold?'

For the first time, Kitty reacted. 'What could Dr Penfold do? He can't bring Jethro back. Everyone's useless. There's nothing anyone can do.'

'He could give you something, love.'

'Give me something? What?'

'Something to stop you feeling so . . .'

'Feeling so?' Kitty's eyes were drying. There was a dangerous glint which Tatiana, oddly, found reassuring. 'Do you want me doped, drugged, so I can't feel anything? Is that what you think best for me? Oh – leave me alone.' She turned her head again and began once more to weep, but silently, shuddering quietly and intermittently.

Tatiana sat. She looked at the clock. Ten o'clock.

At half-past ten Kitty roused herself a little and said, 'Are you still there?' Tattie had turned out the lamp beside the bed and was sitting with the curtains drawn back and the light of the full moon shining in from over the sleeping garden, bright and white across the room.

'I think you slept a little,' she said.

'No, I never slept,' contradicted Kitty. 'How could I sleep?'

Tatiana did not argue. 'Would you like a little something now?' she asked, but Kitty shook her head again, and simply turned her back on the girl, turned so that she could see out of the window into the red glow that was London at night.

'If anything has happened to Jethro,' said Kitty very quietly, 'I don't want to be – here – any more.'

'That's a terrible thing to say, Mother, What about us?'

But Kitty simply stared at the moon.

'What about Antony?'

Kitty sighed. 'Antony's a big boy now. He doesn't need me.'

'We all need you,' said Tatiana gently.

'I don't want a life without Jethro.'

Tatiana bit back the reply that Kitty had been living a life without Jethro for a good year and she seemed to have managed, albeit a little grimly. But she did say, 'Yes you do, darling. You're a sticker.'

Kitty turned a tear-stained face to her. 'Nobody ever runs quite true to form,' she began. 'None of us know how the other . . .' Then she began to weep again. She cried quietly for a long time, until the door opened a crack and Nina looked in.

'The reporters have all gone,' she said.

But the news brought no reaction of any kind from Kitty, whose body, beneath the duvet, was convulsed intermittently. The girls sat together on the bed, Tatiana's shoulders sagging.

'You feeling all right?' Nina asked her sister.

'No.'

'You go to bed and I'll sit with her.'

'I haven't the heart even to go to bed,' Tattie whispered. 'The thought of getting out of one's clothes and . . .'

'Then doss down in them, my love. Just get some shut-eye.

You need it. Do you think you've got a temperature again?'

'I don't know. Probably.'

Nina put a hand on Tattie's forehead and said, 'You're boiling. Go on, you idiot. You've got a fever.'

Tattie laughed. 'Here we are, all fussing each other . . .'

'I don't want anyone to fuss me,' Kitty said from the pillow, and the girls smiled at each other in the moonlight.

Nina turned on the bedside lamp but Kitty quickly said, 'Turn it off. I can't bear the light. Turn if off.'

'Would you like Antony to come home from school if they'll let him, darling?'

'I don't want Antony. What can Antony do?'

'I think he feels very cut off down there. He's worried and miserable. He wants to be here.'

'It's better for him at school,' said Kitty. 'I don't want him. I don't want any of you.'

'Go on,' whispered Nina to Tatiana, smiling. 'Take a hint. And a couple of aspirins too!'

Tattie slipped out and back to her own room where, wearily, she undressed and climbed into bed without brushing her teeth or taking out her ear-rings or hanging up her clothes. She still found it difficult, though, to fall asleep, lying there thinking, confusedly, about Jethro and also about John, whether she loved John or whether it was time to part. She wondered what he had done with his evening after she had left. Where he was now. Back in his flat, no doubt, with his feet up and a glass of beer beside him, watching some stupid late-night movie on the television. She thought of his warm, hospitable little body enfolding his cello on a large lit platform and as she lay longer she wanted to be enfolded too.

Strangely, she too now began to cry, very softly. She cried herself to sleep.

Paula showed John the letter from the Wing Commander in East Anglia and asked what he thought. He scratched his head.

'It looks as though he did something untoward,' he agreed. 'But what?'

'Could he have had a memory lapse?' suggested Paula.

'Not Jethro. No way. His memory's faultless.'

'Did he just play badly?'

He shook his head. 'He wouldn't know how to "play badly" as you put it. He might have failed to give of his absolute best, if he was under strain and stress, but Jethro's worst is light years away better than many big names consider their best. No, something odd must have happened. Something really odd. You see, this man's trying to reassure him and says some of them were coming up to the South Bank. If he'd done anything really heinous they wouldn't say that.'

'He couldn't have been . . .' she flushed – 'drunk, I suppose?'

'Jethro? Before a recital? Hardly. Why – have you ever known him get drunk?'

'No,' she admitted. 'He's got a hard head. And he'd never touch a drop of alcohol the day of a recital or a concerto. Sometimes after . . .'

'Could he have been rude to anyone?' John put in suddenly. 'You know him. If someone really rubbed him up the wrong way. Could he have said something out of turn to one of the Music Club members. I wouldn't put that past him.'

'I suppose he could,' she said doubtfully. 'Although he always said he could never afford to despise his public and people at things like that always seem to love him. I don't think it's terribly likely.'

She paused. 'Then there's this,' she said, handing him the Bayswater telephone number she had found on the other side of Jethro's note about Cardiff. 'I rang it and got a recorded message from a secretary to somebody called Dr Courtney, but I haven't the faintest notion who Dr Courtney is. I tried to find out the address but the girl on the exchange wouldn't give it to me when I gave her the number, and although I looked right through the Courtneys in the book I couldn't find it. I tried to ring Kitty, in case she knew, but she was engaged every time I rang. Then when I tried the number again there was no answer. I know it isn't his doctor. He's called Penfold. And the solicitor's in Holborn or round there, not Bayswater.'

'You think it was some professional geezer?'

'I don't know what I think.'

'You ought to pass it on to the police, oughtn't you?'

'I suppose so.' She rose.

'Would you like me to do it for you?'

She sat down again, limply. She seemed to sag right into the chair. 'You don't know how nice it is to have someone kind.' She wanted to say 'a man', but she thought he might misunderstand her.

John had a little chat with the policeman the other end of the telephone and came back to the table feeling very useful indeed. He was glad he had come. This poor little thing needed support. Kitty had the girls and they had each other, but here was this sweet creature, kind of lost. He wondered how Jethro could put her through all this. He put out a hand and touched hers across the table, meaning to imply solidarity, no more, but she didn't respond except by a weak smile, and he picked up an orange from the bowl instead. He made a terrible mess in peeling it. Shyly, she took it from him and stripped away the pith with expert fingers, handing the segments across the table. One, she popped in her own mouth.

'What a nasty time you're having,' he said.

She looked at him with dry eyes.

'You must be frightened, but keep your pecker up. I have a feeling . . .'

'I'm not frightened any more. I think. I'm not sure what I am. I feel – blank.'

He looked enquiring.

'It's as though. . . . I've gone through all the feeling and now I'm just left, empty of any more. I think – if Jethro walked through that door now, I'd simply get up and make him a cup of tea. I'm too tired to go overboard with joy, just like now I'm too tired to go overboard with worry. I don't like feeling this way.'

'It's natural,' he said, wiping the orange juice from his mouth. He thought what a pretty mouth she had, soft with slightly buck teeth and moist lips.

'Maybe it's being pregnant,' she said.

He did a double-take. 'When?'

'Oh – it's ages off. I've only just realised.'

190

'What does Jethro . . . ?' John reeled at the thought of Jethro's reaction.

'Jethro doesn't even know. I never told him about being late and it wasn't until after he'd gone that I stopped to work it out.'

'You've seen a doctor?'

'Not yet. But I'm sure. Quite sure. One knows these things,' she said brightly.

'I don't know what to say. Without Jethro. . . . Do you want it?' It sounded such a bald question as he asked it.

'Very much,' she said. 'Very very much.'

'Even if Jethro didn't ever . . .'

'Even if Jethro didn't ever – but he will. I expect.'

'What a brave girl you are!' he said. He came over quite emotional. 'You're going to need friends. I'm glad I came over.'

She smiled.

'I'll come around again when I get back from Brighton, shall I?'

'Brighton?'

'I'm off tomorrow. I'm playing Spohr and a little Schubert with the Krommer Concertante, in the Pavilion.'

'When do you get back, then?'

'Normally I'd come back that night, after the concert. But as it happens Natalia's lending me her little flat in Lewes Crescent right over the weekend, so I shan't be seeing you until early next week.'

'You mean Kitty's mother. The Russian lady?'

'That's right. Lovely old bird. Generous to a fault. And the flat's a real duck.'

'I've never seen the Pavilion,' said Paula. 'Not inside, that is.'

'Everybody ought to see the . . .' – a thought bounded into his mind and bounced – 'Why don't you come down? Do you a power of good. Just at the moment. There's room in the flat.'

Paula went very red, right up to the tips of her ears. 'I don't see I could do that,' she said.

He helped himself to an aged walnut, then cracked it open. Inside it was dry and withered. He tried again. 'Perhaps not,' he agreed. 'Pity.' He looked at his watch now and said he supposed he ought to go back and get some sleep if he was playing tomorrow.

'I'm surprised you're not practising tonight,' she apologised. 'It was good of you to come all the way over here, and it's quite late. But I don't think I can exactly offer you a . . .'

'No, no. Can't imagine what the Press would find to say about that! Can you?'

He expected her to laugh, but instead she looked at him gravely with large brown eyes.

'Tell you what,' he suggested, 'I'll give you a ring from Natalia's flat and find out how you are and whether there's been any news.'

She rose. 'Thanks ever so,' she said. The 'ever so' must have slipped out. It was a long time since she had said 'ever so'. But John never even noticed. 'But I expect that if there was any development you'd probably see it in the papers almost before I knew it myself.'

'That's a point,' he agreed. And it wasn't until he was on his way home in the taxi that he stopped to think that Tattie would be the first person to ring him were Jethro found. Which led him to remember that Tattie was planning to spend the weekend with him in Lewes Crescent. Somehow it seemed to have gone clean out of his mind.

Nina rang Dr Penfold at his home number about midnight and asked if she could possibly run round to the house and pick up something to calm Kitty and help her to sleep. She had dickered with the idea of ringing the surgery number to ask for an emergency visit from whichever doctor might be on duty, but she knew David and Holly Penfold well enough to be confident they would not think ill of being disturbed in this event.

'I'll come right round,' said Penfold on the telephone. 'I'm not on duty as it happens and it'd be better for me to see your mother myself. I don't know how she'd take to a strange face just now.'

'I do feel badly about this,' said Nina when he arrived. 'Turning you out on your free evening.'

'Did me a service,' said Penfold. 'We're entertaining my

mother-in-law and she doesn't seem to believe in going to bed. Holly and she are still watching some ghastly video. The old lady's down from Hexham for three weeks and that's three weeks too long. She spends her life complaining we won't let her watch any "nasties". I wondered whether Kitty'd suffer any delayed reaction. She's been so dreadfully stoic up until now and that kind of behaviour under shock always makes me uneasy.'

'Know something?' he threw out as he climbed the stairs, carrying his black bag. 'I have never – ever – been called in to visit your ma before! Jethro – yes – countless times. With a toe ache or – more properly, a finger ache. Do you remember that time he brought me over in the middle of my dinner because he thought he had dermatitis on his hands and it was simply a heat-rash because he'd been sun-bathing. But Kitty. That's another matter.'

'She doesn't believe in doctors.'

Penfold laughed, but at Kitty's bedroom door he paused for a moment and whispered 'Does she still sleep in here? Now?'

'Of course,' said Nina. 'Where d'you expect her to sleep? In the dog's basket?'

She opened the door. There was Kitty, alone in the great French bed, her hair black upon the pillow, her long body curled into a hoop.

'She's still in her clothes,' said Nina. 'She wouldn't undress. Tatiana put her to bed, but now she seems to have got some bug and she's gone to bed too.'

The most recent cup of tea Nina had made her mother stood, untouched, on the bedside table. Kitty never raised her head, but the tears simply flowed, unchecked, unstoppered, silently, as though she had lost all hope of ever stopping. 'It's like the "Sorcerer's Apprentice",' said Nina. 'My least favourite piece of music.'

David Penfold sat down gently on the bed beside her.

'That should at any rate give her a night's sleep,' he said, as Nina let him out into the lamp-lit street again. 'Dole out the pills nightly until she seems to have got the situation under control and give me a ring – whatever happens – in three days.'

'She'll probably refuse to take them,' said Nina. 'Tonight's an exception. Tonight she'd probably take the whole lot! Where did you leave them?'

'My God!' cried Penfold and leapt up the stairs again, throwing open the door of Kitty's room to find her standing – in her bra and pants, a spare figure – at the dressing table with the small plastic container in her hand. Quietly he took them from her and led her back to the bed. Sobbing, shuddering, she allowed herself to be propelled. He laid the covers softly over her and, leaving her door open, ran down again to Nina, who was waiting in the hall. He was shaking a little himself as he handed them over.

'I'm not saying anything, Dr Penfold,' she said.

'You don't have to. It was an aberration and had she . . .' He flinched.

'That's useless kind of talk.' She put them in her pocket. 'It didn't happen. By tomorrow she wouldn't want it to happen. I think tonight it's exhaustion as much as anything. You know – the kind of exhaustion that makes sleep out of the question.'

'Yes I know,' he said. 'But you shouldn't. You can't let this take over. Life – your life – lives – they have to go on.'

'I'm not falling apart.'

'This malaise of Tatiana's . . . is it all part and parcel, do you think?'

'What? Hysterical?'

'I didn't quite say that.'

'I'm glad. 'Cause it certainly isn't. She's simply had a virus, or a touch of whatever's been going the rounds, and went back to work too soon, I should think. All this doesn't help but no – Tattie's no hypochondriac.'

He smiled.

'Dr Penfold,' she asked. 'If Father was suffering from anything – you would tell us? Naturally. Wouldn't you?'

'As you say. Naturally.' He put a hand on her shoulder. Upon an impulse, she stretched up and kissed him. He seemed disconcerted. He hesitated before continuing, then collected himself. 'I've had the police enquiring, you know. And your pa's agent. It would help them if I could produce a certificate to say he had some terminal illness. Then we could all say the strain of the knowledge had been too much for him.

But I'm afraid I can't oblige because he hasn't and we can't. There may be insurance complications about the concert he missed in Manchester.'

'And – and his state of mind?'

'The state of your father's mind! My God – what a formidable thought. Would you say you understood it?'

'Yes,' said Nina simply.

'Oh well – you artists!'

'I'm not an artist.'

'Tiddlypush.' Course you are. Holly listened to that play on the wireless you were in just before Christmas.'

Nina smiled. 'I'm in a lot of plays. After all, I'm on the Beeb Rep and I'm professional, reliable and moderately experienced. But I've managed to escape the theatrical temperament.' Suddenly she laughed. 'It's Mother who ought to have had a sizzling career in the theatre, not me. I'm dull. It's tragic he stopped her.'

'Did he really? he asked.

'Of course. He never wanted competition for the bright lights.'

'Pity. She might have been very good,' he said.

'If she could stand the pace.'

'Ah . . .'

'You don't think he's gone right round the twist, do you?' she asked.

'No more than usual.'

'And there's really nothing physically wrong?'

'Nina – I've not seen him for – oh – getting on for a year.'

'But then? Blood pressure on the high side, but not dangerously so. I told him to be sensible. Take it a bit easy.'

She burst out laughing. 'What a bloody silly thing to say,' she said.

'Sorry.' He sounded mildly but not very offended. 'Hey – what's happening?'

They both froze to footsteps and a sound of rustling paper round the side of the house by the kitchen entrance.

Very softly Nina opened the door and they both sniffed the silence. Now there wasn't a sound except for the rumble of traffic and the metallic thud of a record from a neighbour's house. A car sped past and disappeared taking its sound with

195

it. Nina turned back to look at him and started along the path, which led to the side gate. He crept after her. Together they peered through the trellis at the top of the gate. Penfold drew his breath in sharply and the man at the dustbins stopped dead, still, statue-still, with one arm among the refuse. A mountain of paper lay on the garden path beside him. A torch held in his right hand shone into the bin. He turned and stared at the gate. Two faces showed slatted through the trellis and he turned the torch upon them, yellow.

Nina burst the gate open and leapt upon him. The shock of anything so female and so slight hitting so hard knocked him reeling against the kitchen step, where he stumbled across the dustbin lid and fell, dropping his torch, which David Penfold picked up and shone straight into his eyes. He blinked, half shuttering his lids.

'So?' barked Penfold. 'And who are you?'

'He's a journalist,' said Nina, panting, as she knelt upon the reporter in a most uncomfortable place. 'I recognise him. He was one of that lot hanging round the gate this afternoon. I thought they'd all gone. My God!' She spoke quietly. She hardly raised her voice at all. 'You're disgusting! And what did you expect to find in this lot?' She kicked the smelly contents of Kitty's kitchen garbage around the step with her foot. The spine of a trout shot into his face. He wiped it away.

'Get going,' said the doctor.

'There could be a clue somewhere in this lot,' protested the man. 'You could be grateful to me.'

But Nina simply picked up the dustbin by its two handles. The lid still lay by the step, drunkenly. She picked up the bin and emptied it over the reporter's head and slammed back into the house.

Dr Penfold drove away home after he had seen the man out of the gate and well down the road. He tailed him slowly as far as the underground station in Maida Vale. It had been an infinitely more interesting evening than anything he could have hoped for, and he woke Holly to tell her about it.

Chapter Thirteen

Tatiana and Nina met blearily over the giant Nescafé tin in the morning.

'You going to be able to minister to Mama today?' asked Tattie, dissolving a codeine tablet in orange juice. 'I don't think we ought to leave her alone if we can help it.'

'You've forgotten,' said Nina. 'I'm working.'

'Remind me.'

'Read-through for weirdo Radio Three play about a coal-miner with an obsession about tortoises.'

'How unbelievably boring.'

'Actually it has its moments.'

'I feel like death.'

'Stay at home.'

'Can't.'

So it was that Natalia was invited to come round to Loudoun Road to sit by her distraught daughter's bedside and relieve her grand-daughters. She wore a knitted suit in apricot-coloured bouclé wool with matching stockings. She let herself and her dogs in with the key Nina had left under the bay tree tub, hung her cream cashmere coat in the hall and climbed the stairs to Kitty's bedroom to find it empty, the bed thrown back and unmade, Kitty's nightie on the floor. The curtains had not been drawn. She pulled them back and went to look for her daughter, going from room to room quietly on plump feet. The sense of unease and attendant slight nausea would not have been apparent to an observer. Calmly she opened and closed doors. Evenly she called Kitty's name. Nobody would have guessed she had any cause for concern.

At the bathroom she hesitated for a second, her hand on the doorknob, before entering. But there was nobody there. The bath was none too clean, the mat rumpled and damp, and a wet black towel in a heap on the floor. The cold tap was dripping as it had been for months, a small trickle-stain of brown London water deposit straggling down the basin. She turned it off with as much strength as she could muster, but it still dripped; she hung the mat over the bath and the towel on the rail, then went back into the bedroom and looked down upon the dormant garden over which the winter sun never flitted.

She went downstairs again and as she descended she became aware for the first time of a smell of gas. She hurried, speeding up her normal pace but yet not running, into the kitchen. The dogs followed.

However, it was empty. The Nescafé tin stood on the table with the lid off. The washing machine was running its final cycle and into the spin it came as she crossed the room. A gas jet, unlit, was left on.

Natalia turned it off and went to the telephone. For a while she stood with her hand on that; then took her hand away and went home, putting the key back where Nina had hidden it.

She walked back to the Finchley Road to catch her bus. She might ring Tattie at work once she got home, although, on the other hand, she might not. The girls worried over-much about their mother. Nobody seemed to waste time worrying about *her*, for which she was grateful.

It was a blue, balmy day for February, croci and iris reticulata already appearing in some of the gardens. A squirrel scampered over a wall ahead of her and was gone, shooting along the branch of a sleeping cherry. The dogs showed mild interest. Within a month the curtain would go up upon spring. And would Jethro have come home?

It must – she thought, as she boarded her bus with a hand from the conductor, who belied a villainous appearance – be good in Brighton today. She hoped the weather would hold for John Sorensen, to whom she had lent the flat quite on impulse when she heard he had an engagement down there and would like to stay over for a short break. She never let her flat and very seldom lent it, and she was not quite sure why she had done so now, unless it was because she had a faint suspicion that John was Tattie's boyfriend.

She pondered briefly upon where Kitty could have gone. Possibly to Masius, Jethro's solicitor, whom she had been threatening to persecute. Or to Roger Dilke? Theo? Who else? She realized, looking out of the bus window at the high wall of Lord's Cricket Ground, that she knew very little of Kitty's private life. The dogs sat together on her soft lap and gently she fondled their ears, thinking.

As she walked into her flat the telephone was ringing. Nevertheless she released the dogs from their leads and slipped off her court shoes before crossing the carpet to answer it. She never bothered to do that in Kitty's house where grit and the world outside was ground daily into the carpets, but at home she behaved from habit, without fluster.

It was Theo.

'How nice!' she said. 'I enjoyed it too.'

'My car's been returned.'

She considered the full meaning. 'You mean, Jethro's come to you?'

'No. I mean simply what I say. The car's back but not with Jethro.'

She waited for him to explain. 'Yes, dear?'

'The first I knew was that I had a card in this morning's post telling me to pick it up from a multi-storey near Victoria, and in the same envelope, the garage ticket.'

'The card was in Jethro's hand?'

'No. Not unless heavily disguised and I think I know his writing well enough to see through that. It was brief and to the point – simply told me where to go to pick up the car and said the keys had been left with the attendant in a sealed envelope. It had been there since yesterday evening, about six o'clock. And by the way – the card had been posted nearby according to the postmark.'

'Any apology?'

Theo managed a laugh. 'Jethro apologise?'

'You say it wasn't from him.'

'I said the card wasn't actually written by him. I still know it was Jethro who took it initially. He never made any secret of that.'

199

'Who have you told so far?'

'The police, of course. And I left a message for Roger, but he's at EMI. I think he had some vague feeling Jethro might turn up for the recording session, which of course Roger had cancelled. I knew he wouldn't.'

'What about Kitty? I've just been over there because the girls said she was quite unwell last night and they had to go to work. They said it had all got on top of her suddenly. But when I got there she wasn't in, and I was wondering whether she might be with you.'

'Nothing like that,' said Theo. 'I wasn't sure whether to tell her about the car because I understood from Irene that she was getting into a state and I thought I'd talk to you first.'

'Has he – spoilt it in any way, Theo? I mean – he hasn't scratched your nice paintwork or anything?'

'Miraculously, no. Thanks for asking. No, it's come home in much the same condition as it left me. There's only one thing. There was a piece of scrap paper on the floor – it must have dropped there when he was driving – with a telephone number on it. I rang the number . . .'

'Of course,' said Natalia.

'It was a psychiatrist called Courtney. North of the park.'

'A psychiatrist!'

'Yes, but, he knew nothing of Jethro. The thing led nowhere. Of course he'd heard of him and seen the bits in the papers, but Jethro wasn't a patient of his or anything. I might say I had some difficulty even finding that much out. The girl wasn't going to put me through to him at first and she wouldn't give me any information at all, but I insisted and finally the doctor came through, a bit frosty at first, but when he realised who it was I was concerned about, he thawed.'

'So he is a doctor?'

'Oh yes. When it became apparent I couldn't find out anything from him I rang Penfold, you know, Jethro and Kitty's doctor, and asked him if he knew anything about this man – and more specifically, whether he'd ever referred Jethro to him. He hadn't and he didn't know the chap personally but he looked him up and rang me back and said he seemed quite a reputable shrink, analyst, whatever you call them.'

'How very mysterious.'

'Do you think I ought to tell Kitty now – if only to find out whether she knows anything about this Courtney.'

'I think I'd wait for today. See what else the day brings. Let's talk again tomorrow. Again, I suppose you told the police?'

'Naturally.'

'Do you think it might be worth speaking to the Paula woman?'

He hesitated. 'I wasn't going to mention that. But I have done so. I rang her. She had also found the same telephone number in her house, on the back of something about a Cardiff concerto. She'd kept ringing the number but only found a message on the answering machine. She's as puzzled as we all are.'

'I think,' said Natalia, 'it sounds as though poor Jethro was wondering whether to make an appointment and hadn't actually done so. Yet. Or maybe he has and they hadn't picked up that he was a new patient booked in ahead. Theo! What about that?'

'I thought of that. I suggested it and the girl looked right up in the appointments book until April or beyond. No. He wasn't there.'

It wasn't until Natalia had put the telephone down and gone through to the bedroom for her pink slippers that it suddenly occurred to her that if Jethro had made an appointment to see Dr Courtney in the future, he would be most likely to have made it under another name.

Guy Knight, the accountant for Messrs Allan, Marvell and Dilke, Concert Agents, sought more contact with the musicians than he felt came with his corner of the job. And so, as he had a meeting scheduled at Glyndebourne, he offered to drive John plus cello down to Brighton.

Thus they were, that pale pre-vernal Thursday morning in February, driving along the road which cuts through the South Downs and into the back of Brighton. They were, of course, discussing Jethro. They had been talking about Jethro all the way from Clapham Common.

'I have this theory . . .' said Guy, overtaking, in one, an L-driver in a Ford Fiesta, an old man in a yellow Toyota and a Christian Salveson long vehicle. John grasped the sides of the passenger seat. '. . . that Jethro Manning is a very insecure man.'

'Most real artists are insecure,' said John. He felt extremely nervous. One had to weigh the saving of the fare against the stress of being a passenger and he was definitely returning by train.

'The higher you climb the further you fall, eh?' suggested Guy, cheerily. 'Half these pianists seem neurotic as old women about their hands.'

'Not only pianists.' John looked down at his own, in their thick black leather gloves. He played with the gauntlets. He found he was experiencing a fantasy about fighting his way out of a burning car. Diffidently, he touched his seat belt. The flint wall dividing the traffic lanes made him especially nervous.

'You drive with spirit,' he said to Guy.

'Thanks.' Guy seemed pleased. 'It's not often you can put your foot down in the south of England.'

John couldn't really see what the south of England had to do with it, but he had a picture of Guy racing up the A1 past Scotch Corner.

'Funny you don't drive,' said Guy.

'I've never felt it necessary,' muttered John.

'Jethro Manning drives. He nicked poor old Theo's Rover when he made his get-away on Sunday. Probably in Monte Carlo by now! Drives like the clappers, I wouldn't wonder. What d'you reckon?'

John was not at all sorry when Guy pulled up outside Lewes Crescent. He looked anxiously over his shoulder at the cello as though he half expected it to have suffered from travel fatigue. Guy tried to help him out with it, but John found he felt protective, even possessive, towards it, and he clutched it to him as Guy stood by the car door.

'Well . . .' he said.

'Well!' said Guy.

'Would you like to come in?' asked John. He did so hope the answer would be 'no'.

'That'd be nice,' said Guy. 'Shall I carry that?'

John shook his head and fumbled for Natalia's keys.

'Natalia's place is very cosy,' he said as he led the way up the staircase that rose with delicacy from the tiled communal hall. 'She believes in creature comforts. Everything tends to be pink and tasselled in her world.'

'You make it sound like a French bordello,' grinned Guy.

'She will have left it with cushions plumped up and a bottle of San Patricio in the fridge – sorry, a pale dry Cortado on the sideboard at this time of year, next to the port she keeps for her male friends. She has this "thing" about leaving the flat each time as she would like to find it the next time she puts the key in the lock.'

'Frightening lady!' said Guy.

'Nothing about Natalia is frightening,' contradicted John, gaining confidence as they reached the right landing, although he was considerably out of breath. Guy leaped up beside him and a little ahead.

He put the key in the lock and opened the door. He wiped his feet on the mat inside the hall and nodded to Guy who followed suit obediently. He felt pleased.

If Natalia's Baker Street flat was voluptuous as a double pink paeony, the Lewes Crescent apartment was pink-washed, fresh, young, the walls and curtains a matching pearly blush, shot like a sunrise, swagged and braided in oyster. Over the fireplace hung an impressionist painting by a Sussex artist, of a discreetly rosy sky fading across a sea whose wavelets lapped lightly upon shingle you could almost hear shuffling to and fro on the beach.

The sitting room carpet, a modern design hand-woven in fondant colours to Natalia's order, lay upon pale sanded and varnished pine boards; and deep, exquisitely comfortable chairs the tone of Jersey cream stood upon the carpet, inviting collapse into their succulent cushions. Against the wall stood a long low dog basket, lined in deeper rose pink. A mirror placed near the door, where Natalia could review herself before leaving the room, was of pink-shaded glass and deliciously flattering.

It was an altogether charming room, and so it did seem odd when, after John had laid his cello down on the sofa and his leather strapped suitcase on the floor, Guy picked up a thick man's sweater, none too clean, from a chair and held it up towards John.

'The old lady seems to have been entertaining!' he said, flinging it over the back of the chair to sit down.

John returned from the window, where he had been viewing the blue and placid Channel, and picked it up. There was a hole in one elbow and the crew-neck was frayed. He frowned. He felt confused. 'Coffee? Tea?' he asked.

'Do you suppose she keeps beer in the fridge as well as sherry?' suggested Guy. 'I could do with an ale.'

John, obligingly, pottered through to the kitchen.

'God Almighty!' He stood at the door, staring at the scene facing him. Guy joined him. 'Messy old lady,' he commented. 'So now where's the gracious living?'

While John, wearing rubber gloves he found on the draining board, wiped the table free of crumbs and put the top on the Sussex honey and shovelled the congealed bacon fat and tomato skins into the bin, Guy wandered off to seek the lavatory. He came back saying, 'I've had a look in the bedroom and I reckon someone's living here!'

John, still wearing his rubber gloves, followed Guy. He felt deeply disorientated and upset, looking at the unmade bed, the socks on the foor, the unwashed rose-sprigged mug on the bedside table. The pink telephone lay on the bed among the rumple of Natalia's rosy silk sheets. He replaced the receiver and put it back on the fitted telephone table the other side of Natalia's bed.

John knew that the first priority was to get rid of his travelling companion. 'You've been more than kind,' he said. 'I've brought you right out of your way.'

'Think nothing of it.'

'Still,' said John, thrusting a can of beer at him from Natalia's fridge, 'if whoever this is comes back there's going to be a lot of time wasted on explanation and sorting out and one of us is going to have to find a hotel. Meanwhile I've got to practise before tonight. So would you think me very inhospitable if I . . .'

'Why didn't you say?' Guy opened his can and gulped the beer down. 'I'm off. Let me know what the squatter boyfriend's like when you've met him. Well, well . . . how the other half live!' And off he did indeed go.

John took his case into the little cubicle Natalia reserved for her house guests. He unpacked thoughtfully, hanging his tail coat and trousers in the wardrobe, laying out his dress shirt and tie on the bed, unwrapping his black shoes from their plastic bag. He carried his spongebag through to the bathroom and stood looking down into the bath with distaste. Taking the scourer he scrubbed away at the black rim crusting from the bath and wiped the handbasin free of scum and evidence of tooth-cleaning. Natalia's fleecy pink towel with appliqué carnations was not actually on the floor but flung, very wet, over the heated towel rail which, John observed, was hot. He straightened the matching bath-mat and propped up the cork mat beneath that, mopping up a lake of water just seen under the basin. He noted with some interest that the shaving mirror was still steam-wet as though the bathroom had not long been left, and on it he wrote 'Jethro Manning needs a Nanny!!!'.

He wondered about all the people he might possibly telephone at this point. As he took himself back into the sitting room and began to lift the cello from its case he came face to face with the fact that he would prefer to phone Paula to any of them. He couldn't tell why. It was simply so. Tattie could be abrasive. Roger could be angry, even angrier. Kitty could be distraught. He decided not to ring anyone – yet.

For an hour and a half he practised, but without true concentration, an ear half cocked for a key in the lock. He kept looking at his watch. He tried to stop himself, to set sensible periods between the trips he made to the window to look out upon Lewes Crescent below, but the tension eroded his ability and he began to be anxious that when it came to tonight he would be below par. He wished he could feel angry, like Roger. He simply felt as though he were dreaming, and his strength and vitality seemed to be draining from him.

The Krommer Concertante, although well established already after two years together in engagements, could not afford to rest on their laurels and reputations are as easily lost as won. This evening would be heavy with wealth and a little light on sensitive, listening appreciation, a reception, musical entertainment and buffet supper served to captains of industry and their ladies on the occasion of the retirement of Sir Terry Jacks, out-going Chairman of the CPBPE (Council for the Promotion of British Production Enterprise). The Royal Pavilion made, of course, a splendid setting for such events, even though much of it was still and would be under scaffolding and plastic sheeting for some time yet as a result of the prolonged restoration programme; but the Concertante knew that half their audience would be there for the party and not for the music, which was, in fact, an elegant concession to Sir Terry, himself a devotee of the arts and a passable amateur flautist. What was more important was that the giant manufacturing company Gimingham Castle Laminates of which Sir Terry had been Chairman before he came to the CPBPE, had been a notable patron of modern music, offering a considerable award to the winner of the 'Composers for Britain' competition.

John made himself an omelette and chips from Natalia's stores, and rang for a minicab to take him and his cello to the Pavilion. The Concertante were scheduled to meet at two-thirty p.m. for the afternoon rehearsal, but as yet he was unsure whether they would be able to use the Banqueting Room, in which they were performing, for the full rehearsal time, or whether they would have to make do with some small chamber not open to the public for a mini-rehearsal before they could sound out the acoustics of the hall itself.

The cab dropped him at the doors and as he humped his cello out and paid off the driver he was accosted by an upper-class drunk with a dog, who told him not to enter the Pavilion's 'Halls of Decadence'. 'Don't, old man – don't I beseech you,' pleaded the man, wavering on the end of a lead. Relieved to see two members of the Krommer waving at him through the glass, he mumbled his polite excuses and hurried in.

'Be it on your own head, you silly bugger,' boomed the dog-owner after him.

'Come,' said Marigold, the red-haired viola. 'Come see! I *must* show you the Prince Regent Awakening the Spirit of Brighton. He looks the spitting image of you!'

206

'I know him well,' smiled John.

'We can rehearse in the Banqueting Room from three-thirty to five-thirty,' said Edgar the horn. 'Until then they're letting us use a suite of closed rooms for a run-through. OK?'

'OK,' said John, shambling through the Chinese halls, hung with mirrors, the walls sumptuous with pink linen painted to pretend to be a grove of waving blue bamboo in leaf. He followed Marigold up the cast iron staircase, under the lanterns. He made a resolution now, for the rest of the day, to forget Jethro.

Rehearsal went well and he surprised himself by the way he had contrived to pull himself together. After a short tea-break the musicians took themselves down to the Banqueting Room. Marigold stood staring up into the dome at the giant plantain foliage and the vast winged dragon hovering over the sparkling great star of mirror glass from which was suspended the chandelier itself, a shower of crystal from which six further dragons rose, a lotus flower in tinted glass issuing from each throat. She looked first up into the dome, forty-five foot high, then round the hall at the porcelain, the pictures, the ormulu and the gilded wood. 'Wow!' she said. Marigold was American.

'No further news about Jethro Manning, is there?' asked James, the leader, as they broke up. The question seemed to be directed towards John, who was assumed to have access to the Mannings, and he simply shook his head.

'Very tragic business,' said James, shortly.

John left the Pavilion, discomforted, with an hour and a half to spare before he need return, booted and spurred, for the concert. The drunk with his dog was now sitting splayed out on a bench, apparently exhausted, for this time he made no attempt to waylay John. John wondered whether such a man had a home to go to. Stylishly shabby but not destitute, he thought.

Walking back to Lewes Crescent, the sea dark and mysterious below and Brighton twinkling wintrily behind him, John regretted that he had not brought his dress suit with him and changed in the Pavilion. He had thought that the walk would freshen him, but now he had changed his mind, scared of any confrontation before the performance, of any crisis which

207

could throw him and disturb his concentration. When the house in the Crescent came into view he looked anxiously to see whether there was any light on at the level of Natalia's flat, but there was no sign of life. For a strange moment he did not know whether he was relieved or made more anxious. If lights had been blazing, how could he have forced himself into the house and up the stairs and through the apartment door. What would he have done? He could hardly have run away from the clothes he had to wear tonight and yet – and yet he would have wanted to turn on his heel and walk fast back towards Brighton. At any time, Jethro was strong meat but now, after what had happened. . . .

John squared his shoulders and smiled at the fluttery feeling in his breast. He took the stairs slowly, without Guy to impress, and when he came to the door he could not, for one terrible moment, find Natalia's key. If he had left it behind at the Pavilion! But he traced it at the bottom of his deep coat pocket, nestling in Kleenex, and brought it out.

The flat was in darkness. He turned on the light in the hall and went straight through into the bedroom where he himself was sleeping, pausing only to run the bath tap in the bathroom. The mirror had dried with his writing still legible upon its surface. 'Jethro Manning needs a Nanny!!!'

Something made him look into Natalia's bedroom on his way back to the bathroom, toddling along wrapped in his own large white towel. He stood like an astonished statue at the door. The bed was made, the cover pulled tidily up and the cushions in ice pink, ice green and ice blue arranged with precision up at the bed head. At first glance, the room wore the air of a recently vacated hotel bedroom. Something made him lift up the edge of the bedcover to see how the bed was made beneath it, and he was not surprised then to see that it had hardly been 'made' at all, that the sheets and blankets had simply been dragged over, unsmoothed, to give an illusion that the bed had been made.

Thoughtful, he lay in the hot steamy water, pondering.

Before he left for the Pavilion, he went into the kitchen and opened the door of the fridge. It was empty. No food there at all except half a packet of lard and a packet of UHT milk.

He called the minicab number, booked a taxi which never

208

came, and then had to walk fast, panting, puffing, heart thumping, back to the Pavilion. Every now and again, in his desperate state, he raised a thumb at a passing car, but nobody took any notice.

The audience was more responsive than the Krommer had anticipated, portly, elderly, well-heeled, but not unmusical for the most part. Or maybe it was simply that the Pavilion itself, glittering with light, infected them with some germ of aesthetic vivacity. 'Aren't they sweet, just darling?' whispered Marigold of the stoutish ladies from Sussex and the home counties in their long-preserved and seldom worn veteran long dresses.

'How many at your estimation?' asked Edgar, while he threw back a glass of water during a brief interval before the Schubert.

'I'm told we have close on two hundred and fifty, which is all it will hold,' James told him. 'Come on. Back we go.'

It was as John was just settling on to his seat that he heard a woman in a dark red velvet dress, matching her face, say to her neighbour 'And I said to Sidney, that's Jethro Manning!'

He was thrown completely off his stride. He knew, after the first few phrases, not only that he had never before opened so badly, but that it was going to go on. Panic made him sweat. Beads of fear came out on his brow. 'This is mad – this is crazy – this is only a tuppenny-halfpenny party at the Brighton bloody Pavilion,' he told himself, but it didn't seem to make any difference. He felt the audience freeze before him. Of course he was imagining it all, but nevertheless, he felt them freeze. And by the time he came to the final bars of his part he hated Jethro with an anger he had never felt before, not for anyone.

He hurried away from the others and mopped his face in the gentlemen's lavatory. Tears of chagrin started to his eyes and came popping out on to his chubby cheeks, to be mopped furiously away. 'Damn Jethro,' he swore, doing up his zip and coming out to face the others.

What astonished him was that nobody else seemed to realise he had played badly. Nobody at all. James said, 'Well, that seemed to go OK,' in a self-satisfied way. John thought he was living in a mad world.

Following the throng through into the Great Kitchen for the buffet supper, he found he was talking to himself. He stopped dead, overtaken by embarrassment, and found that somebody had put a glass of red wine into his hand. He took it at a gulp and was then even more confused to find that his glass was empty, which it remained for some time as he wandered around, trying to avoid Marigold who was by now becoming a little bit of a bore. Standing under the copper palm tree leaves topping the columns supporting the ceiling, he searched around the spits and the tables and the food and the five-hundred-piece 'batterie de cuisine' to see if he could locate the women who had been sitting in the audience and whom he had heard speak of Jethro.

At last he saw the woman in the red dress and managed to ease his way through the crowd of eating, drinking industrialists and their wives to reach her. At one point he passed a tray of full glasses and managed to exchange his empty one. He stuffed the occasional canapé into his round mouth as he went and then, as luck seemed to have turned, managed to swill down the wine and grab yet another before the woman turned from the man to whom she was speaking and addressed him.

'Splendid evening,' she boomed. 'Are you enjoying it?'

It struck him as odd that she should ask this, without at any point seeming aware that he was one of the entertainers. She made no effort to thank him for his part in the music or comment upon the players. It took away his momentum and left him unable to ask the question he had been reserving for the moment after the one when he would have smiled and inclined his head. He was already managing to forget how bad he had felt his own performance to have been. The heat and the hum had quite banished any feeling of chagrin or self-criticism and he was beginning to discover a rosy glow diffusing the shame. The only thing that still obsessed him was Jethro.

He opened his mouth unsure still what he was going to say and found that he had come straight to the point.

'I heard you mention Jethro Manning,' he said.

'Oh yes?' she replied. She seemed to have forgotten.

'He's a friend of mine.'

'Ah.'

210

'I wasn't sure whether you were saying . . .'

'He's the pianist who's disappeared, isn't he?' asked a man who had just arrived at her elbow.

'He's in Brighton,' she gave as an answer, and then threw back a sausage roll which sent her into a paroxym of coughing, so that everyone's attention was temporarily diverted finding her another glass of wine to drink. She indicated to John that she would like him to pat her back, which he did, finding it remarkably hot to the hand.

'How do you know?' asked the man once she had stopped.

'Where?' demanded John. Several people turned and glanced at him because he had so raised his voice.

'I saw him on the station last night. He came off the London train. I was meeting my husband in. I told Sidney but he wouldn't believe me. He often doesn't. It's so stupid. Sidney's so slow, he misses everything.'

'Did you . . .' John felt quite shaky. 'Did you tell the police?'

She opened her eyes wide. 'Why would I do that?' she asked.

'He *is* missing,' said the other man.

'If he's missing I suppose he wants to be missing,' she commented, with some coldness. 'One gathers he has a perfectly horrendous wife and a peculiar mistress and they're at each other's throats all the time. I should think the poor man deserves to get away. Of course I didn't tell the police.'

'His wife's a marvellous woman . . .' began John, going rather red. 'She's always been a great support to him.'

Now everyone stopped talking and turned to look at him and the woman in red.

'. . . and Paula Kingston – the . . . the "other woman" . . . is . . . sweet,' he ended up. He went quite scarlet. The group seemed to freeze on him. Overwhelmed, he squeezed his way out and in escape found himself pounced upon by Marigold, who handed him her glass and said, 'Do drink this, John. I've had too much. I'm getting drunk.'

Almost without thinking he took the glass and drank her wine. The room had become quite suffocating and he found that she was leading him out and through towards the South Drawing Room where several groups of people were standing around chatting and laughing. Silently he and Marigold

211

walked the length of the room towards the Saloon. He began to feel cooler, happier. He stumbled momentarily and Marigold steadied him at the elbow. He turned and smiled at her. Perhaps there was something to be said for her after all. She was certainly very pretty.

And then she spoke. 'Something very funny happened to you tonight, didn't it?' she asked, chattily.

His heart fluttered. Maybe it was too many canapés, or maybe it was what Marigold was going to say. His eyes beseeched her not to.

'I suppose it was just an aberration,' she went on. 'It does happen sometimes. I'd hardly have known it was you. I told a woman at the supper that you usually play fine. I told her – anyone can have an off day.'

He looked at his watch. 'It's time I was going,' he said.

'D'you want a lift back to London? There's room in our car.'

'I'm staying in Brighton,' he said shortly. Then he burped. It was extremely humiliating. He felt urgently that he had to get out – quickly.

This was all ludicrous, eating sausage rolls and becoming inebriated on bad red wine. He had to find Jethro.

He went for his coat and then he went out to find Jethro. He quite forgot that he had left his cello behind.

On the Thursday morning, as John and Guy were on the road to Brighton, Paula was in her darkroom when she heard the front-door bell ring.

The very thought of reporters flustered and upset her; and John had told her, before he left last night, to ignore them. In the end they would go away, he had said, like wasps in October. She rather wished he hadn't gone to Brighton.

There was no way she was going to answer the door to anyone for ten minutes, until she had finished processing the black and white film from Monday's jobs in Petersham and at the theatre. It had taken her long enough to force herself to get down to work again, the demands of the past few days having eaten away at her nervous energy and induced a kind of stupefaction, an apathy in which all she seemed to be able to do was to make ineffectual attempts to reach key people by

212

telephone and stare out of the window from behind Aunt Virginia's curtains at the sorry little band of Pressmen chatting desultorily at her gate, breaking off intermittently to make a dash for the bathroom, although now it no longer seemed possible to throw up the meagre diet upon which she had subsisted since Tuesday's luncheon at the Manning's.

The bell rang again. It made her jump. What kind of a person would do a job like that, she asked herself? Invading and alarming distressed women in the so-called seclusion of their homes?

Stoically she continued, able for the first time since Sunday night to concentrate upon something other than Jethro. After a few minutes of silence she decided they must have given up, and would be, once more, huddled round the gate or in the porch, whiling away hours of professional boredom.

It was when she was loading the next film on to the spiral for processing that the darkroom telephone rang. Normally she would answer this extension. That was, after all, why she had had it fitted. But at this moment her hands were full and, fussed, she was forced to allow it to ring. It could be Dilke with news. It could be the police. Or might it be the bank? It could, she supposed, be John telephoning from Brighton. It could even be Jethro. Could it? She had not thought to set the recording machine. She found her jaw was working and tense as she heard the last ring fall away into silence.

Before long she was able to turn on the light. She took off her rubber gloves and opened the door into the hall, where the cat sat, with its eyes closed, under the radiator. It ignored her.

She closed the darkroom door behind her and walked through into the living room, over Aunt Virginia's Chinese carpet to the bow window, and peered through the net. To her surprise all the reporters had gone and the road was empty, apart from the usual lines of parked cars. In a strange way she felt almost unnerved, deprived that they had gone. What did it imply? Had their editors lost interest in Jethro already? Or was there any further information to which she was not privy? Could it have anything to do with the telephone call?

It was then that she noticed that the car parked immediately outside her own hedge was occupied. Someone was sitting at the wheel. And that someone was Kitty.

Chapter Fourteen

Paula brought in the coffee on Aunt Virginia's tray with the two Persian kittens on it. She didn't stop to think. She had been so shocked at the look of Kitty.

'Woolie's best,' she apologised as she set it down on the inlaid occasional table from somewhere East. 'My aunt's.'

'Pretty,' said Kitty absently and Paula gave her a curious glance, but it seemed to be in good faith.

Kitty was staring through the folding doors into the dining room and the Polynesian paintings. Paula turned her head too. 'She travelled a lot,' she explained. 'She was a missionary.' She waved an arm in the direction of a shrunken head in the hall.

She knew Kitty wasn't listening although she nodded politely. It was terrible to see this woman, drained of all colour, without the civilising mask of make-up, hair loose and lying round her shoulders, eyes without lustre. She looked, not simply older, but ten years older. And what was worse, she had made no attempt to present herself before her rival. The black trousers and polo-neck jersey, without relief, did nothing for her.

'You see,' said Paula, 'I couldn't even answer the darkroom telephone because my hands were full of film.'

'It didn't matter,' said Kitty.

It seemed that, having failed to raise Paula by the door bell, she had gone down the road to the call-box and then come back to sit and wait, apparently until Paula returned or opened up.

'The Press were so ghastly yesterday and early this morning, it never occurred to me they'd just leave. I assumed they were still here, battering on my door.'

214

'We didn't have any this morning,' said Kitty. Her voice was flat, tired, expressionless. 'They've all moved over to Abbey Road. Apparently word got about that Jethro might turn up at EMI.' She almost smiled. The whites of her eyes were pink.

The cat stretched by the hall radiator, rose, and stalked into the living room with its tail straight up, rigid, like a furry pole. Its buttocks moved majestically, its little anus aggressively displayed. Passing Paula it jumped straight on to Kitty's knee.

'I hate cats,' said Kitty. 'That's why they always come to me.'

Paula picked him up. His claws dug into Kitty's jumper and dragged as she tried to pull him away.

'You wouldn't have a Mars Bar by any chance, would you?' Kitty asked as Paula came back from putting him out into the back garden.

'Er – no. Sorry.'

'I just have this yearning . . .'

Kitty gave a dry little laugh like a rattle as Paula looked sharply at her. 'No. I'm not pregnant!'

There was a hesitation before Paula said, 'I am.'

'Was Jethro pleased about that?' asked her visitor with a sudden healthy glimmer of former malice.

'He never knew. No. It wasn't what made him go.'

There was another pause.

'Or a tin of condensed milk?' suggested Kitty.

Paula shook her head.

'I feel' – she flopped an arm about, like a rag doll – 'as if I have no strength left. My knees have given up, my limbs are water and all my energy seems to be running out of my fingers like sand.'

Paula left the room and came back with a box of Turkish Delight. 'Someone gave me this for Christmas,' she said. 'One of Jethro's pupils, I think.'

'They used to bring me bath oil,' said Kitty. 'The bathroom at home's full of bath oil.'

'We ought to do a swap,' murmured Paula.

She opened the box and Kitty helped herself. 'Mm,' she said, biting into it. 'Rose water. That's the taste and the scent. It's rather comforting.'

'I'm not dotty about it,' remarked Paula.

Kitty took some more and she followed suit.

215

'Funny, isn't it? Us sitting here stuffing ourselves with Turkish Delight. Like women in a harem!' said Kitty.

Paula smiled.

She's pretty when she smiles, thought Kitty. Aloud, she said, 'That's a concept that would appeal to Jethro!' And her lack-lustre eyes danced blue for the first time. Then she sighed, deeply. 'Oh dear God,' she whispered. 'If only he would come home.'

'God? I didn't know you . . .'

Kitty looked at her and then, to Paula's horror, she began to cry.

Kitty stayed with Paula all day until tea-time. Some of the time she spent lying, wrapped in Aunt Virginia's rust-coloured mohair rug on the sofa, drifting in and out of sleep. And it was not until Paula had driven her home in her own car and been sent back to Barnes in a taxi on Kitty's insistence and at Kitty's expense, that she realised with quite shocking clarity that if Jethro walked through the front door she would not want him.

She sat in the big chair in the living room for a very long time on her return. She sat wondering what and who her baby would be like.

And then the telephone rang.

It was John, from a public house on Brighton front. She looked at the clock. It told her that the time was ten to eleven.

'You all right?' enquired John.

'I'm fine. How did the concert go?'

'Terrible. I was appalling.' Two pints of Guinness had brought back realistic memories and he was considering drowning his shame in a third when the barman called 'Time!' He wondered right up to the moment when he said 'goodbye' to Paula, whether he would tell her that Jethro was probably in Brighton. But he said nothing. Except, on impulse, 'It's a pity you're not here.'

John woke late with a head and a mouth on Friday morning. It took him a moment to register where he was, but when he remembered why it was that he had woken feeling so uneasy he waddled through to the telephone in his pyjamas and rang

216

the Pavilion to make sure his cello was safe and ready for him to pick up later in the day.

He drank his orange juice in his bath and ruminated upon the fruitless search of last night, which had taken him on a trail of closing pubs and unwelcoming hotel porters, round revolving doors, up and down the lower promenade in and out of seat shelters where huddled figures sat wrapped in army surplus coats, heads sunk on rheumy chests. The sea had roared up and down the shingle then; and it had roared all night, shifting and shovelling the wet stones. A wind had blown up in the early hours. He had listened to it lying warm beneath Natalia's soft blankets, his limbs eased by her Monogram.

He hastened back into town. It was imperative he find Jethro before Tatiana arrived tonight in her white mini. He felt that Tattie, blazing into Brighton, could send out vibrations so redolent of 'Manning' as to hurry Jethro away, along the coast or inland or over the water to France, maybe. Indeed, for all John knew he might already be half-way across the Channel from Newhaven's little harbour, or tucked up in an hotel in Dieppe.

Assuming that Jethro was still in Brighton, it would make sense to start, at noon, in the Star and Garter, known as 'Dr Brighton' to those who knew, a hostelry which John himself had left late last night at the suggestion of the landlord. It was a place where he and Jethro had sat on occasion, ruminating into Sussex Bitter, at one of the old barrel-tables, rising only to replenish tankards or play 'The Mystery Trail'. They had come once with Kitty, years ago, before the girls were of drinking age. She had sipped disdainfully at Campari, glaring at the regulars who so quickly became Jethro's friends, complaining that all men were children and mentally arrested at that. Jethro had pinched her and said she had been born old. Kitty had walked out. John remembered it well. And the men had stayed on, lugubriously content, groaning together at the reassuring banality of the mottos painted across the beams, witty as jokes from Christmas crackers. 'Marriage is a great institution for those who like institutions', and 'A philosopher is a man who can look at an empty glass with a smile'.

'Ho-ho,' Jethro had intoned. 'Ho-ho,' John had echoed sadly. Later, Kitty had come back and literally kicked them

217

out, saying they made her sick. She'd said it wouldn't have killed John to have paid for a few rounds, either, when she turned out Jethro's empty pockets.

'Hey-ho,' sighed John, watching the clientele, so jocular from habit and good manners. The lad at the bar was a new face and couldn't remember whether a man answering to Jethro's description had been here recently.

After only a pint and a few solemn retrospections, John got up and left by the side door, where the wind caught him and nearly blew him across the promenade. He stopped, wrapped his scarf more tightly around his neck and then saw the man standing looking out to sea, his gloved hands on the railings. He had his back to John, but John knew that straight proud back anywhere.

His heart leapt. Excitement and alarm! The quarry found so soon! Puffing, holding his coat together, he dodged across the road between the moving and the standing traffic and came up behind the large figure.

Up the beach below them roared the waves, smashing up the shingle in the menacing surf, pounding up the pebbles in a ferment of furious foam and dragging them back into the turbulance.

John hesitated. Was this the moment to invade his friend's reverie? Suddenly he felt overwhelmed with diffidence. Whatever private stress or distress had removed Jethro from his own familiar world, he now seemed a person apart, lost in meditation, contemplation of the ocean. To disturb him seemed a violence, almost like awakening a sleep-walker; and who could say what repercussions it might have.

The gale was blowing up banks of dark cloud from the south-west and the blue of the morning retreated in disorder towards the Downs. John felt chilled, and shivered. He didn't care for the sea in this mood. Not like Jethro, who always said the ocean was the great healer. The waves thrilled Jethro. They frightened John. Jethro sometimes shouted at them, roared back at all that majesty shattered into mere foam, at the walls of water building up again, thundering and plundering, gathering up all in their enormous arms and carrying it back away from the sea's safe edge, back into the fathoms upon fathoms of the deep, cold enormity out there, where only the surface trembled under the wind and the ocean lay still, guarding its treasures, forever receiving, forever throwing up its gifts.

John stood, quite humbly, waiting. It would be better not to disturb the great man at his own peculiar devotions. In time he would turn and they would walk back together to 'Dr Brighton's'.

Now John could see the fishermen at the end of the Palace Pier, sitting on their absurd little stools, lines dangling into the sea. He could see the pillars of spray breaking against the girders.

He shuffled his freezing feet and Jethro turned.

Only it was not Jethro. It was a man with a moustache and green-flecked eyes. John scurried away.

Now he felt at a low ebb. And cold. The front was bleak, the wind searching every corner as windows began to spring into life with light. John, hands deep in his pockets, wandered through the Lanes with reduced hopes and a sense of fatigue. He began to feel that his arrival in Natalia's flat had scared Jethro away and now he must have left the coast. He could be anywhere. Paris, by now. Brussels. Milan.

Even on a February afternoon with a brisk gale blowing up the Channel, the Brighton Lanes were full of people, wandering aimlessly alone, or in clusters, stopping to press their noses to an intriguing window full of silver and jewelry. Students from the University of Sussex meandered along with records under their arms from the shop in the square; Americans, French and Dutch hurried anxiously from shop to shop, vaguely aware that bargains were an anachronism.

It was only a quarter to three, yet John felt it was time for tea-cakes or cinnamon toast or something with nostalgia value, and it was as he was looking around for a 'cosy café' which might conceivably offer these, rather than Black Forest Gâteau and other nasty foreign habits, that he passed a window, and a moonstone drop pendant displayed within it caught his eye. For some obscure reason it made him think of Paula. He stopped. He had no intention of buying it for her. It would be a very peculiar thing to do, even if he had money to throw around on pendants for girls. But he liked to imagine her with it around her soft neck. How odd. It would be lost on Tattie, go unnoticed. Tatiana's requirements were either a complete absence of feminine frippery – or else something magnificent, astounding. Yet on Paula this could shimmer with gentle mystery. He puckered his brow at the complexity which was woman. And was this moonstone? Opal was unlucky, was it not? But he was sure this was no opal.

The window was packed with gems, precious and semi-precious. John leaned closer to the grille, screwing up his eyes. Through the battery of gold and silver, of chains and rings and things for personal adornment, of cream jugs and sugar bowls and tongs and coffee spoons and ladles and paper-knives and paperweights and coasters, whisky decanter labels, gin decanter lables, table-napkin rings and christening mugs – through all this he could just see into the lighted interior of the shop. A spotlight shone on to a desk where a seated woman examined something under a glass. She had raven black hair to her shoulders and exceedingly red lips.

And in the chair beside her sat Jethro.

For what could only have been a second John and he exchanged a look of astonished recognition, which immobilised John. Then he gasped and felt for the handle of the door. As he tried to turn it, it seemed to stick, heavy, warped in the damp salt air. He rattled and turned and pushed and it swung open, releasing a peal of bells, a positive tumbling torrent of silver music.

John stood inside on a patched Persian carpet, facing a heavy brocade curtain at the rear of the shop. The woman raised her hand from the spot of light on the table, and said, 'Yes, dear?'

John stared at the empty chair where Jethro had been sitting. 'Yes?'

Within the shop he could see that the black hair was artificial, a dyed raven fall from a grizzled parting. The scarlet lips were smudged, the outline of the mouth blurred and the teeth, now parted as she smiled, aglint with gold. Her large white hands, soft and puffy, were freckled with grave-marks. And she wore a stale heavy scent with a good deal of musk-substitute in its chemistry.

'There was somebody here,' said John.

'Somebody here?' she repeated. She laughed and at that moment all the clocks in the shop, clocks John had never noticed when he entered, began to chime for three o'clock. It was an eerie, metallic sound, a clamour of chimes.

'There's nobody here but you and me,' she said.

'Jethro . . .' John felt hot, steaming, a little shaky.

'Can I help you?' she offered.

He pulled himself together.

'I . . . I'd like to see the moonstone pendant in the window,' he said.

For a second she looked unsure.

'The one on the silver chain,' he said. 'Next to the crucifix.'

'Ah yes.' She smiled and again there was a flash of teeth. She glanced over her shoulder towards the curtain. It was a momentary gesture, but enough.

She had no alternative but to rise, and when she did so she revealed her bulk. A heavy, cumbersome woman in a thick ethnic skirt, red woollen stockings and Noddy slippers. She eased herself out of her chair and through the small space between the table and a glass-topped display cabinet and in doing so she knocked over the lamp. As she bent to pick it up John, wide enough of girth himself, contrived to push through the gap on the far side of the table, behind it, and through the curtain. It took her a moment before she had raised herself, held the lamp in her hand, and shouted 'Stop, stop! Thief! Police!'

Behind the curtain it was dark. John felt for a switch, found one miraculously and flipped it. The shop the other side of the curtain was plunged in darkness. He heard her dismay, her fumbling, her few swear words as he stumbled over something – a box – a crate of something. A bottle rolled across the floor. He trod on a can. And then as his eyes became adjusted to the lack of light he realised that he was in some sort of a box-room, a store-place. There was nobody there, but a door stood ajar without, a sliver of light beyond. He pushed it open and found himself at the foot of a staircase, lit, apparently, from a window above.

Now he could hear talking in the shop. He ran, heart working hard, up the stairs, which were uncarpeted, making something of a clatter. At a bend with a half-landing there was a fire-door, semi-glazed, showing the dusky afternoon light outside. He pushed. It opened. He ran along a wrought-iron balcony and down a fire-escape and found himself in a yard. All around him were high brick walls with small fronted windows in them. Somewhere a lavatory flushed. He squeezed past some dustbins and through a narrow alley and found himself once more out in the Lanes.

John gasped, leaning against a wall. He staggered, reached out and grasped the arm of a silver-haired Kentucky gentleman who exclaimed, smiled and disentangled himself, saying 'Hey-there!' or some such courtesy.

Collected and with regained breath, John took his bearings. Now, doggedly, he made his way round to the shop front again. But when he came level with it, he saw that the door was bolted and barred, the grille padlocked, the CLOSED notice was on the door and inside, the shop lay in darkness. He pounded upon the door but nobody came.

He remembered his cello just as his taxi was turning up above the Aquarium, and directed the cabbie back to the Pavilion. He felt extremely discouraged. It had never occurred to him that Jethro, if they came face to face, would deny him. It gave him a very strange feeling. He supposed that when he got home to Lewes Crescent he should phone the Brighton police. But at the moment, slouched in the back of the cab clutching his cello, the thought was insupportable.

He looked at his watch. It was tea-time indeed and there were to be no tea-cakes or cinnamon toast today. The sea, below, sounded hostile. Had it not been for Tattie's imminent arrival, he would, he thought, have caught the next train back to Victoria.

Once in the flat he turned on the lights, drew the curtains and put the kettle on to boil, in order to comfort himself with Natalia's Lapsgang Souchong. And then, the lust for tea-cakes being so uncontrollable, he ran down the stairs again and out, round the corner, to the small provisions shop he had discovered on his previous visit.

In the absence of tea-cakes he bought a sliced loaf and some powdered cinnamon. By now the wind had blown the sea into a fury, a frenzy. John hurried back indoors, and more slowly, up the stairs. He had left the door on the latch, and slammed it behind him as he bundled into the kitchen with his purchases. Then he turned to the kettle, which he expected had turned itself off automatically while he was out. He picked it up and, to

222

his surprise, found it light, empty. Lifting the lid, steam scalded his hand and he cried out in pain and alarm. 'What the hell . .?' he began, then picked up the teapot on the table to find it full.

He had not expected her at this hour. She must have taken the afternoon off, and the realisation that his solitude was over came as a shock, not altogether pleasurable. He had wanted a quiet hour to recover from the day's events before deciding how much to tell her and who, if anyone, to telephone in London.

'Hello,' he called, putting out two cups and fetching a lemon from the rose bowl. 'You're early.'

He heard footsteps on the landing, and looked quickly towards the door. They were not Tatiana's.

John filled up his own glass. He felt he needed and deserved it. But Jethro put his hand over his and shook his head as John leaned forward with Natalia's decanter.

'You must forgive me,' said John. 'I'm taking a little time to adjust. I feel a bit bemused.'

Jethro was sitting opposite him, upright on a hard chair, a half-finished glass of mineral water in his hand. John crossed his own neat little feet and sank further into the cushions.

Jethro put his own glass down and sat with his hands gripped tightly together on his knee.

'You don't do things by halves, chum, do you?' commented John after a while. 'I mean. Was it really necessary to go off without warning?'

'There wasn't any other way,' said Jethro slowly. 'If I had cancelled engagements ahead and given Roger due warning I'd have had so much pressure put on me it would have been impossible. I couldn't have coped. It would have destroyed me.' He frowned. 'You know. The moment Kitty heard she'd have been round in Barnes breaking up Paula's house and saying she'd ruined my career and she was an assassin and God knows what. Even without that, Paula would have been wringing her hands and looking guilty and saying it must have been her fault. Between the two of them . . .'

'I think Paula's pretty sensible,' said John.

223

'Do you?' asked Jethro.

'But what a thing! Just to ditch the Hallé with no notice!' John could not help bristling. 'It was an extraordinary thing to do.'

'I forgot Manchester,' said Jethro simply.

'Forgot!'

'Yes.' Jethro's locked fingers twitched a little. 'They were, after all, extraordinary circumstances.'

'I'm still not quite clear . . .'

'You don't understand, do you?' demanded Jethro suddenly, and passionately.

'Well – perhaps not entirely . . .'

'I simply knew that if I went on as I was going I would break. God, man – it was hell enough getting through that Queen Elizabeth Hall recital. The only way I did so was simply to con myself into believing I wasn't there at all – that I was playing for myself at home. I willed myself. I looked out there at them. . .'

'I was one of them,' complained John gently.

'. . . out there at them. And thought to myself – you're not there, none of you, damn you. You're all illusion. No reality. No substance. A sea of masks. Does that sound mad?'

'Well . . .'

'There was no other way.'

'Why did you change the programme and take out the Mussorgsky?'

'I didn't feel like Mussorgsky.'

'And did you feel like Scriabin?'

'Yes.'

'And since none of us audience were really there at all, you felt like indulging yourself and the spirit of Scriabin?'

'Something like that. Yes.'

'But why, Jethro?'

'I'm not in the witness box, you know,' said Jethro stiffly. 'May I have some more water?'

John took a stern hold upon himself. He must now, he realised, be careful not to destroy the advantage he had with Jethro actually sitting there, in person, talking, and in no way risk sending him running away into the shadows again. 'Sorry,' he said humbly. And waited for what seemed a long time before Jethro continued.

'I had always known I had high blood pressure,' said Jethro.

'Had Penfold told you?' John had not intended to interrupt.

Jethro looked at him, pityingly. 'What doctor ever *tells* you your own blood pressure. They just take it and stay silent. It's only *your* body.'

'They how did you know?'

'I'm not a fool,' said Jethro.

John was silent.

'Anyway, eventually I did get this little Paki doctor in Hammersmith to concede that it wouldn't do me any harm to slow down a bit and cut back on the booze. I knew what that meant.'

'It could be said of any of us,' said John, filling up his own glass.

'Remember, I'd seen it first hand.'

John looked enquiring.

'My father.'

'Your father had a stroke, had he not?'

'Exactly.'

'The Paki doctor wasn't necessarily saying you were a candidate for a stroke. Not yet.'

'But I have this tingling.' He held up his hands for John to see.

'Does that mean . . .'

'Maybe I've already had a slight stroke.'

John started. He felt quite alarmed and somehow suddenly on dangerous ground. The body in which he sat didn't seem quite so safe as it had before this conversation. 'Is that likely?' he said, in what he hoped was a dismissive voice.

Jethro shrugged. 'Could be. One doesn't always know. Anyway, I saw my father completely paralysed down the right-hand side of his body. He couldn't speak. He couldn't communicate with us although I'm sure he understood every word we said to him. I used to push him up and down this bloody front here, up to Hove and back again . . .'

'That's why it seems a funny place for you to have come back to now, doesn't it?'

'Does it? Does it?' growled Jethro. He put his hands back loosely on his knees and looked at them.

'Do they tingle – all the time?' asked John a little timidly. It was quite mad, but he was sure he could feel his own hands begining to tingle as he spoke.

'Yes.'

'Now?'

'Yes.'

'And *his* hands were affected?'

'One. It. . .' Jethro's voice shook – 'it used to quiver a little, sometimes.'

'I can see . . .' began John, tentatively.

'Can you? Can you?' There was a quiet, intent, constrained ferocity in Jethro.

'A little,' conceded John.

'But you think it's pure neurosis on my part, don't you?'

John shook his head vigorously.

Jethro looked at him with mild contempt. 'If that was going to happen to me I didn't want to be among people who expected things of me. I had to get away.'

'To Brighton.' John nodded.

'It was the natural place to come,' said Jethro. 'Apart from anything else, I needed Meryl.'

'Meryl?' John hesitated. 'Not the woman in the shop in the Lanes?'

'Who else?'

John reflected as to why anybody, especially Jethro, who came warm from Paula's bed, could need Meryl.

'She's the only person who can put me in touch,' said Jethro.

John stared at him. 'Do forgive me, old friend. With whom?'

'With those who have gone before,' said Jethro quietly.

There was a moment. Then John said 'You don't mean . . .?'

'Specifically my mother.'

'Grief!' said John.

'I've known Meryl for years. She's kept me in contact with Mummy for a long time.'

The word fell oddly from Jethro's lips. John stared at the large, impressively built man sitting there. 'I didn't know you believed in – er – things like that,' he said.

'I never wanted Kitty to know. She'd be sceptical about the spirit world. Can't you imagine how destructive she could be, without even trying? And Paula. She's so conventionally

226

religious. She's easily shocked by anything outside her own narrow comprehension of the C of E and Evensong at twilight.'

John thought, quietly, what a peaceful companion Paula might make.

Jethro rose and began pacing around the room. It made John nervous, but he didn't want to interrupt the flow as Jethro continued.

'Mummy never wanted me to study for the piano, you know. She knew it would lead to disaster, tragedy, disillusion, destruction . . .'

John opened his mouth, but closed it again. He wanted to say 'Bollocks' rather rudely, and something else about 'Mummy', and a word to the effect that the only disaster was of Jethro's own making.

'She saw all this time and money and hope spent on me, while Kiki . . .'

'Hope's not rationed,' said John.'And who's Kiki when she's at home?'

Jethro looked away. 'My sister. She was . . . she was a Mongol child. Mummy virtually gave up her life for Kiki, kept her at home, wouldn't hear of her going into any kind of a "place".'

'It can't have been easy for you,' said John, quietly.

'But I was a part of the trouble,' said Jethro, with some violence. 'Can't you see? I was using up the resources. That was Dad's fault, really, for encouraging me, for pushing me . . .'

'Oh come off it,' said John. 'He didn't have to *push* you. He couldn't have held you back. You were a natural.'

'If he hadn't given me the opportunities – taken me to Paris.'

'He'd have had a delinquent on his hands. It's what you were meant to do.'

'Mummy insists that is not so. I could have done many things, been many people.'

'You can only be Jethro and what you are. You're not seriously telling me you regret it?'

'He was punished,' said Jethro.

'What!'

'Just like I'm being punished. That's what Mummy's saying now.'

227

'Then someone ought to shut her up. And fast. Make a start with that Meryl woman.'

'She's why I had to come to Brighton. Now do you see?'

John pondered. This was not at all easy. And Jethro's pacing up and down by the window, up and down, was making his own head thump and beat for a start.

'Doesn't your father ever speak up?' he asked suddenly. 'Doesn't Meryl ever tune in to your poor old Dad? Oh no – I'd forgotten. He's lost the power of speech!'

Jethro stopped dead in his tracks and turned. 'Well yes,' he said, ignoring the last remark. 'Yes, actually. He – he came through for the first time about a month ago.'

'And about time. You'd been down here to see Meryl even then?'

'I've been coming down for years.'

'Does Kitty know about it? Or Paula?'

'I told you, no. It's quite beyond either of them.'

'To that shop?'

'To Meryl's flat, above. Dad said – he said I ought to go and see a psychiatrist.'

'Your Dad had something there,' muttered John.

'He kept going on about it. He got quite excited.'

'And did you?'

'Not at first. You see, Mummy said it was nonsense. She said he was up to his old tricks again trying to manipulate my life. She became very angry and upset and told me not to take any notice of him. At one session they were both trying to come through together.'

'Regular ding-dong,' said John. But Jethro never smiled.

'In the end it was Meryl who persuaded me to make an appointment with a man called Courtney in London,' Jethro went on.

'Good on Meryl!' said John with some enthusiasm. 'I've misjudged her! And have you see this man yet?'

'Yesterday. I used another name. Collins. I drove up to London and left poor old Theo's car in a garage. Meryl wrote a note for me. I didn't want him tracking me down. I don't know, quite, why I ever took his car. Impulse. Couldn't face trains and people the evening I left.'

'What was Courtney like?' asked John. 'Any good?'

'Early days,' said Jethro shortly. 'We'll see.'

'You intend to go on seeing him?'

'I'll give it a run.'

'And is your mother going bananas about it?'

For the first time Jethro smiled. 'Aye,' he said, 'but Dad's pleased as punch. He says the shrink'll get me back on the concert platform in no time!'

John found, to his dismay, that he wanted to weep. He sniffed and blew into his hanky.

Jethro sat down. He seemed calmer until John told him that Tatiana was on her way down to Brighton, and then he leapt up.

'I must go,' he cried.

'Your daughter won't eat you.'

'I couldn't face any of my family. Not yet,' he added. He picked up his coat, which he had thrown over another chair.

'What do you intend to do?'

'Do?'

'Are you going to stay in hiding? What do you want me to do?'

'I suppose it does seem a little pointless,' conceded Jethro, after thought.

'Do you want to be in Brighton? To keep chatting to your parents. Or do you think it might be more to the point to be in London for convenience. The shrink,' he added. He was scared of going too far.

'It could be.'

'You could stay with me.' As he offered he blanched at the prospect of Jethro in his flat for more than twenty-four hours.

Jethro actually grinned. 'It's a pressing invitation,' he said. 'You've gone quite pale, dear boy.'

John began to protest.

'I don't want to go back to Paula,' Jethro interrupted. 'I find her – enervating.'

John kept his own feelings about Paula to himself.

'She's so damn passive,' said Jethro.

'A matter of taste, I suppose,' said John, a little gruffly.

'And Kitty would kill me off quickly – at the moment. I couldn't take Kitty.'

'So?'

'I'll go to my darling mama-in-law!' Jethro's face relaxed. 'I'll stay with Natalia in her pink heaven until I can face . . .'

'Who?' asked John, ill-advisedly, perhaps.

'The world,' said Jethro.

The telephone rang.

'And now I'm going back to Meryl's flat for the night,' said Jethro as John went to answer it. 'Before my exhausting daughter gets here.'

'No need,' said John when he came back. 'That was Tatiana to say she's not coming. Her bug's worse and she feels lousy and frankly, if I'm reading correctly between the lines, she's cooling off me.'

'Are you her lover?' asked Jethro.

'Well – er – I'm not sure any longer.'

'I suppose I ought to challenge you to pistols.'

'I shouldn't bother. Not these days.'

'You're too old for her.'

'She's old enough to look after herself. She's light years older than you, Jethro. When you're dead and gone you could come zooming in through half the mediums in China and she wouldn't let it worry or divert her one centimetre.'

'Wouldn't she?'

John shook his head.

Jethro sighed. 'Did you tell her?' he asked.

'I thought that might not be what you would want,' suggested John.

'You thought right,' said Jethro, taking off his coat and sinking down, now, into one of the more comfortable chairs. Although his hands were again tightly clasped, the rest of his body sagged, relaxed, inert.

Oh well – thought John – it's a start.

In the morning John took Jethro tea in bed and found him already up, pacing his room.

'You see, you see . . .' he began with no preamble, as though John had a private line to his thoughts '. . . she seemed so compliant, so tolerant. She never jumped up and down and made a noise.'

'I presume,' said John, sitting heavily in Natalia's corded silk

230

chair so that it creaked, 'we are talking about Paula, not Kitty?'

Jethro ignored him and carried on. 'I was so drawn to the soft contours of the woman – and I'm not even talking of her body. No hard edges. No sharp edges. No abrasive thoughts coming up to knife you in the back when you were least expecting them. It seemed very seductive at the time and then . . . you'd be amazed,' he said, coming and standing close in front of and over John's chair in a way so intense that John started to feel a little claustrophobic, 'how boring that could get!'

'I can't say I see why.' John sounded as he felt, huffy.

'Mm,' grunted Jethro, walking away across the room as suddenly as he had come, running the tap in Natalia's basin and splashing his face and the surrounding carpet generously. Briskly he dried his face on a tiny towel with cream satin appliqué camellias. 'Seemed quite seductive. Poor Paula,' he added, after a moment.

'Are you going back to her?' asked John, somewhat stiffly.

'Dunno.'

There was a silence.

'Kitty makes you work for it,' said Jethro.

'I imagine so.'

'Paula gives it all. It's all too bloody easy!' Passionately he flung himself on the bed. Then he raised himself on one elbow and reflected, 'I wonder which'll wear better in the end.'

John wanted to hit him. It seemed to him a deplorable way of looking at women. But the thinking part told him to be very careful.

'Tell you one thing . . .' said Jethro, '. . . there were times – on the pillow with Paula – even then – I kind of missed Kitty, damn her. But you know, once you've done something . . . made a real stand . . . difficult to U-turn. Have Kitty say, "I knew – all along I told you so!" She likes to be right, you know. She thrives on being right.'

'Don't we all?'

Jethro didn't answer.

'Would you like me to ring any of them and say . . . say you're OK?' John put to him.

'You could.'

'Could I? Well – who?'

'You could ring Paula.'

231

'That's an idea,' said John, colouring.

'And I suppose the unfortunate Roger. Put him at rest.'

'If that's possible,' murmured John. 'Poor devil!'

'And old Theo.'

'Ah yes – Theo.'

'Tell Natalia I'm coming to stay for – for an indefinite period.'

John smiled. 'I'll do that.'

'Maybe I'll ring Kitty myself,' said Jethro, after thought.

On the way to the station, John made the taxi stop while he ran, puffing, into the Lanes and bought the moonstone pendant for Paula. He explained to Meryl what had happened but she said she already knew because she had received a message from the spirit world.

'Is Jethro going to be all right?' he asked her, as he was on the point of leaving.

She nodded, mysteriously, smiling. Her ear-rings were small silver mobiles.

Natalia groomed the dogs and did a marathon 'shop' at Selfridges Food Store and filled the flat with flowers. She bought two large boxes of Kleenex for Men and laid in a stock of toilet paper, remembering Jethro. She prepared a goulash and threw tit-bits of beef into the dogs' bowls, at which they sniffed suspiciously as though they were laced with arsenic.

She had her hair done and finished with a pearl-pink rinse and made up the spare bed. And then, she took Uncle Evgeny's photograph off the piano. Jethro would never tolerate anything on the piano, not even a single rose.

She lifted up the lid and looked at the yellowing, ivory keys. Gently, very tenderly, she ran her fingers over them as she had been taught as a young girl.

Chapter Fifteen

From the nursery upstairs the insistent, angry scream made conversation difficult. Jethro fidgeted irritably with the tuna mousse on his plate. It was overly rich and creamy, and had the look of something improvised in an odd moment between 'feeds', jabbed at indiscriminately with gherkins, which Paula ought to have known he detested. Kitty, who had painted her nails crimson and carefully for the occasion, smiled with serene dignity, but keeping all the while a close eye on Jethro. So far, things had gone well, and she didn't want him souring the 'entente'. She continued, above the baby's crying, treating it rather like coughing at a concert, to tell John about the flat Tatiana had just moved into with Alerick. John's distraction failed to disturb her. She ignored it.

'With Sally in New York, you see . . .' she said. '. . . You remember, she married that viola with the curly beard. . .'

Suddenly John rose and spoke to his wife. 'Don't you think perhaps,' he suggested, '. . . if we brought him down?' He turned to Kitty. 'He's a sociable little lad,' he said.

Paula nodded, vaguely.

Jethro wondered why they had come out here to dine in this colourless house in Barnes. He couldn't really recall with any substance a time he had felt differently about all this – he looked around – all those boring watercolours of Paula's hung on the walls and the Dralon sofa. Had he really made love upon *that* only three years ago? Another existence. He yawned.

He was feeling moderately good these days. The agents were promoting his new Queen Elizabeth Hall in five months from now, and before that he had his US tour ahead with all the challenge that offered. He always enjoyed America and the Americans. Sometimes he horrified Kitty by saying they might go and live out there. His programme for the States was a good balance of strong virtuoso stuff and the kind of sensitive lyricism for which he had become increasingly renowned since the last South Bank recital. People was saying Jethro Manning had mellowed and revealed entirely new aspects of himself, that he ran very deep. This was, perhaps, to be expected after a substantial period in psychotherapy, of which his public soon became aware, for the Mannings had never found it easy to live and move and have their being incognito.

At first he had been uncertain about the sessions with Dr Courtney, and somewhat on the defensive. However, the consulting rooms were a civilised venue, with their sane white walls; the charcoal tweed upholstered chairs were comfortable, looked down upon by the four refined David Gentlemans in their stainless steel frames and grey-green mounts, and he liked Courtney himself, a quiet fastidious man with Heseltine hair just greying. There was nothing nutty about the image, and Jethro grew to look forward to his visits once he became used to them, feeling in some way proprietory about Courtney, so that when he arrived to find the previous appointment leaving, or left to find the following person arriving, he was annoyed as though by a trespasser.

The therapy took the form of an exploration of his early introduction to piano playing and the valuation of his 'gift' within the home, the extent to which it was honoured, indeed celebrated by his father and, conversely, resented by the mother, who had never failed to make him aware of the unfairness in life that one child should receive so much largesse at the hands of fortune and the other so little.

Talking exposed such raw places in Jethro's psyche that he surprised himself, on his second visit, by weeping uncontrollably as apparently submerged memories were evoked. The doctor sat quietly attentive, recipient of so much pain. Now, for the first time, Jethro came face to face with something he had disguised from himself, the deep repugnance and dislike he had felt for his poor sister. As a child it had been possible to flinch away from such unbearable truth by simply retiring into his world of sound. The best way to deaden the rather brutish, simple grunts and noises she used to make while eating or pushing around the toy carpet sweeper their mother gave her to play with, was to shut himself away with Beethoven, whom he was sure would have understood. He never admitted to such feelings of distaste, amounting almost to hatred, even to his father, who was perceptive enough to imagine the stress the boy suffered, but too reserved, too cautious to invite real confidence in anything but the field of music, to which they could freely admit together. Thus much was suppressed and the young Jethro lived with his guilt. He thought himself to be very wicked but assumed this to be the price of genius. He ingratiated himself as far as he was able with his mother, eagerly fetching and carrying and running errands and thus bringing his parents yet again into conflict because his father counted time spent away from the piano as time wasted, but Jethro never felt convinced of any great affection from her.

When his sister died he was appalled at the well of despair into which his mother sank and wanted only to run away. Again, music seemed to provide the answer. When his father's stroke hit, at such a time, the shock might have virtually paralysed his performance at the Wigmore Hall début, but it did not. He played magnificently to a wildly appreciative audience and afterwards, stunned by his own success, by the reviews which acclaimed him, he could only feel that perhaps, after all, he had no heart. In vain did Kitty assure him that it was partly for his father he had played so well, that this was the greatest 'gift' he could have given the man so suddenly locked in the silent world of his wheelchair. He felt, instead, that there must be something basically missing within him, a capacity for human feeling which had, perhaps, been strangled by his own talent. Thus his own talent began, just occasionally, to assume the nature of something evil to his imagination.

He talked his way through the first year. And quite early on, Courtney suggested that the neurosis had been born of a need to find a way out of his problem. Jethro carried a terrible load of guilt. He felt at the deepest and quite unacceptable level that he had sold his soul and the only answer he had been able to find, it seemed, at a point of adult crisis, had been to be physically *unable* to perform. Thus the tingling and tremors in his hands. Not imagined, but induced. This was not an unusual syndrome, Dr Courtney told him, which was not particularly flattering and irritated Jethro. It seemed there was even a word for his condition – 'secondary gain'. He was unsure how much he liked having a label attached to his own sense of confusion, but he did have to admit that it made sense of much he had not fathomed.

Slowly things had improved and he had been able to play Natalia's little piano, at first intermittently, tentatively, during one of her tactful trips to Selfridges Food Store; but increasingly with passion, and allowing her to sit quietly listening, the dogs on her knee. At last came the time again when he was able to move back into the concert scene, Roger Dilke guardedly welcoming to him, his audiences moving him deeply by their warm response. After the first major concert he held Kitty in his arms in the Green Room and did not even attempt to hold back the tears.

He must watch the eating and drinking in America, without Kitty to nag at him. She had decided not to come on his tour because all this private therapy had been costing a fair amount and however much Jethro had begun to earn again, it never went all that far with Nina's jobs being intermittent and Antony at Oxford now, with champagne tastes. Jethro wasn't on a strict diet or anything, and the blood pressure seemed to have settled down, but he watched himself more carefully than he had done in the old days and Kitty had taken to filling his glass with Perrier instead of wine as the evening wore on.

Kitty flitted into his conscious mind and suddenly the corners of his mouth softened. They had indulged themselves in a stupendous row that very morning, the first time they had felt safe to do so for a long while, and Kitty had thrown a bowl of fruit salad at him. It had made them both feel better.

Paula looked at him. She wondered what he was thinking. She wondered whether by any chance he was thinking about her, and flushed slightly.

Now John came down with his son in his arms. John beamed and the baby seemed mollified, now mercifully silent.

'Now you just stay there, Clinton,' he said, propping him

236

up on the sofa against cushions, 'and be sociable.'

Jethro thought what a stupid name Clinton was for a baby.

Kitty went on talking. Now it was about Nina and her break into television in the current BBC 'sit-com'. Paula had her chin cupped in her hand, and looked thoughtful, attentive, although she was not in fact listening to a word Kitty was saying and if addressed directly or questioned would have jumped guiltily. John gazed at her. He thought how beautiful she was. Beautiful beyond compare. Then he glanced at his son, and smiled, held out a hand which the baby gripped by the first finger, staring at the company unwinking, unblinking. Suddenly it was silently sick down its babygro. John took out his hanky and mopped it up. Jethro looked away quickly.

'Hello, sweetheart!' said John, as the door opened and the three-year-old Sophia crept in, dressing-gown cord dangling. 'Hey – come here! You'll trip over that. Let Daddy do it up.'

The little girl closed into John's warm arm and looked at Jethro across the table. He broke open his roll on the ecru tablecloth and took no notice of Sophia. He felt no kinship, felt no stirrings, and nobody had felt it appropriate to tell him. His mind, now, was elsewhere, in Baden-Baden where he would be next week. He was silently listening to Ondine in his head.

Sophia climbed on to John's knee and he held her, stroking her soft, flyaway, fair hair. He was glad she had Paula's hair. There was, he thought, little of Jethro at all about her to disturb the sense of ease within his domestic life. He loved the cuckoo as much as his own fledgling.

Kitty saw him anew and suddenly she realised what a lovely man he was and what Tatiana had allowed to slip out through her fingers. A pearl. 'Too nice for any of us, by far,' thought Kitty, whose new realism was disturbing to some of her older friends, like Theo.

'Ah well . . .' she reflected to herself, rising politely to follow Paula into the kitchen where nappies spun merrily round in the tumble-dryer, exuding warm air and nursery vibrations. She tripped and stumbled on Sophia's toy telephone, trailing the wire on her heel as she carried through the wreckage of the tuna mousse. Paula stooped, picked up the toy, and the two women smiled at each other.

237

When Jethro and Kitty came home to Loudoun Road, he went straight to the big black piano in the music room, lifted the lid and began to play a Bach prelude.

Upstairs, as she undressed, Kitty listened. So far as one could tell, Jethro had quite forgotten the hole in that room when the piano had been taken to Barnes. She lay on her bed and accepted the music.

She closed her eyes, but yet she could not obliterate Sophia's image and pale gold hair. That was something she simply had to accept, that from time to time the child's presence would invade her own heart and peace of mind. She was relieved it was so like Paula. She wished in a way she could sort out her feelings more clearly towards the little girl, come to terms with the conflict of emotions which attracted and repelled her to Jethro's third daughter, the girls' step-sister. But with any luck the two families need not converge again for some time. It had been civilised of Paula to ask them to dinner, but it would not be necessary to return the invitation for a while. Both Jethro and John were busy enough for face-saving excuses to be made.

She turned off the light and lay listening to her husband in the dark. She fell asleep while he was still playing.

Dear Reader,

You have been reading a Piatkus Paperback, one of a new range of novels which we hope will offer you what you want – an enjoyable, well-written story with realistic characters which leaves you feeling good at the end (though we don't promise that it will always be a happy one).

If you have enjoyed this book, please recommend it to your friends and look out for our distinctive pink, grey and cream covers in your local bookshop. If you don't see them, please ask the bookseller to order them for you.

Among other novels we are publishing at the moment are *Sisters* by Debby Mayer, the story of an independent young woman who unexpectedly finds herself guardian to her eight year old half-sister, *To the Tenth Generation* by Rita Kashner, a powerful novel about a mother and son set in Israel, and *An Honest Woman* by Anne Christie, about the breakdown of a modern marriage.

We would love to hear from you with comments about our new series and if you would like to be put on our mailing list please send a large stamped addressed envelope to

    Piatkus Paperbacks
    5 Windmill Street
    London W1P 1HF

Thank you for reading us.

Judy Piatkus